JAT

MW00627928

Aditya Narayan Dhairyasheel Haksar was born in Gwalior and educated at the Doon School and the universities of Allahabad and Oxford. A well-known translator of Sanskrit classics, he has also had a distinguished career as a diplomat, serving as Indian high commissioner to Kenya and the Seychelles, minister to the United States, and ambassador to Portugal and Yugoslavia.

His translations from the Sanskrit include the *Hitopadesa* and the *Simhasana Dvatrimsika*, both published as Penguin Classics and *Shuka Saptati: Seventy Tales of the Parrot*, published by HarperCollins India. His latest work is *A Treasury of Sanskrit Poetry*, which was commissioned by the Indian Council for Cultural Relations, and released in 2002.

JATAKAMALA
Stories from the Buddha's Previous Births

Translated from *Arya Shura's original in Sanskrit*
by
A.N.D. Haksar

With a foreword
by
His Holiness the Dalai Lama

HarperCollins *Publishers* India
a joint venture with

New Delhi

First published in India in 2003 by
HarperCollins *Publishers* India
a joint venture with
The India Today Group

Copyright © A.N.D. Haksar 2003

A.N.D. Haksar asserts the moral
right to be identified as the author of this work.

HarperCollins *Publishers*
1A Hamilton House Connaught Place, New Delhi 110001, India
77-85 Fulham Palace Road, London W6 8JB, United Kingdom
Hazelton Lanes, 55 Avenue Road, Suite 2900, Toronto, Ontario M5R 3L2
and 1995 Markham Road, Scarborough, Ontario M1B 5M8, Canada
25 Ryde Road, Pymble, Sydney, NSW 2073, Australia
31 View Road, Glenfield, Auckland 10, New Zealand
10 East 53rd Street, New York NY 10022, USA

Typeset in 11/14 Simoncini Garamond
Nikita Overseas Pvt. Ltd.

Printed and bound at
Thomson Press (India) Ltd.

P.M.S.

For
B.
with love

Contents

THE DALAI LAMA

foreword

Stories of the previous lives of the Buddha are found in many Buddhist traditions. Although each tale presents an example of the future Buddha's perfection of some virtue in his long career as a Bodhisattva, these stories are not restricted to Mahayana literature, for versions of them are also found in the Pali canon. I feel this is important evidence of the continuity that exists between the Hinayana and Mahayana traditions.

These stories of the Buddha's previous lives have had great impact wherever they have been told. They have been a major inspiration for a wealth of Buddhist works of art. They are also widely cited as examples of the fundamental values of the Buddhist path, for they tell vividly how the Bodhisattva put generosity, morality, patience and other positive values into practice. On the one hand his inclination to implement these virtues stems from his having cultivated the awakening mind, the altruistic aspiration to attain enlightenment for the sake of all sentient beings. On the other, his steady practice of such perfections, as a source of merit and insight, contributed to his eventual achievement of the enlightenment he sought.

For those of us who are the Buddha's followers these stories contain the practical lesson that the path to enlightenment is long and arduous, requiring immense determination, courage and effort. However, they also show us that much of the Buddhist path, indeed of nearly all spiritual paths, consists of putting fundamental human values into practice. You don't even have to be religious to do this. I am sure we all have countless opportunities to be generous, to be patient, to take a moral stand, but what distinguishes the Bodhisattva is that by seizing those opportunities wherever he can, he continuously makes his life more meaningful.

This present work is a new translation of a celebrated Sanskrit collection of thirty-four stories of the Buddha's previous lives known as the *Jatakamala*. Arya Shura, who is regarded as one of India's greatest Sanskrit poets, composed it about seventeen hundred years ago. It is widely respected as exemplary in both form and content.

I am particularly happy that Mr A.N.D. Haksar, who has led a distinguished diplomatic career, has made this new translation into English for the modern reader. Not only do these beautiful tales have a timeless quality to them, but also the qualities of compassion, friendliness and concern for others are no less important now than when the stories were written. Moreover, I am personally well acquainted with this text from its Tibetan edition and have read and taught from it many times. It is a book of which I am very fond, for it is a Tibetan tradition that the Dalai Lama should teach one of these stories at the culmination of the Great Prayer Festival that is celebrated every Tibetan New Year. Therefore, I have no doubt that many readers will derive great pleasure from this book and, should they be so inclined, will find in it a source of practical inspiration to make their lives more meaningful too.

15 December 2001

Introduction

THE *JATAKAMALA* OF ARYA SHURA IS A WORK WELL KNOWN BOTH in sacred Buddhist and in classical Sanskrit literature. Its creedal repute is matched by its literary quality. Its tales of goodness and righteous conduct are couched in the elegant language which characterized the early kavya genre. Combining picturesque prose with polished verses, they can be read no less for their timeless message of compassion and concord than for the colourful, often tender and sometimes dramatic, imagery with which it is presented.

Scholarly opinion places the composition of the *Jatakamala* around the fourth century AD.[1] It seems to have been current well into the next millennium. Some of its stories and stanzas appear in the Ajanta cave frescoes which are dated to the sixth century.[2] At least three later commentaries on its text are extant.[3] The Chinese pilgrim I-Tsing mentioned it among the works he found popular in India during his travels at the end of the seventh century.[4] Its translation into Chinese took place between the tenth and the twelfth centuries.[5] Translations are also recorded in Tibet where the work as well as the author were held in high esteem.[6] Both figure in two celebrated anthologies of Sanskrit poetry, respectively from eleventh-century Bengal and fifteenth-century Kashmir.[6A]

Manuscripts of the *Jatakamala* name Arya Shura as the author. So does the record of the Chinese translation, which is confined to fourteen of the original tales.[7] As with many other writers of ancient India, little is known about him as an individual. The work testifies to his erudition and literary skill, and to his religious faith in which he had perhaps been ordained as a monk. The first part of his name could thus be an honorific. This seems clear from the Kashmiri anthology where he is mentioned with a Buddhist title, as Bhadanta Shura. He is considered the author of another work which was translated into Chinese in AD 434, and of some others, three of which survive only in Tibetan translation.[8]

Arya Shura is known in Tibetan tradition as a saintly teacher as well as an honoured writer. Lama Taranatha's seventeenth-century account[9] indicates that he had intended the *Jatakamala* to be a longer work but died before this could be accomplished. It also describes him as an authority on prosody, and with various other names, including Ashvaghosha. Most modern scholars do not identify him with that earlier poet, though some see in his writing the influence of Ashvaghosha's famous verse-biography, the *Buddhacharita*.[10] According to another opinion, Arya Shura was one of the Buddhist savants who began to use Sanskrit as the language of their work from about the third century AD.[11]

*

The title *Jatakamala* is usually translated as a garland or series of birth-stories. The work is a collection of thirty-four such tales. Literally, 'jataka' means the story of a previous birth. The connotation is better understood in the light of some underlying concepts which for many are also articles of faith.

The first of these is the concept of rebirth: that every being has passed through many lives before the present one, and is likely to pass through many more in the future. Further, that these lives are not limited to the human species or confined to this world.

The second is the concept of karma: that a chain of cause and effect binds together every being's past, present and future lives, so that the circumstances of each are affected by the totality of those which have preceded it. It is postulated that each being is born with a balance of merits and demerits accumulated from the actions of previous lives, and this determines how comfortable or painful, elevated or base the present one will be. Implicit in this is the assumption that good or bad deeds in the present life will secure corresponding results in the future.

In the context of Gautama Buddha having attained the ultimate perfection during his earthly existence, it would follow from these concepts that he must have performed surpassingly good deeds in countless past lives. This is the basis of the jataka tales of his previous births. He features in them as the Bodhisattva – another concept which needs some elucidation here.

In the words of the Indologist A.L. Basham, the term 'Bodhisattva, literally meaning "Being of Wisdom," was first used in the sense of a previous incarnation of the Buddha.'[12] Later the term acquired an identity of its own. Bhikshu Sangharakshita describes the Bodhisattva as 'the heroic being who, practicing the ten perfections throughout thousands of lives, aspires to the attainment of Buddhahood for the sake of all sentient beings.'[13] The future Buddha does not seek that exalted state, it should be noted, for any personal consideration. His sole concern is to help others and to alleviate their sufferings. He would forego even his own salvation for the welfare of the world. This selfless goal of high altruism is spelt out in Arya Shura's very first tale:

> 'My intent has no purpose
> apart from helping another:
> not competition, nor wish for glory,
> nor gaining heaven or a kingdom,
> not even the ultimate bliss.'

This ideal is exemplified in the stories of the *Jatakamala*, which also has the title *Bodhisattva-avadana-mala* or a garland of the Bodhisattva's good deeds. In these tales he appears in different incarnations: as a ruler or a merchant, a teacher or a student, a hermit or a monk, a loving father and husband or a respectful but determined son. He is also born as an ape and an elephant, a hare and a deer, a swan, a woodpecker and a fish. In one existence he is the king of the gods, in another a blind old boatman; in one a celestial sage, in another a wild buffalo. In each he typifies one or more virtues taught by the Buddha: moral conduct and charity, compassion and forbearance, courage and wisdom, veracity, patience and friendliness towards all creatures. Thus the stories are also homilies on the *paramitas*[14] or perfections of the Bodhisattva. This appears clear from their concluding portions, which are in the nature of comments and directions for future sermons or discourses. Some scholars[15] consider these to be later additions for monastic and congregational use by preachers and divines; if so, this also points to the continuing popularity of the work in the centuries after it was written.

As stated in his prologue, Arya Shura's stories are taken from the Buddhist canon and tradition. This is also the case with other similar collections. The jatakas have been preserved in the Pali canonical work *Khuddaka Nikaya* of the *Sutta Pitaka*, which was compiled in the fourth century BC and probably reduced to writing some three hundred years later. There they occur in verse form which was later elaborated in prose commentaries, given their present shape in the fifth century AD by Buddhaghosha in Sri Lanka. These commentaries, which constitute the main corpus of the stories, comprise 547 jatakas.[16] They are written in simple Pali in contrast to the cultivated Sanskrit used by Arya Shura perhaps a century earlier. His *Jatakamala* is a select anthology unlike the comprehensive compilation of Buddhaghosha, and its tales also differ in detail and presentation, apart from language and style. The source of both, however, is the same collection of birth-stories which had developed from the time of the Buddha. As twelve of Arya Shura's thirty-four tales are not found in the Pali jatakas at all,[17] they also constitute a valuable supplement to the latter.

*

In modern times the *Jatakamala* was among the works which received early attention when Indological studies gathered pace in the West. Its manuscript copies were first acquired in 1828 by the British Assistant Resident in Nepal. Further manuscripts followed, and two jatakas from them (tales 6 and 13) were published in subsequent years.[18] A critical edition of the whole text came out in 1891, prepared by the Dutch Sanskritist Hendrik Kern and published as the first volume of the newly started Harvard Oriental Series. Its translation into English by fellow scholar J.S. Speyer appeared in 1895, published by Max Mueller in his 'Sacred Books of the Buddhists' series.

Max Mueller expressed the view that Kern's edition would probably remain the final one.[19] Various manuscript sources of the *Jatakamala* have begun to be scrutinized anew during the last two decades,[20] but any authoritative revision of Kern's text is yet to emerge. Nor has there been any further translation of the full work into English since that of Speyer more than a century ago, though translations have appeared in Bangla, German and Hindi.[21]

The present translation is intended to bring this once acclaimed ancient work before today's general readership in modern English. The Buddhist jatakas, better known in translations from the Pali,[22] need equally to be available in those of the tales preserved in Sanskrit. Both convey through lively stories the message of respect and caring for others, humans as well as animals, which is of no less importance in our times.

This translation is based on Kern's edition of the original Sanskrit text, and on two versions published in India.[23] These contain minor corrections together with Hindi translations respectively by Prof S.N. Chaudhari and Dr J.C. Mishra, which I have consulted with profit but not necessarily followed. I have also benefited from Speyer's learned literal translation and his erudite notes and introduction, though departing from time to time from his pioneering interpretation of the text.

My translation endeavours to combine fidelity to the original with the requirements of modern English usage. It also seeks to maintain the reverential tone of the original. While occasional archaisms have been used to this end, no attempt has been made to replicate in English, a language very different in grammatical construction and literary convention, Arya

Shura's metric variations or the compounding, paranomasia and other figures of speech which embellish his Sanskrit verse and prose in the kavya manner. Nor have I tried to read any esoteric meaning in his words, treating them more in their literary rather than a scriptural dimension. The word dharma, which has multiple meanings, has mostly been rendered as virtue, righteousness or the right path; sometimes, specially when the reference is to the faith enunciated by the Buddha, it has been left in the original form.

Apart from the prologue, which is formed of four stanzas, the stories of the *Jatakamala* are written in a mixture of prose and over fourteen hundred verses in a variety of poetic metres recognized in classical Sanskrit. These verses are of five broad types: gnomic; laudatory, chiefly of the hero's virtues; descriptive of scenes; narrations of action; and substantive utterances by the Bodhisattva. The bulk of them have been rendered here in prose to maintain cohesivenessness and continuity in the narratives and dialogues which could otherwise have been cumbersome in translation. Occasionally they have been rendered in free verse, where such renditions seemed to fit harmoniously into the translated whole, to convey some flavour of the original.

*

The first translator of the *Jatakamala* had high words of praise for it as literature. 'It has perhaps been the most perfect writing of its kind,' Speyer wrote in his introduction. 'It is distinguished no less by the superiority of its style than by the loftiness of its thoughts.'[24] The work has also been criticized by some historians of Sanskrit literature[25] for its extravagant treatment of the Bodhisattva's sacrifices and virtues, which according to them have been so magnified as to appear unreal and tedious. This supposed defect is, however, in keeping with the tradition of ethical exhortation in ancient Indian writing, and was probably deemed a merit in times when the Bodhisattva's deeds were upheld as ideals for emulation.

Taranatha recounts a legend that Arya Shura was himself inspired by his hero's example in the first tale to offer his own body to a starving tigress. Another tale in this collection describes a similar sacrifice performed by an elephant for the sake of some men in distress. The theme of universal compassion, which recurs in these and other tales, is interspersed with the evocation of other ethical ideals. Responses to human predicaments are the subject of stories such as those of the righteous king in love with the woman who turns out to be the wife of his minister, the virtuous prince obliged to give up his family, and the dutiful student asked by his teacher to steal in a supposedly good cause. Others dwell on the harmony possible between man and animal, on the challenge of dealing with evil, and on the power of truth and goodness. An attractive feature of these tales is the rich variety of their setting and characters. Often described in fascinating detail, the former range from forest scenes to a festive city, from the tumult of battle to a storm at sea, and from philosophic disputations to the beauties of the harem and horrific scenes of hell. The cast of characters includes gods and demons, kings and bandits, hermits and merchants, apart from children and animals. The tales of the *Jatakamala* were thus devised to be enjoyable as well as edifying.

*

I would like to express my deep gratitude to His Holiness the Dalai Lama for his illuminating foreword to this book. It makes clear the relevance of the Jatakamala's message for our times and his own familiarity with the work. I am grateful to Renuka Chatterjee for giving me extended time to work on this translation despite repeated unavoidable delays. It was completed eventually at the homes of my children, Sharada and Vikram, to whom my thanks are due, and specially to my daughter-in-law Annika for her assistance with the computer. I am also grateful to Vikrant Mahajan for editing the manuscript and to Mihir Chanchani for designing the cover. For my wife Priti, who read the drafts and helped me in more ways than can be counted, no words of gratitude can ever be adequate. I have dedicated this book to her for our fortieth wedding anniversary which marks the year in which it was completed.

New Delhi   A.N.D.H.

Prologue

OM! SALUTATION TO ALL THE ILLUSTRIOUS BUDDHAS AND THE Bodhisattvas!

Glorious were the Sage's deeds in previous births. Endowed with excellent virtues, they were auspicious and renowned, charming and irreproachable. With devotion will I praise these wonderful deeds, and with an offering of the flowers of my own poetry.

These admirable deeds are signposts which point the way to the essence of the Buddha. May they render tales of goodness ever more delightful, and bring peace even to the hard-hearted.

I attempt here to narrate the marvellous deeds of the best of men, in accordance with scripture and tradition. I do so, considering that it will be of benefit to the people, and may also make my words more pleasing to hear.

None could attain the splendour of his virtues; not even those who strove for themselves.[1] For what he did was for the sake

of others. His fame burns bright in the fitting name, The
Omniscient.[2] With bowed head do I salute that one without
equal, together with the dharma and the sangha.

1

The Tigress

ONE SHOULD HAVE THE UTMOST FAITH IN THE LORD BUDDHA for, even in his previous births, the Lord considered all beings as himself and had immense affection for all creatures.

Thus has it been heard from my guru, a devotee of the Three Jewels,[1] who was esteemed by his own teacher for his accumulation and practice of virtues. He would extol this heroic deed of the Lord in a previous birth.

The Lord was then a Bodhisattva. In keeping with his extraordinary vow, he favoured the world with a stream of compassion, charity, kindness and succour. Once he took birth in an eminent brahmin family, which was pure of character and devoted to its duties.

The birth rite and the other sacraments were administered in due order to the Bodhisattva as he grew up. Intelligent by nature, industrious and eager to learn, he was well tutored and soon became adept in the eighteen sciences, and a master of all the arts which accorded with his family tradition.

The brahmins came to regard the Bodhisattva as a personification of the scriptures. The princes considered him a respected ruler, and the students a helpful father. For the common people he was a veritable king of heaven. His merits brought him great wealth, honour and fame. But these gave him no pleasure. The practice of dharma had purified his mind. He was also familiar with the renunciant life. Observing that desires were the cause of many evils, he shook off worldly life as something unhealthy, and chose to live on a wooded hill.

There, detached, with wisdom tranquil,
he put to shame the world of men
which, to evil deeds addicted,
knows not the peace which comes with virtue.

The friendly calm which flowed from him
entered, as it were, the hearts
of even beasts, who gave up mutual
violence, and lived like hermits.

His pure conduct and self-control,
compassion and contentedness,
made him loved by even strangers,
for all the world was dear to him.

His wants were few, he knew no cant,
he sought no glory, gain or pleasure,
he caused the minds of even gods
to fill with adoration for him.

His merits had won the hearts of men;
now, hearing of his ascetic life,

they left their families and sought
salvation in his tutelage.

He taught them as best as he could,
pure conduct and self-control,
heedfulness and inner calm,
friendliness and a focussed mind.

His disciples became numerous. Most found fulfilment. The
blessed way lay open, and people embarked on the goodly path
of renunciation. When the doors to disaster had thus closed,
and the pathways to perfection become high roads accessible
to all, the great soul once went forth to see and enjoy this scene
at leisure.

Accompanied by Ajit, a disciple, the Bodhisattva wandered
about the mountain caves and groves which were suited to the
practice of yoga.

There, in a hillside cave, he saw
a young tigress, freshly whelped,
so sick with pain of giving birth,
that she could scarcely move.

She was famished, it was clear,
from her gaunt belly and sunken eyes;
even at her tiny cubs
she stared, as if at food.

They snuggled, thirsty, to her teats,
fearless, trusting in their mother:
she snarled at them ferociously,
as if at some stranger.

The sight filled the Bodhisattva with compassion. Though calm and composed, he trembled at another's pain like a great mountain in an earthquake.

'My child! My child!' he exclaimed to his disciple. His words were full of sympathy and concern:

> 'Look at this worthless worldly round!
> Hunger makes this animal break
> the bonds of love maternal:
> she seeks to eat her own offspring.

> 'How painful is, alas, the fury
> of love for one's own self,
> that even makes the mother seek
> her own child as her meal!

> 'Who would want to nurture
> that enemy called self-love
> which leads one to embarking
> on deeds even like this?

'Go quickly, therefore, and find something to stay the hunger pangs of this tigress, so that she does not hurt her cubs or herself. I too will try to prevent her from doing anything rash.'

'Very well,' said the disciple, and he went off to look for food for the animal. Having sent him away on this pretext, the Bodhisattva said to himself:

> 'Who should I hunt for flesh,
> when all my body is here?
> Uncertain is finding another,
> it may also impede my duty.

'This body is not the self. It is
transient, worthless, home to suffering,
ungrateful, and even unclean.
Not to rejoice at its use for another
is hardly a sign of wisdom.

'We ignore others' pains because
of obsession with our own pleasures,
or because we cannot help. But I
have no joy when others suffer,
and to help them I am able.
Why should I then be indifferent?

'If I were able, but ignored
even an evil doer in pain,
my heart would burn
in the thought of that sin
like dry grass in a forest fire.

'Therefore will I cast this wretched
body from the mountainside,
make it lifeless, and thus save
the tiger cubs from their mother
and the tigress from infanticide.

'What is more, I will do this
to guide those eager to help mankind;
to urge the laggards, cheer the generous;
the minds of the virtuous to attract;
to dishearten the hosts of Mara,[2]
and gladden those who love the Buddha;
to shame the selfish, full of spite and greed;

to assure adherents of the blessed path;
astonish those who sneer at charity,
and bring joy to the charitable
by clearing the highway to heaven.

'"When will I be able
with these limbs to benefit others?"
This old wish I will now fulfil,
and soon attain enlightenment.

'My intent has no purpose
apart from helping another:
not competition, nor wish for glory,
nor gaining heaven or a kingdom,
not even the ultimate bliss.

'With this, may I always be
able to remove the suffering
of people, and to give them joy
at the same time, like the sun
which dispels darkness and gives light.

'It matters not
if I am thought of
in virtue's context,
or cited in the course of talk;
may I ever, in every way,
do good to the world
and bring it joy.'

Having thus made up his mind, and delighted at helping
another, even with his life, the Bodhisattva discarded his body

to the amazement of even the calm minds of the gods. At the sound of it falling down, the tigress cut short her effort to kill her cubs. Curious and annoyed, she looked in that direction and, seeing the sage's lifeless corpse, she pounced upon it, and began to devour it straightaway.

Meanwhile the disciple had returned without finding any meat. He looked for his teacher, and beheld the tigress devouring the Bodhisattva's lifeless body. His grief and sorrow at the sight were overshadowed by his wonder at the deed which had caused it. As was appropriate, he gave expression to his great respect for the sage's virtues:

> 'Behold this noble soul's compassion
> for the suffering, and indifference
> to his own comfort. He has exalted
> the good, and done down the wicked.

> 'Behold his fearless prowess,
> his love, supremely virtuous,
> his body, full of merits,
> now venerable all the more.

> 'Gentle, and patient as the earth,
> he could not bear to see the pain
> of others; his valorous feat
> lights up, alas, my frailty.

> 'The world now has him as Protector,
> we should not grieve at this:
> Mara sighs today for certain,
> fearful of defeat.

'All homage to that noble refuge for all creatures,' said the disciple, 'the immensely compassionate, the Bodhisattva for the sake of all beings.' And he reported the incident to his fellow disciples. They, and all the heavenly beings, marvelled at the Bodhisattva's deed. The ground, where lay the treasure of his bones, was covered by them with a shower of garlands, scarves, ornaments and sandalwood powder.

One should, accordingly, have the utmost faith in the Lord Buddha, for, even in his previous births, the Lord had immense affection for all creatures, and considered all things as himself. And one should rejoice at having faith in the Lord, as this will make it more firm.

One should also pay respectful attention to dharma, which has been brought to us through hundreds of hardships. As for compassion, one should remember that it engenders the inclination to help others and builds up excellence of character.

2

The Shibi King

HEARKEN WITH RESPECT TO THE BLESSED DHARMA, WHICH the Lord brought here for our sake through hundreds of hardships. Thus has it been heard:

At the time when the Lord was still a Bodhisattva, because of the merits he had accumulated by a long discipline, he once became the king of the Shibis.

From childhood itself, the king was modest and given to honouring his elders. The people loved him. Intelligent by nature, he had broadened his mind by learning many sciences. Endowed by fortune with the royal attributes of energy, discretion and majesty, he looked after his subjects like his own children.

The king possessed all the qualities needed to pursue the three human ends of virtue, wealth and pleasure. Glory, which is a mockery in the arrogant, a calamity in the foolish, and a heady wine for small minds, was for him no more than a name. What pleased this noble, kind and wealthy monarch was to look at the beaming faces of mendicants when they received what they sought.

The king delighted in charity. He had alms halls equipped with cash, grain and all other perquisites built throughout the city, and showered gifts on seekers like the rainclouds of the Golden Age. In keeping with the nobility of his mind, his almsgiving was purposeful, courteous and timely. There was food for the hungry and drink for the thirsty. There were couches and seats, garments and meals, perfumes and garlands, silver and gold, for those who sought any of these. People marvelled and rejoiced on hearing of the king's munificence, and came to his country from various places. They came happily, like wild elephants to a great lake, for they had not found such scope for their entreaties anywhere else. They came from all directions, pleased at the prospect of some gain.

These mendicants came in the unkempt garb of travellers. The king, however, received them as if they were friends returning from exile. His eyes widened with joy on seeing them, and their words of entreaty gave him immense pleasure. His satisfaction in giving surpassed theirs in receiving. And these recipients spread the fame of his charity, so that it overshadowed the pride of other kings, just as the scented elephant's[1] odour does the spoor of other elephants.

Once, while touring the alms halls, the king observed that the supplicants had decreased in number as their wants were fulfilled. This gave him no satisfaction, for it restricted his charitable work. The fact was that no request exceeded his disposition to give; while the supplicants were satiated on meeting him, he remained athirst to do even more charity.

When the earth came to know the king's generous thought on giving – that he did not care even for his own limbs – it trembled like a woman who loves her husband. The tremor shook Sumeru, the lord of mountains, who glitters with the glow of numerous gemstones. 'What is this?' wondered Shakra, the king of the gods. On realizing that it was the king's extraordinary thought which had caused the earth to quake, Shakra marvelled greatly. 'Has the king thought thus in the exuberance of his great joy at giving,' he said to himself, 'or has he bound himself to charity with the firm resolve of giving away his own limbs? Well, I will test him.'

On the following day, the king was seated in the assembly, surrounded by his ministers. The usual proclamation had been made, summoning the supplicants to declare what they sought. Stores of gems, gold, silver and cash in the treasurer's care had been opened. Boxes filled with all kinds of cloth had been unsealed. A variety of fine carriages had been brought out, with different kinds of well-trained draught animals harnessed to them. Hosts of supplicants had begun to arrive. Among them was Shakra, the lord of the gods, who appeared before the king in the guise of an old and blind brahmin.

The king's gaze was steady, pleasant and gentle. Filled with friendliness and compassion, it seemed to welcome the new arrival with an embrace. 'What do you wish for?' the royal attendants asked the brahmin. He approached the king, gave a benediction, and said:

'Old and blind, O best of monarchs,
I come from far to supplicate
for one of your eyes, O lotus-eyed king,
as even one is adequate
for completing this life's jounrey.'

The king was overjoyed at the prospect of his heart's desire being realized. But he wondered if the brahmin had actually made the request, or if he had imagined it because of his constant preoccupation with the thought. Anxious to hear the pleasing words again, he asked the supplicant:

> 'Who has sent you, noble brahmin,
> to come to me and seek an eye?
> Giving it is very difficult,
> who expects that I will do it?'

The king's intent was understood by the lord of the gods, who stood there disguised as a brahmin. 'I have come here to beg you for an eye on the instruction of the lord Shakra,' he said. 'Fulfil his expectations and my hopes with this gift.'

The invocation of Shakra's name convinced the king that, by the god's favour, the brahmin would regain his eyesight in this way. 'I will fulfil the wish with which you have come here, brahmin,' he replied gladly, in words calm and clear. 'You want one eye from me. I will give you both. Then go wherever you please. Seeing you with these bright lotus-like eyes, people will wonder if you are the same person or someone else. They will marvel greatly as they recognize you.'

The king's ministers were agitated and distressed on realizing that he had decided to give his eyes away. 'Mercy, sire!' they expostulated. 'Too great a joy in charity has led you to overlook the adverse consequences of this misjudgement. You cannot donate your eyes like this. For the sake of one brahmin you cannot disregard all the rest of us, and let your subjects, who flourish in comfort, burn in a fire of grief.

'Give away money, the symbol of prosperity, brilliant gems, milch cows, carriages drawn by trained animals, or handsome rutting elephants. Give away houses fit for all seasons, brighter than autumn clouds and resonant with tinkling ankle bells. But not your own eyes, for you are the one eye of the world.'

'Moreover, great king,' the ministers added, 'how can the eyes of one person possibly be affixed to another? Even if this were possible through divine influence, why your eyes? Furthermore, sire, what will a poor man do with eyes which will reveal to him only the prosperity of others? It is better to give him money than to do something rash.'

The king replied to the ministers with soft and conciliatory words. 'Having declared a gift,' he said, 'to think of not giving it is to bind oneself again in the noose of cupidity which had earlier been broken. Who can be a greater sinner than the person who promises to give, but changes his mind out of miserliness? There is no atonement for one who encourages the supplicant's hopes with promises to give, but dispenses only harsh words of refusal.

'As for the question why this person does not get his eyesight back by divine influence alone,' the king continued, 'you should know that all effects need a cause for their accomplishment. Even providence needs a cause. Therefore you gentlemen should not obstruct my resolve to make this great gift.'

'Our submission, sire,' said the ministers, 'is that you may gift goods, grain and jewels, but not your eyes. In making it we are not tempting you into any impropriety.'

But the king persisted: 'One should give that which is solicited. A gift unwished for provides no pleasure. Of what use is water to someone who is drowning? So I will give him what he has asked for.'

The chief minister then spoke out. The king loved and trusted him most of all. Setting aside all formality out of affection for his master, he said to the king:

'O don't do that!
You have dominion which outrivals

Shakra's own prosperity.
To gain that, it needed, not a little
of penance and austerity.
With it, and with religious rituals,
you won fame and immortality!
Yet you are bent on spurning it:
what can be this policy,
and the aim with which you proffer
both your eyes in charity?

'Your sacrifices have assured you a place among the gods,'
the chief minister added. 'Your glory has spread to all the
quarters of the world. Your feet are radiant with the glow from
the crowns of vassal kings. What is it that you now wish to get
by giving away your eyes?'

'I am not doing this to gain an empire,' the king replied
courteously, 'nor heaven or salvation or even glory. My concern
is to be of help to the people. I wish therefore that the trouble
this man took in approaching me should not go waste.'

The king then had one of his eyes gradually taken out,
undamaged, in the manner prescribed by the surgeons. It was
bright and lovely, like the petal of a blue lotus blossom, and
he presented it with great gladness to the supplicating brahmin.
Shakra, on his part, performed a miracle whereby the king and
his court saw the eye established straightaway in its new abode.
Overjoyed to see the brahmin with one eye functioning, the
king gave him the second eye also.

The brahmin's visage was now complete with both eyes. The
king's looked lake a like of lotuses bereft of its blooms. But he
was pleased, though his citizens were not. In the city and in
the palace, the earth was wet with tears. As for Shakra, he was
both amazed and delighted to note the king's unshakable

resolve to attain perfect realization. 'What courage, fortitude and benevolence!' the god marvelled. 'I can hardly believe what has happened, though I have seen it with my own eyes. It is not right that this great man should suffer thus for long. I will try to tell him of some method for getting back his eyes.'

The wounds, where the king's eyes had been, healed in due course. The grief in the palace and the city also abated. One day the king sat by the lake in his garden, seeking to be alone. The lakeside trees were bent under the weight of their beautiful blossoms. Bees hummed in the soft, cool and scented breeze. As the king sat upon a couch, Shakra appeared before him.

'Who is there?' the king called out.

'I am Shakra, king of the gods,' Shakra replied. 'I have come to you.'

'Welcome,' said the king. 'I am at your disposal. What is the purpose of your visit?'

Addressed with such courtesy, Shakra said to the king: 'Choose a boon, royal sage! Ask for whatever you wish!'

The king was astonished. A giver, and unused to treading the mean path of supplication, he replied proudly: 'I have abundant wealth, Shakra, and a large and powerful army. But, being blind, I now wish only for death. I can no longer see the faces of those who importune me, their eyes brimming with pleasure and satisfaction when their wishes are fulfilled. That is why death is dear to me.'

'Give up such thoughts!' said Shakra. 'Only good people achieve a state like yours. But I would like to ask Your Majesty a question. You are in this situation because of your supplicants. Yet they remain close to your heart. Tell me frankly why this is so, and free yourself of this condition.'

'Why do you press me to praise myself, sir?' said the king. 'Listen, nevertheless, chief of the gods: if the entreaties of supplicants have always pleased me as if they were blessings, may one of my eyes be restored.'

The power of the king's veracity and accumulated merits was such that, as soon as he uttered these words, one eye reappeared on his face. It was like the petal of a blue lotus flower studded with a piece of sapphire. Delighted at this amazing occurrence, the king addressed Shakra once more: 'If I was happy to give both my eyes to the person who asked for one, may my second eye also return to me.' And, no sooner than he had spoken, his other eye also reappeared, as if rivalling the first.

> The earth then shook
> with all its mountains,
> the sea overflowed
> across its borders,
> while drums celestial
> rolled a constant,
> deep and pleasing beat.
> Then the sun shone
> pure, autumnal,
> and the sky turned
> clear and lovely,
> and from it fell,
> in whirling cascades,
> strange flowers tinged
> with sandal powder.
> Gods and nymphs,
> wide-eyed with wonder,
> came there then;
> a soft breeze blew,
> and gladness filled
> the hearts of people.

Supernatural beings praised the king's extraordinary deed. Full of joy and wonder, their auspicious voices were heard everywhere. 'Behold the purity of his heart!' they exclaimed. 'O what magnanimity and mercy! What indifference to his own comforts! We salute him for his valour and fortitude. With his eyesight restored, the world once again has a protector. His long accumulated store of merit is for certain infallible. He has indeed won a victory for dharma.'

'Well done! Well done!' said Shakra, adding his praise. 'The intent of your pure heart was not unknown to me. That is why I returned your eyes to you. They will now have the power of unimpeded vision for a hundred miles in all directions, transcending even mountains.' Having spoken thus, the king of the gods disappeared.

The king returned to his capital. The ministers followed him, their eyes wide and their hearts filled with wonder. The city was festive with flags and banners, and, as the people looked on, the brahmins welcomed him with benedictions and hosannas. Then, seated in the assembly hall, and surrounded by the ministers, the brahmins, the city elders and the country folk who had come to greet him, he taught them dharma on the basis of his own experience.

'I obtained these eyes with divine powers,' he said, 'because of the merit which accrues from charity. With them I can see for a hundred miles in all directions, even through mountains, and I can see things as clearly as if they were nearby. Considering all this, who can remain indifferent to satisfying supplicants with whatever he has?

'There is no method for man's advancement better than charity, born of compassion for others, and done with modesty. I gave away my human eyes and obtained divine eyesight in this life itself. Therefore, O Shibis, make your wealth meaningful by gifting or using it. This is the path for glory and happiness in this world as well as in the next.'

> Wealth is meaningless and mean,
> its worth is but in charity
> to help men on this worldly scene:
> and thus spent, it comes to be
> a treasure true which will endure;
> or it will perish, it is sure.

Hearken with respect to the blessed dharma, which the Lord brought here for our sake through hundreds of hardships. This story should be recounted to explain the Tathagata's[2] greatness and his abiding compassion, and to demonstrate the merits which hearing it yield in this world itself. Gathered with respect, these merits will bear delightful flowers of glory in this very life.

3

A Bit of Gruel

No GIFT GIVEN WITH A PURE HEART TO A WORTHY RECIPIENT IS
ever small, for its results are always great. Thus has it been
heard:

While he was a Bodhisattva, the Lord once became the ruler
of Koshala. As king he had energy, discretion, majesty and all
the other royal virtues in ample measure. But their splendour
was surpassed by that of his heaven-sent fortune. Adorned by
it, these virtues shone like moonbeams in an autumn sky.
Fortune also embraced the king's vassals like a mistress, while
spurning his foes, however proud. It did so as the vassals loved
the king, while his virtuous mind would not permit the
suppression of even his enemies.

One day the king remembered his previous birth. Greatly
moved, he distributed even more gifts in charity, which is the
primary source of happiness. He gave them to shramans and
brahmins, to beggars and the poor. He also cultivated good
conduct ceaselessly and observed the rules of fasting on holy
days. Desirous of attracting the people to a better life by
teaching them the power of good works, the king would further

recite with joy, both in the assembly and in his inner apartments, the following two verses:

> 'In former times we only heard
> that service to a holy sage,
> however small, was bound to yield
> results not unimportant.
> Now, behold the fruit immense
> of a saltless, dry and coarse,
> burnt-brown bit of gruel!

> 'This army, dark with elephants,
> with horses gay, and chariots;
> my sole and sovereign sway on earth;
> ample wealth, a noble spouse:
> see, all this glory is the fruit
> of just a bit of gruel!'

Though consumed with curiosity, the ministers, brahmin elders and leading citizens felt unable to ask the king why he recited these verses repeatedly. At last the queen herself became curious after hearing the constant recitation. 'O King,' she asked when an opportunity presented itself in the assembly, 'you always recite these verses as if with a heart full of gladness. But mine is filled with curiosity. If you think I deserve to know it, please tell me why you keep repeating these stanzas. It must be something public, for secrets are not talked about in this manner; and that is why I ask you.'

The king looked lovingly at the queen. 'You are not the only one moved by curiosity,' he said with a smile. 'All these ministers, too, are extremely curious when they hear my words without grasping their purport. And so is the whole city and the palace. Listen why I recite what I do:

'Like someone who wakes up from a sleep, I have remembered my former birth and life. I was then a labourer in this very city. Though of good character, I was very poor. I eked a meager livelihood by working on hire for people who had risen high only because they had money.

'Insults, fatigue and dejection were part of my work. Yet I was afraid of losing it, as I had a family to support. One day, as I was about to go to work, I saw four monks seeking alms. They had subdued their senses, so that the glory of monastic life itself trailed behind them.

'Saluting them with a heart full of faith, I humbly offered them some gruel, which was all that there was at home. It is because of that gift that the glow of other kings' crowns today lights up the dust at my feet. Thinking of this, my lady, I recite what you have heard. To do good works and to meet holy Arhats[1] is now most satisfying to me.'

The queen's eyes widened with wonder and delight. Looking at the king with great respect, she said to him: 'Good works should indeed yield such results. Your Majesty esteems such works because you have seen their fruit with your own eyes. That is why you are opposed to evil deeds, disposed to earning merit, and given to looking after your people like a father. You shine in the glorious fame of your great charities. Rival kings remain under your sway. With your righteous policies, may you long protect this earth girt by the wind-swept sea.'

'And why not, my lady!' replied the king. 'I will make every effort to remain on the blessed path, the pleasant signposts of which I have already seen. People wish to give after having heard about the fruit of charity. I have experienced them myself. So how can I not give?'

Looking tenderly at the queen, the king observed that she was radiant with an almost divine splendour. Wishing to know the reason, he asked her: 'You stand out among womenfolk like the crescent moon among the stars. Tell me, my dear, what did you do to obtain this sweet result?'

'My lord,' said the queen, 'I too remember something from my former birth and life!

'I remember it as an experience from my childhood,' the queen continued on the king's repeated urging. 'I was a servant girl, and I humbly gave a portion of rice to a sage whose mind had been stilled. Then I went to sleep, and woke up here. This is the good deed I remember, Your Majesty, and by it I have gained the earth and a husband like you. You say that nothing done for a person with passions stilled can ever be inconsequential, and this is exactly what the sage also said.'

The assembled courtiers marvelled at this conversation, which demonstrated the results of meritorious actions. Perceiving that it had gladdened and impressed them with regard for good deeds, the king addressed them briefly:

'Having seen the immense results of even a little work of piety,' he said, 'who indeed will not apply himself to such works through charity and good conduct? A person who has sufficient money, but foregoes the glory of charity because miserliness clouds his mind, is not even worth looking at.

'Wealth is of no use, for, like it or not, it has to eventually go. If one can gain some merit by giving it up in the proper way, who will follow the path of selfishness, especially if he knows the benefits of virtue? For happiness, fame and many other benefits are to be found in charity.

'Charity is a great treasure which always abides with us. Thieves and the like cannot take it away. It clears the mind of the dirt of greed and selfishness. It is a vehicle which relieves with comfort the fatigue of life's journey. It is an intimate friend who provides all kinds of pleasure.

'Abundant wealth or brilliant dominion, physical splendour or residence with the gods, all that one can wish for may be attained through charity. Knowing these benefits, who will not give?

'Charity is said to be at the root of riches and dominion. It is the piety of the prosperous. But even a rag given by the lowly in charity is a gift to be commended.'

The king's persuasive words were greeted with great respect in the assembly. All those present were inspired to engage in charity. Thus it is, that nothing gifted with a heart full of faith to a worthy recipient can ever be considered small, for its results are always immense. With a happy mind should one give gifts to the noble sangha, and obtain great joy, thinking that a similar or even greater fortune will accrue to one before long.

4

The Merchant Prince

THE GOOD EVEN DISREGARD DANGERS IN WISHING TO GIVE for charity. Who indeed should not then give if it is safe to do so? Thus has it been heard:

When he was a Bodhisattva, the Lord was once born as a merchant prince. Virtuous effort and fortune's favour earned him great wealth. Fair dealings and good character secured him deep respect among the people. He had been born in a noble family, and had burnished his mind by learning numerous sciences and skills. The king also honoured him for all his qualities.

The merchant prince was charitable by nature. Delighted supplicants praised him everywhere by name. His fame spread in all directions, exalted by his heroic deeds of charity. No mendicant had any doubt whether he would give or not. All importuned him boldly, as his good deeds were well known. He had not accumulated wealth for his personal pleasure, nor out of avarice or any rivalry with others. He just could not bear to see the sufferings of those who supplicated him, and was unable to refuse them.

Once it was time for the great man's dinner. Bathed and anointed, he had been served a variety of dishes prepared by highly skilled cooks. At that moment a mendicant seeking alms approached his house. It was a Pratyeka Buddha.[1] All his sufferings had been burnt away in the fire of wisdom.

Desirous of increasing the merchant prince's store of merits, the Pratyeka Buddha came and stood at his door. Calm and gentle, he stood there quietly. Without any apprehension or agitation, he stood there with his eyes downcast, gazing at the ground no further than a yoke's length, a begging bowl in his hand.

The perfection of the prince's charity was intolerable for Mara,[2] the evil one. In order to obstruct it, he created a hell between the threshold of the gate and the point where the venerable mendicant stood. This was a frightful abyss many fathoms deep, full of fierce leaping flames and dreadful sounds. Terrible to behold, it was filled with hundreds of people writhing in agony.

Observing that a Pratyeka Buddha had arrived as a seeker for alms, the prince said to his wife: 'My dear, please go yourself and give sufficient alms to the noble one.' 'Very well,' she replied and proceeded with all kinds of food offerings to the gate. But there she saw the hell beneath the wall, and turned back suddenly, her eyes filled with fear and distress. Her husband asked what the matter was, and she told him what she had seen.

'How can the noble one go away from my house without receiving alms?' the prince said to himself with some agitation. Anxious to give alms to the great soul, he disregarded what his wife had recounted, and himself went out with the food offerings. Near the gate he too beheld the most fearful hell in between.

'What could this be?' the merchant prince wondered. And when this thought crossed his mind, Mara emerged in front of him, displaying his marvellous celestial form as he flew up into the sky. 'O master of the house!' he said, speaking like a well-wisher, 'this is the hell named Maharaurava – the most terrible. It is the place for those who wish to give away their wealth out of addiction to charity and greed for words of praise from supplicants. They have to stay here for many thousands of years, for it is difficult to escape from this place.

'Of virtue, wealth and pleasure, the three goals of human endeavour,' Mara continued, 'wealth is the prerequisite. To destroy it is the same as destroying virtue. How can anyone who destroys virtue in this way not end up in hell?

'You have sinned by destroying wealth in pursuit of charity,' Mara added. 'That is why this hell has appeared here to devour you with its flame-tongued mouth. It is better that you turn your mind away from charity, so that you do not hurtle down and join all those other almsgivers who writhe and weep so piteously. Those who receive alms, on the other hand, are freed of the error of giving wealth away, and obtain a place in heaven. You too should exercise restraint and give up these efforts at charity which block the path to paradise.'

'This wicked one is indeed trying to put obstacles in my work of charity!' the prince said to himself. Then, without departing from courtesy and cordiality in keeping with his true nature, he gave a firm reply.

'It is out of kindness and concern for my welfare, that Your Honour has pointed out this noble path to me,' said the prince. 'This disposition for compassion towards others is particularly appropriate for divine beings like yourself.

'But it is better to treat an ailment before or just after its appearance. If faulty treatment has already made it incurable, further efforts to remedy it can only be destructive. I suspect that my addiction to charity is past cure. That is why I am unable to give it up inspite of your well-meant advice.

'You say that wealth is a prerequisite of virtue, and giving it away in charity is therefore unrighteous. But my small human mind cannot understand how wealth without charity can lead to virtue. For, if wealth is just stored, it can be stolen by thieves or be lost by flood or fire.

'And when you try to restrain me by saying that givers go to hell and recipients to heaven, it only strengthens my efforts to give more. May your words not be in vain, and may my supplicants indeed go to heaven! For, you must know that I give for the welfare of others, and not to seek any pleasure for myself.'

Then Mara addressed the merchant prince once again. 'It is for you to consider,' he said, 'if my words are meant for your benefit or are just idle talk. Then do as you wish. But, happy or regretful, you will remember me with respect.'

'Your pardon, sir!' the prince exclaimed,

> 'Most willingly do I descend
> into this hell, fiercely blazing,
> its flames licking my lowered head,
> rather than neglect a beggar
> whose entreaties show his love,
> and it is time to honour him.'

Speaking thus, the prince fearlessly stepped into that hell. He relied on the power of his own fate, knowing that charity can never be evil. Nor did he heed his family and attendants who tried to stop him, for his wish to give had become even stronger.

> Then, by the power of his merit,
> there sprang up in that waterless
> hell a lovely lotus flower
> whose bright rows of stamen teeth
> seemed to mock the wicked Mara.

The prince stepped on the lotus blossom born of his merits, and went up to the Pratyeka Buddha to whom he gave alms with a heart full of faith and joy. The holy monk manifested his own satisfaction by rising up into the air, where he shone like a cloud radiant with lightning. As for Mara, his hopes were dashed. Crestfallen and dejected, he promptly disappeared, together with his hell.

Thus it follows that the good even disregard dangers in wishing to give for charity. Even fear cannot make them take the wrong path. Who indeed should not then give if it is safe to do so?

5

The Unconquerable

NEITHER THE HOPE OF WEALTH NOR CONCERN THAT IT MAY BE
lost will turn good people away from charity. Thus has it been
heard:

As a Bodhisattva, the Lord was once a merchant prince of
good family. He had many virtues. He was liberal and honest,
humble and modest, learned and wise. In affluence he was like
Kubera, the god of wealth. Hospitable to everyone and always
engaged in works of charity, he was devoted to the public good
and a most excellent almsgiver. As he never succumbed to
selfishness and other vices, he was well known by the name
Avishahya or the Unconquerable.

Both he and his supplicants delighted in meeting each other.
Neither had any doubt that their wishes would be fulfilled. He
could never refuse a supplicant, for compassion left no room
in his heart for clinging to wealth. Knowing wealth to be a cause
of great calamities, and liable to perish, he was overjoyed when
supplicants took it away from his house.

Shakra, the king of the gods, was amazed to hear of his
generosity and charity. Wishing to test the firmness of his

resolve, the celestial ruler caused some of Avishahya's reserves of bullion and grain, jewellery and apparel to disappear every day. Concern at the depletion of his wealth, Shakra thought, may tempt the merchant prince to be selfish. But the great man was committed to giving alms. No sooner than his goods vanished like drops of water drying in the sunlight, did he bring out even more for gifting, almost as if his house were on fire.

Shakra's astonishment continued to increase as the merchant prince remained intent on charity despite the erosion of his assets. At last, one night, the king of the gods caused all of Avishahya's wealth to disappear, but for a single sickle and a coil of rope.

Next morning, on waking up as usual, Avishahya beheld his mansion, emptied of all its contents. There was no money, food or apparel, nor any servants. The house was a melancholic sight, silent and desolate, as if it had been ravaged by demons. He went around it, wondering how this could have happened, and found that only a sickle and a coil of rope remained.

'Has someone, used to earning a livelihood by his own efforts, and unaccustomed to begging, thus shown favour to my house?' he wondered. 'If so, my wealth has merely been put to good use. But if, instead of being utilized, it has simply been destroyed by someone who could not bear to see me flourish, it is then my bad luck and a great pity. I always knew that fortune is fickle, but what pains me is the trouble this will cause to my supplicants. Long used to the ease of courteous charity, they will be like thirsty travellers at a lake gone dry.'

But Avishahya's calm composure left no time for dejection and distress. Himself unused to begging, he could not bear to solicit others in his present condition, not even those whom he knew well. He understood how hard this could be, and it increased his compassion for supplicants even further. In order to welcome them suitably, he took the rope and sickle in hand, and would every day gather grass, by selling which he could earn something for attending to those who came to him for alms.

Shakra observed that, even in absolute poverty, this great man did not give way to despair but remained intent on charity. Filled with wonder and admiration, the king of the gods then appeared in the sky in his marvellous celestial form in order to dissuade Avishahiya from giving alms.

'Master of the house,' said Shakra, 'your wealth has not been taken away by bandits or kings, nor lost by fire or flood. It is because of your excessive charity that you are in your present state, so distressing to your friends.

'Therefore I say to you for your own good: curb this addiction to charity. If you do so, even in your present condition, you will regain your former prosperity and splendour. Constant expenditure, even though in small measure, leads over time to the depletion of what has been earned. Accumulation, on the other hand, makes it grow like an ant hill. In view of this, discipline and restraint is the only way for those who wish to increase their wealth.'

But the prince extolled the practice of charity, and told Shakra:

'O Shakra of the thousand eyes!
Ignoble deeds are hard to do
for the noble, even though
they may be in dire straits.
Therefore, may I never have
such wealth, as for which I must be
a person who is miserly.

'Can a person, who is proud
of his family's honour, hurt
the sufferers who seek relief
from their lot of misery
in begging, which is hard as death,
with words of curt refusal, flung
like thunderbolts from cloudless skies?

'How can someone like myself
accept wealth, a horde of gems,
the rule even of paradise,
if they cannot help to brighten
the faces of my supplicants,
ashen with the pain of begging?

'Possession is a problem,
a disaster in disguise:
it increases selfishness
and not the generous spirit;
it deserves to be given up
by someone like myself.

'Fleeting as a lightning flash,
cause of many problems, and
a mean and petty thing is wealth.
But giving is a source of joy:
which noble one will ever seek
refuge therefore in selfishness?

'Shakra, you have shown your sympathy for me with your
words for my welfare,' Avishahya continued. 'I am gratified.
But my heart has got used to the joys of giving. How can it

be satisfied with a wrong path? Please do not be angry with me, for I have little strength to go against my own nature.'

'O master of the house,' replied Shakra, 'the course you describe is all right for someone who has a high position, sufficient wealth, and various large enterprises well under way; whose treasury and granary are full, and whose future is assured. It is not appropriate for one in your condition. Look, one should first gain wealth through honest work, either by using one's own wits or by following family traditions of good reputation. Thus is the splendour of rivals surpassed, honour gained even from the king, and fortune's much-desired favour won. From time to time one may attend to the people's welfare and hearten friends and relatives. Nobody will point a finger if one then goes in for charity or the pursuit of pleasure. But wishing to give without having the means only brings trouble, as with the nestling which wants to fly before its wings have grown.

'Therefore, restrain yourself and concentrate on earning wealth,' Shakra added. 'Meanwhile, put aside your desire to donate. There is nothing ignoble in not giving if you have no possession.'

'Do not insist so much, Your Majesty,' the prince responded.

> 'Even when one's self-interest
> seems greater than the good of others,
> one should forswear wealth, and give:
> for pleasures of prosperity,
> however sweet, cannot compare
> with the satisfaction which comes
> in vanquishing one's avarice
> and giving all in charity.

'Wealth alone leads not to heaven
nor cures such ills as venality;
giving earns both fame and merit,
so who will not do charity?

'One who, moved by compassion,
wants to save the world besieged
by age and death, is even willing
to give his very self for this;
and has no time to taste of pleasure
when others suffer: what will he
do with this prosperity?

'Moreover, O king of the gods,
Knowing that our life's duration,
like our wealth, is transient,
we should not care about our riches
when we meet a mendicant.

'When a chariot marks out a track on earth, another follows it, and the next one does the same with greater confidence. I am not inclined to spurn this good first road to follow a wrong path. If my wealth increases once again, it will certainly attract more supplicants. But, even in my present condition, I will give what I can. For, Shakra, may I never default in the practice of charity.'

Shakra, the king of the gods, was delighted at these words. Looking at Avishahya with great respect and affection, he praised him and said: 'Excellent! Most excellent! People seek affluence, even by disreputable, base and terrible actions, because they are obsessed with their own pleasures, seduced by fickle minds and careless of the dangers involved. But you did not care for the loss of your wealth and comforts, or even for my temptations. You displayed your inner greatness by your steadfastness in wishing to help others. How your heart shines with generosity! It has been cleansed of dark selfishness and, even though your wealth is gone, the hope of its recovery has not spoilt you by making you reluctant to give.

'I could no more shake your resolve for charity, than can the wind the snow-white mountain peak,' said Shakra. 'And it is not surprising: such is your compassion that you grieve in the grief of others and wish well to the whole world. I hid your wealth only to spread your fame through this ordeal. For, even a splendid gemstone cannot attain the reputation and value of a jewel without being tested. Now, like a great cloud which fills up lakes, rain down your charity on supplicants. And forgive me for what I did. By my favour your wealth will never deplete again.'

Having thus praised the prince, Shakra restored his wealth and disappeared. So it is, that neither the hope of riches nor concern that it may be lost turns good people away from charity.

6

The Hare

IT IS THE NATURE OF THOSE WHO ARE GOOD AND GREAT-SOULED
to give of whatever they can. This is to be seen even in beasts.
Should not a human being then be charitable? Thus has it
been heard:

There was a certain forest region which ascetics visited from
time to time. It was filled with delightful thickets of reeds, vines
and trees laden with flowers and fruit. A river adorned its
boundary, the waters pure and blue like turquoise. The ground
within was covered with a carpet of grass, pleasing to the touch
and beautiful to behold. In that place, the Bodhisattva was
once a hare.

The hare had a pure disposition. Small animals did not fear
him. Endowed with a handsome body, ample strength and great
energy, he wandered about the forest, unchallenged, like a king
of its denizens. With his own skin and fur for an ascetic's garb
of animal hide and tree bark, and with blades of grass to satisfy
his need for food, he lived there gloriously, like a sage. The
friendliness which suffused his every thought, word and deed,
made even wicked animals his friends and disciples.

The hare's loving kindness and many other virtues had in particular won the hearts of an otter, a jackal and a monkey, who became his constant companions. The four lived happily in the forest, like brothers whose love is based on mutual kinship. Unlike the usual nature of animals, they had ceased to be capricious and had forgotten how to steal. They sought repute and adhered steadfastly to the rules of righteous conduct. Even the gods marvelled at their virtuous activities.

One evening the hare sat with his companions who had come with great respect and reverence to hear him discourse on dharma. The newly risen moon was almost full. With the sun on the far horizon, it shone brightly like a silver mirror without a handle. Noticing that it was in the fourteenth day of its waxing phase, the hare said to his comrades: 'The moon seems to be smiling in its almost full beauty as it informs good people about the Poshadha festival. It is clear that tomorrow will be the day of the full moon. All of you should therefore observe the rules of Poshadha, and first honour any guest who comes on that day with some special and lawfully obtained food, before eating anything to sustain yourself.

'Look,' the hare continued, 'all meetings end in separation. Whatever goes up must come down. Life is as fleeting as a flash of lightning. Therefore one must always take care, and try to increase one's store of merit by charity adorned with character. For merit is the ultimate support for people caught up in the difficult cycle of existence.

'If the moon outdoes the lustre of the stars with its radiance, and, if the sun overwhelms other luminaries as it blazes, it is due to the virtues of merit. If proud princes and ministers bear humbly and happily, like well-trained horses, the yokes of their kings' commands, it is because of the power of meritorious deeds.

'And those who have not accumulated merit,' the hare added, 'are pursued by misfortune even if they stumble along the path of practical wisdom. Misfortune overtakes them, as if angry at having been spurned by those who have an abundance of merit. Therefore give up the path of sin, which leads to disrepute and misery, and apply your minds to gathering merit, the means to happiness and prosperity.'

'Very well,' said the companions on thus being admonished, and, after saluting and circumambulating their teacher, they departed for their homes. But the hare began to worry soon after they had left. 'If a guest arrives,' he said to himself, 'my other friends will have the ability to entertain him in one way or the other. I alone am in a pitiable condition. I can hardly offer a guest the bitter blades of grass which I bite off with my teeth. Alas for this helplessness! What is the point of living if, instead of being a matter of joy, the arrival of a guest becomes a cause for sorrow?

'This mean and worthless body is incapable of entertaining a guest,' the hare cogitated further. 'How should I dispose of it so that it benefits someone?' And then realization dawned upon him. 'But I do have something which is unexceptionable, easily available, within my power and fully suitable as a guest-offering,' he thought. 'It is my own body! Then, why should I worry? There is no need, O my heart, to feel sad and miserable. I have an excellent means of hospitability, and I will entertain who comes with this little body itself.'

Having made up his mind, the hare felt a deep contentment, as if he had secured some immense gain. As his heart opened itself to this flood of thought, the gods also manifested their pleasure and power. The sea-girt earth trembled, as if overjoyed. Divine trumpets sounded in the sky. The horizons shone bright and clear. Lightning laughed in the clouds, which rumbled softly and showered a rain of flowers. A mild breeze blew, laden with fragrant pollen from blossoming trees, and spread as if a silken canopy in happy reverence of the great soul. And the gods praised his marvellous resolution with amazement and joy.

But the mind of Shakra, the king of the gods, was filled with wonder and curiosity. Wishing to ascertain the hare's true intention, he assumed the form of a brahmin on the following day. It was at noon, when the sun was at its zenith and its rays at their sharpest. The forest reverberated with the shrill sound of cicadas, as shadows contracted and birds ceased to fly.

It was a time when heat and fatigue had sapped the energy of all travellers. Shakra appeared as a brahmin who had lost his way and was worn out with hunger, thirst and distress. He began to weep and wail loudly, not far from where the four animals lived. 'Help me, good people!' he cried. 'I have lost my companions, and wander alone in this dense forest. I am tired and famished. My sense of direction is confused. I cannot tell the right path from the wrong, nor say where I am headed, all by myself, in this wilderness. But I am miserable with the heat, thirst and fatigue. Will someone help me?'

His piteous cries shook the hearts of the four friends. They rushed out in alarm and, observing the sad state of the traveller gone astray, approached him politely with words of assurance. 'Do not think that you are lost in this forest,' they told him. 'With us, gentle sir, you are as if with your own disciples. Favour us, therefore, by accepting our hospitality today. Tomorrow you may go wherever you please.'

Taking the traveller's silence to indicate his acceptance of the invitation, the otter quickly produced seven rohit fishes. 'These seven,' he said, 'were either left behind by the fishermen, or they jumped on to the ground out of fear. I found them lying there as if they were tired and asleep. Please make a meal of them and stay here.'

The jackal too brought such food as he had procured. 'Here is an iguana, good traveller,' he said respectfully, 'and there is a pot of curd left behind by someone. Favour me by partaking of these, and stay in this forest.'

Then the monkey came forward with some ripe mangoes. They were soft and round, bright yellow in colour, as if painted with orpiment, and very red around the stalk-ends. Joining his hands together in a salutation, the monkey said: 'O best of seers, what I have is ripe mangoes, delightful water and cool shade, as pleasant as good company. Enjoy these and stay here.'

Finally, it was the turn of the hare. Approaching the traveller with all courtesy, and gazing at him with great respect, he invited the man to accept his own body. 'A hare grows up in the forest,' he said, 'and has neither lentil beans nor sesamum seeds or grains of rice to offer. But I have this body. Cook it on a fire and use it for a repast while you stay in this hermitage today.

'The arrival of a person in need is a festive occasion,' the hare added. 'One offers whatever one has to satisfy the visitor. I have nothing more than this body. Please accept it, for it is all that I have.'

'How can one like me kill someone else?' replied Shakra. 'Not to speak of someone like you, who have displayed such friendliness towards me.'

'What you say is entirely appropriate for a kind brahmin,' the hare responded. 'But sir, for the sake of doing me this favour, would you wait here while I look for some means for this favour to be done?'

Shakra, the lord of the gods, understood the hare's intent. He created a fire of burning coals, the colour of molten gold.

Smokeless, it was full of tiny flames scattering many sparks. The hare, who was searching everywhere, also saw this blaze. 'I have found the means for you to do me that favour,' he said happily. 'Now you can fulfil my hopes by making use of my body. Look, great brahmin, to have something to give, the wish to give it, and a guest like Your Honour – such a combination of opportunities is not easy to come by. Let it be fruitful with your support.'

With this request, the great-souled hare saluted his guest with all respect and courtesy. Then,

> He looked upon the flaming fire
> like one who spies a sudden treasure,
> and entered it with utmost joy,
> like a single swan which enters
> a lake abloom with smiling lilies.

The chief of the gods marvelled greatly at this sight. Resuming his own form, he showered celestial flowers on that great being and praised him in words which please both the ear and the mind. Taking him in his own divine hands, which had the lustre of lotus petals and sparkled with finger rings, Shakra displayed him to the other heavenly beings. 'O gods and denizens of paradise!' he exclaimed. 'Behold and rejoice at the wonderful and virtuous deed of this noble personage! How fearlessly and hospitably did he give up his body today! Those who are less steadfast tremble even at forsaking the remnants of a sacrificial offering. What a contrast it is, between his animal species and his generous charity and his keen awareness! He puts to shame, it is clear, all those who lack respect for meritorious action, both gods and men. How permeated is his mind with the practice of virtue! His love of righteousness has been proved by the magnanimity of his deed.'

In order to make this great deed known for the benefit of the world, Shakra adorned the spires of the excellent palace, Vaijayanta, and the celestial assembly hall, Sudharma, as well as the disc of the moon with an image of the hare.

> Even now, when the moon is full,
> the likeness of the hare appears
> on its disc, in heaven shining,
> like the image in a mirror.

And that is why the moon, which ornaments the nocturnal sky and makes night lilies bloom, is known in the world as Shashanka or 'Marked with the Hare'.

Having had such an auspicious friend, the otter, the jackal and the monkey also attained heaven after leaving the earth. Thus, it is seen that great beings give of whatever they can, even when they are animals. Should not a human being then be charitable?

7
The Hermit

COURAGE IN RENUNCIATION IS AN ORNAMENT EVEN OF HERMITS, what to say of householders. Thus has it been heard:

When the Lord was a Bodhisattva, and journeyed through the cycle of existence for the good of the world, he was once born in a great brahmin family, distinguished on earth by the purity of its conduct.

The birth shed lustre on the family, like the bright full moon of autumn does on the night sky. In due course the child underwent the natal and other sacraments ordained in the scriptures. He studied the Vedas with their supplementary texts, and all the sacred laws. The fame of his learning spread throughout the world of men. Receiving valuable gifts from donors who held virtue dear, he came to acquire great wealth and prosperity.

Like a great cloud which showers rain upon the land, the brahmin gladdened kinsfolk and friends, dependents and the poor, elders and honoured guests with his riches. The fame of his learning became even greater with his heroic charity. It shone like the moon which, with all its splendour, is more radiant in the pure air of autumn.

But the great soul understood that the householder's life gives no satisfaction. It is filled with illusions, and is fraught with the infirmities of association with evil actions. Always distracted by the acquisition and the safeguarding of wealth, it is the opposite of peaceful. A target for the arrows of a hundred problems, it is, moreover, accompanied by ceaseless toil and fatigue. The life of the renunciant, he saw on the other hand, is free of these faults and consequently happy. It is also suited to the practice of dharma, and a proper basis for commencing it for the attainment of salvation.

So he cast aside, like so much straw, the great wealth he had effortlessly acquired. He gave it up despite its charm as a means for public respect, and devoted himself to the discipline and the rules of penance and renunciation. But his fame did not fade, and those who sought salvation continued to come to him as before.

However, he considered association with householders to detract from the joy of detachment and an impediment in breaking free from worldly bonds. Seeking the bliss of solitude, he therefore repaired to the island of Kara in the southern sea. Sapphire-blue waves played upon its windswept beaches of white sand, and the terrain was beautiful with trees full of flowers, fruit and new leaves. Near the shore there was a lake of pure water. In this spot he established his seat, embellishing it with a hermitage. His ascetic body, emaciated with austerities, gleamed like the new moon in the sky, whose radiance is no less for being a crescent. Thus did he live in the forest, absorbed in his vows and observances. His senses were calm and tranquil. Even the birds and the beasts, whose intellects are limited, realized that he was a sage and emulated his example.

The great soul was habituated to giving alms. Despite living in a forest, he would honour any guests who happened to come there with the roots and fruit he had gathered, with fresh water and hearty words of welcome, and with kindly blessings appropriate to ascetics. He himself lived on the remnants of the forest food left over by the guests, limiting his diet to a quantity no more than sufficient for his sustenance.

The spreading fame of his powerful penance shook Shakra, the king of the gods. Wishing to test the sage's fortitude, Shakra caused all the roots and fruit in that forest suitable for feeding ascetics to disappear. The sage, on his part, gave no thought to why they had vanished. His mind was engaged in meditation. Always content but never insensible, he was indifferent to his body and food. Boiling young leaves of plants, he used them for his meals, and went about as calmly as before, without any craving or eagerness for better food.

> Living is nowhere difficult
> for those who are contented:
> where indeed is there a lack
> of leaves and grass and water?

Increasingly amazed by this situation, Shakra, the king of the gods, concluded that the hermit was much more steadfast than he had thought. In order to test him further, he stripped all the creepers and trees in that forest region of their leaves, as if with a summer wind. But the sage was not disquieted. He gathered the fallen leaves and subsisted on them after cooking them in water. His mind was content with the bliss of mediation, and he went about like one satiated with nectar:

> In ascetics, contentment
> gives glory to their merits,
> as in the wise, humility,
> and in the rich, liberality.

The extraordinary constancy of the hermit's contentment astonished Shakra even more. He then appeared before the sage in the guise of an angry brahmin. It was during the great man's devotions. He had just finished his prayers, offered the libation into the sacred fire, and was looking around to see if there were any visitors, when Shakra materialized as a guest.

The hermit received him with a glad heart. Welcoming him cordially, he told Shakra that it was time for a meal and extended him an invitation. Taking the latter's silence to mean acceptance, the sage's face lit up with pleasure, and, greeting him once again with kind words, he offered Shakra all the boiled leaves he had collected with so much trouble. As for himself, the joy of giving was enough to satisfy him. Returning thereafter to his meditation room, he passed the rest of the day and the night with the same gladness and delight.

On the following day Shakra once more appeared at the time of the hermit prayers, and yet again on the third, fourth and fifth days. On each occasion he was entertained similarly, but with even greater joy. For the longing of good people to give increases with the practice of compassion; it does not decline even in deadly distress.

Shakra was now wonderstruck. He also became uneasy and afraid that the power of the hermit's penance could secure him sovereignty over heaven, merely by asking. Resuming his marvellous divine form, Shakra then questioned the sage about the purpose of his austerities. 'What are you hoping for,' he asked, 'that you have left your kin and tearful loved ones, given up the delights of your possessions, and taken to this painful penance? Wise people do not abandon grieving relatives and easy-to-come-by pleasures, and resort to comfortless penance groves for paltry reasons. What is it that has got into your mind and enslaved it so? Please tell me if you consider me worthy, and dispel my curiosity.'

'Listen, sir,' the hermit replied, 'this is the purpose of my efforts: It is extremely painful to be born again and again, and suffer the calamities of old age, illness and decrepitude. The mind is agitated by the thought that one has to die. I have therefore resolved to save people from these agonies.'

'He does not seek my sovereignty,' thought Shakra, feeling reassured. He was also pleased by the sage's well-said words. Praising them as appropriate, the king of the gods invited him to accept a boon. 'These words of yours, ascetic, are right and well-said,' he told the sage. 'I grant you a boon, O Kashyapa.[1] Ask for whatever you desire.'

The hermit was contentment personified. Indifferent to worldly pleasures, he considered even the act of asking for anything to be painful. 'O first of the gods,' he replied, 'if you wish to favour me by giving me a boon, then this is what I choose:

> That fire of greed, which burns up man,
> and is never satisfied,
> even after he acquires
> power, riches more than dreamt of,
> wives and children, long desired:
> may it never touch my heart.'

Shakra was even more pleased with these well-said words which displayed a mind inclined to contentment. 'Excellent! Excellent!' he exclaimed, praising the hermit as he again requested him to accept a boon. 'These words of yours are also commendable O sage!' he cried. 'In return I am glad to grant you another boon.'

In the guise of asking for a boon, the Bodhisattva then preached dharma to the king of the gods. He pointed out how difficult it is to get rid of the evil passions which afflict man. 'O Vasava, abode of virtue!' he said, 'O king of the gods, if you will give me a boon, then I ask for another small one:

> The fire of hatred, by which men
> are overcome as if by a foe,
> and deprived of happiness,
> of status, fame and even wealth:
> from me, may it stay far away.'

The lord of the gods marvelled on hearing these words. 'Excellent! Excellent!' he cried in wonder. 'Rightly does fame attend upon renunciants like a woman in love. For these well-said words, too, accept a boon from me.'

In the guise of accepting a boon, the hermit now criticized association with those afflicted by passions, for he was opposed to such afflictions. 'May I never have to hear a fool, nor to see or to talk to one, or to suffer staying with one,' he said. 'This is what I ask of you.'

'Those who are in distress are specially deserving of good people's sympathy,' responded Shakra. 'And foolishness, being at the root of distress, is the worst of all conditions. Thus the fool is to be pitied in particular. How can you, who are so compassionate, not even wish to see one?'

'If it were possible to cure a fool,' the sage replied, 'would someone like me make no effort for his benefit? You must understand that he is just not suited for a cure. He follows wrong ways as if they were the right ones, and wants to put even others on them. Unused to modest and straightforward behaviour, he gets angry if he is told something even for his own good. He is consumed by the illusion that he is learned. He is harsh and irascible, even towards those who wish him well. And he is violent in the absence of good manners. Tell me, is there any way of doing good to him? It is because there is none, O best of gods, that even those who are compassionate do not wish to see a fool. He is so unsuitable!'

Shakra was again pleased to hear these words and said: 'For your priceless words I grant you another boon, as gladly as I would offer you a tribute of flowers.'

Pointing out that good people are delightful in all circumstances, the sage then said: 'May I see one who is wise, Shakra, hear him, stay and converse with him. Grant me this boon, O first of the gods.'

'You seem to be very partial to wise people,' observed Shakra. 'Tell me, what have they done for you? What is the reason, Kashyapa, that you appear so eager to meet someone wise?'

The sage replied, pointing to the nobility of good people: 'My heart longs only to meet someone wise because such a person himself treads the path of virtue and also leads others to it. Even harsh words meant for his benefit do not agitate him. He is adorned with sincerity and humility, and it is always possible to have him accept what is to his good. My mind is partial to merit, and so I am inclined towards the meritorious.'

'Excellent!' cried Shakra, pleased even more than before. And, praising the sage, he invited him once again to accept a boon. 'As you are contentment personified,' he said, 'for sure you already have everything. Yet accept a boon. Consider you are doing me a favour by accepting. If a token of love, offered with all devotion and ability with the intention of doing some good, is not accepted it is extremely painful.'

The sage perceived Shakra's strong desire to be of help. Wishing him well, and demonstrating the potency of the wish to give, the sage told him: 'May I have your inexhaustible stocks of food, your tender mind intent on charity and your supplicants of pure character. This is the boon I choose.'

'You are an ocean of well-said words!' cried Shakra. 'All that you have asked for will come to be exactly. I grant you a boon once again.'

'Foremost of all gods!' the Bodhisattva replied, 'if you grant me the great favour of another boon, this is what I choose: O slayer of demons, do not come to me again with such blazing splendour.'

'Do not speak like this, sir,' retorted Shakra, annoyed as well as amazed. 'People seek to see me with prayers and vows, with the rituals of sacrifice and the exertions of penance. I have come here wishing to give you a boon, and you do not want to see me! What is the reason, sir?'

'Do not be angry, king of the gods,' the sage replied. 'Please let me explain. It is not for lack of courtesy, or out of irreverence towards you, that I spoke thus. Your marvellous divine form, though it shines gently, still blazes with splendour. I am afraid that, in beholding even its kindly glow, I may lose sight of my penance.'

Shakra then saluted and circumambulated the hermit, and disappeared forthwith. His power produced an abundance of divine food and drink which the sage saw next morning. He also beheld hundreds of Pratyeka Buddhas invited there by Shakra, as well as many celestial pageboys girded to wait upon them. The sage was delighted to satisfy these holy personages with food and drink, and himself remained content with the diet, meditation and tranquillity appropriate to ascetics.

Courage in renunciation is thus an ornament even of hermits, what to say of householders. The virtuous man should adorn himself with it, and it should be highlighted in giving cheer to the charitable; in censuring greed and hatred, delusion and folly; and in commending association and friendship with good people.

8

King Maitribala

THOSE WHOSE COMPASSION IS TRULY GREAT DO NOT CARE FOR their own pleasures. They suffer in the sufferings of others. Thus has it been heard:

The Bodhisattva was once a king named Maitribala. His glory lay in compassion, and his mind was filled with friendliness for all creatures. Intent on protecting the world, he was endowed in full with charity and self-control, restraint, tenderness and similar virtues which benefit the people.

King Maitribala guarded his subjects with skill. He felt their weal and their woes as his own, both in wielding the sword and in applying the law. His sword was more of an ornament, for other rulers obeyed his orders with respect; but his application of the law was manifest in the measures he took for promoting the people's welfare. He supervised them like a wise and benevolent father, and dispensed rewards and punishments without infringing the rules of righteousness.

Thus did Maitribala rule, taking care of his subjects with truth and liberality, wisdom and patience, increasing with many noble deeds his own store of the merit needed for achieving enlightenment. Once five yakshas[1] came into his kingdom. They had been exiled by the yaksha ruler from his dominion for some offence. They were proficient in killing other people by consuming their vigour and life force.

The yakshas noticed that there was no distress in Maitribala's kingdom. Some festival or the other was always taking place there. The land was prosperous. The people were happy, healthy and content. The visitors wanted to plunder them of their vigour but, despite the utmost effort, did not succeed. For the king's power was so great that his very intent of protecting the people was sufficient to do so.

Unable to rob the life force of any inhabitant of the land inspite of all their efforts, the yakshas consulted each other. 'What is this?' they wondered. 'These people do not have any special knowledge, religious merit or other attainments which can counter our powers. Yet all our attempts have been in vain so far.' They then decided to disguise themselves as brahmins and scout the country.

In a wooded area they saw a cowherd sitting on a patch of grass in the shade of a tree. He wore shoes on his feet and a circlet of wild flowers and fresh leaves on his head. An axe and a staff lay to his right as he sat by himself, twining a rope and singing lustily. 'O-o-o-,' the yakshas stuttered[2] as they approached him. 'O guardian of cows, aren't you afraid to stay all alone in this desolate forest?'

'What should I be afraid of?' asked the cowherd, looking at the visitors. 'Haven't you heard of the fierce nature of yakshas, ogres and ghouls?' they replied. 'Even people who are surrounded by attendants, endowed with learning and religious merit, and equipped with lucky charms, no matter how brave and fearless they might be, can barely escape these creatures who feed on the flesh and fat of men. How is it that you are not scared of them in this lonely, dense and fearful forest?'

'The people here are protected by a great talisman,' the cowherd responded with a laugh. 'Even the king of the gods cannot harm them, what to say of these flesh-eaters. That is why I can go about without any fear: in the forest as at home, at night as during daytime, irrespective of being alone or in a crowd.'

The yakshas became very curious. 'Tell us! Tell us, gentle sir,' they asked respectfully, so as to encourage the cowherd, 'what is this special talisman of yours?'

'Listen,' he replied, laughing, 'this is what our most wonderful and excellent talisman is like: his chest is as broad as the rock of the golden mountain; his face is as radiant as the bright autumn moon; his arms are long and thick, like great bars of gold; and his gaze and gait are majestic, like those of a bull. Such is our mighty talisman, our king.'

Having said this, the cowherd cast a look of indignant surprise at the yakshas. 'It is amazing,' he cried, 'that you have not heard of our king's power which is so well known! Maybe you could not believe what you heard, because it is so marvellous. I wonder if the people, from where you come, are not too confused or indifferent to understand what merit is about. Perhaps they are just unlucky in having remained ignorant of our king's renown. At any rate you still have some luck in coming here from that wild country.'

'Most gentle sir,' asked the yakshas, 'tell us how the king has such power that these supernatural beings are unable to harm the people here.'

'Our great king's power derives from his own nobility,' said the cowherd. 'Look, distinguished brahmins, friendship is his strength. His army with its colourful banners is there only to comply with custom. He knows no anger, does not speak harshly and protects the land properly. Dharma guides his policy, not base politics. His wealth is used to honour the virtuous. He does not depend on the affluence and pride of the wicked. Our wonderful lord has hundreds of other similar merits. Because of them no mishap can harm his subjects. What more can I tell you? If you are interested to know about the king's virtues, it is better that Your Honours go to the city, where you can estimate their extent.

'In the city,' the cowherd continued, 'Your Honours will see how people maintain social order through devotion to their respective duties. Constant security and plenty has made them happy and prosperous. They are polite, well dressed and specially kind to any guests who may come. They adore the virtues of their king, and sing his praises with joy, as if they were reciting some auspicious prayer. You too will come to respect his qualities and are bound to want to see them with your own eyes.'

The yakshas were already resentful of the king as their designs had been thwarted. The well-intentioned and appropriate account of his virtues did nothing to soften their hearts, and they wished even more to harm the king. Having learnt of his love of charity, they went to him at the time of his public audience, and begged for a meal.

The king was delighted. 'Quickly give these brahmins a meal of their choice,' he ordered the men in charge. But, though the repast they were presented with was fit for a monarch, the yakshas accepted it no more than tigers take grass. 'We do not eat such food,' they said. Hearing this, the king came to them. 'What kind of food will suit you all?' he asked. 'O lotus-eyed ruler!' they replied. 'O monarch whose vows are never broken! The food and drink of yakshas is freshly cut human flesh and warm human blood!' And they assumed their own terrible forms, hideous with dreadful fanged mouths, fierce yellow gleaming squint eyes, and ugly flat noses with gaping nostrils. Their hair and whiskers had the colour of fiery flames, and their bodies were as dark as rainclouds.

The king looked at them carefully. 'These are ghouls, not men,' he concluded. 'Obviously they do not care for what we eat and drink. The food they want is most detestable.

'These yakshas are wicked and pitiless in adhering to such a diet,' the king thought further. 'But they harm their own interests thereby every day. When will their miseries end? And how can I procure such food for them, even once, by killing or doing violence to others? At the same time, I do not recall having ever refused suppliants, making their faces wilt like lotus flowers blighted by an icy wind.

'Their faces are pinched with hunger,' the king thought with compassion. 'Yet they do not like the cold and bloodless meat of animals who die on their own. How can I take flesh out of someone living? But these yakshas have come to me. How indeed can I let them go back, disappointed and dejected, languishing with hunger and thirst? So, this is what should be done: I will give them flesh from my own body, bleeding, fresh and plump. This body is like a bad ulcer, always painful and problematic. I will end the troubles it has caused me be putting it to good use.

As he took this firm decision, the high-souled king's face lit up with pleasure. Pointing to his own body, he told the yakshas: 'It is only to benefit the public that this flesh and blood is here. It will be my great and good fortune if it can be used today for serving my guests.'

Even though the yakshas understood the king's intent, it was so amazing that they could not believe it. 'When the supplicant's pathetic entreaty has revealed his own misery,' they remarked, 'it is only the donor who can know what should be done.' Taking this to indicate their assent, the king happily gave orders to summon his physicians for opening his veins. But his ministers were perplexed, and then angry and agitated on knowing that he intended to give away his own flesh and blood. Prompted by affection, they told him clearly: 'It does not behove Your Majesty to ignore the interests of your loving subjects in your excessive joy at giving in charity. Your Majesty knows very well that whatever is harmful to the people is dear to these demons. It is the nature of their species to derive satisfaction from activities hurtful to others. Your Majesty is indifferent to comfort, and bears the burden of kingship only for public benefit. But your decision to donate your own flesh is wrong and should be given up.

'There is no doubt,' the ministers added, 'that these yakshas cannot bear to see the people protected by your power. Their skill in doing mischief thus thwarted, they seek to harm your subjects by cunning. The fat and the like offered to the gods in the sacrificial fire is accepted by them with pleasure, yet these creatures are not pleased with your sumptuous food presented to them with such respect! Though Your Majesty is not obliged to share your thoughts with people like us, our devotion to duty compels us to speak out. How can it be righteous for Your Majesty to ruin everyone else for the sake of these five?

'Moreover,' the ministers said in conclusion, 'why such lack of affection for us? Have we ever held back our flesh and blood from its use for the sake of our master, that he should wish to give his own while ours is still available?'

After listening patiently to their entreaties, the king addressed his ministers. 'Requested specifically for a thing which he possesses,' he said, 'how can someone like myself say falsely that he does not have it or will not give it? Being your leader in matters concerning morality, if I were myself to tread the wrong path, what will happen to my people who follow my example? Therefore, it is only out of concern for you all that I will let go of my body's essence. If I were selfish and mean, what power would I have for doing good?

'As to what you have said out of loving respect and faithful affection for me, that I am indifferent to you in wishing to give my flesh and blood when yours is available, let me set you at rest. My love for you has certainly not been diverted elsewhere or affected by any lack of trust. But it is not befitting to display it by asking you for something which I have in abundance. It would be another matter if what I had were depleted by some turn of fortune or in the course of time. But my limbs are large and well endowed. They have been nurtured only for the sake of supplicants. When they are available, it would be wrong of me to ask you for the same. And how could I bear to give you pain when I cannot do so even to strangers? Therefore I will give of my own flesh. Besides, they have asked me for it, not you.

'Because of your excessive affection for me you have felt impelled to obstruct me in a righteous duty,' the king told the ministers. 'But the way you gentlemen are acting towards my supplicants is not right. Is it good to stop someone from giving food and suchlike in charity in his own interest? Or is it bad? Then how can you question this action of mine? So do not insist anymore, but examine this subject properly, and eschew false ideas as befits my ministers. Indeed, words of approval would become Your Honours more than anxious looks!

'Beggars seeking money for various purposes are to be found every day,' the king added, 'but supplicants such as these cannot be obtained even by praying to the gods. Now that they have come, it would be sheer meanness even to discuss the matter. This body is both impermanent and a seat of sufferings. To be possessive and miserable about it is to descend into the deepest darkness.'

Having persuaded the ministers not to stop him, the king summoned his council and had the physicians open five of his veins. 'Please help me in this pious duty,' he said to the yakshas, 'and give me the great pleasure of accepting my gift.'

'Very well,' replied the yakshas, and, cupping their hands to gather the king's blood, they began to quaff it straightaway. It was dark red, like the sap of the red sandal tree. The royal body was of the colour of gold. As those creatures of the night drank from the king's wounds, he shone like the golden peak of Mount Meru, encircled by dark, low-lying rainclouds tinged with twilight colours. Such was his joy, his great forbearance and the strength of his body, that his limbs did not falter nor his consciousness fade. Neither did his blood cease to flow. 'It is enough,' the yakshas said at last, as their thirst was quenched.

The king was pleased that his body had become a means for serving supplicants. His face beaming with happiness, he picked up a sword with a bright bejewelled hilt and a sharp gleaming blade the colour of a blue lotus petal. With it he cut off pieces of his flesh which he gave to the yakshas. The pleasure of giving left no room for feeling the pain caused by the cuts. It came with each sharp sword stroke, but receded at the glad thoughts, so that it seemed too tired out by coming and going to reach the mind.

So cheerfully did the king satisfy the yakshas with morsels of his flesh that even their cruel hearts were softened. They were filled with wonder and kind feelings to see the king intent on cutting his own flesh, his composure unshaken. 'How amazing and marvellous this is!' they thought with a thrill. 'Can it really happen?' And, banishing any resentment of the king from their minds, they expressed their feelings with praise and salutations.

'Enough! Enough, Your Majesty!' they cried, all excited, bowing to the monarch and begging him to desist. 'Do not torment yourself any more. We are content with your marvellous deed which would win the heart of every suppliant.' And, gazing at him with great respect, their faces drenched with tears of joy, they said: 'Rightly do people proclaim your well-deserved glory. Rightly does the goddess of prosperity prefer to leave her lotus forest and seek shelter with you. If heaven, though guarded by Shakra, does not envy earth, which is protected by your power, surely it is deceived. What more is there to say? The world of mortals is fortunate indeed to have a personage such as you. We are deeply distressed to have caused you this trouble. But people like us have to take refuge with those like you to save themselves.

'Hoping to negate our misdeeds,' the yakshas continued, 'we would like to ask you a question, sir. The kingly state is meant for you, and you have secured it effortlessly. Yet you disregard it. What is the great position which you seek in this manner? Is it sovereignty over the whole earth which you wish to obtain through this penance? Is it the status of Kubera, god of wealth, or of Indra, king of heaven? Or is it the final liberation or absorption into Brahma, the ultimate reality? The goal of your endeavour cannot be very far. Please tell us what it is, if you consider us deserving to know.'

'Listen, then,' replied the king. 'This is the purpose of my endeavour: Worldly wealth needs much effort to obtain and none to lose. If it cannot give the pleasure of contentment, how can it give peace? That is why I do not desire the glory of Indra, what to say of any other.

'Moreover, when I see the helpless creatures of this world beset by so many calamities, my mind can never be at peace merely by the mitigation of my own sufferings. I seek enlightenment through deeds of merit and the conquest of evil passions, so that I may save these creatures from the ocean of worldly existence with its mighty waves of old age, illness and death.'

Bristling with the thrill of joy, the yakshas saluted the king and said: 'Your deed is in keeping with your great purpose. We can therefore say with conviction that the goal of one such as you cannot be far. Please remember us when you attain it, for all your efforts are meant only to benefit others. Forgive us for having troubled you out of ignorance and blindness to our own interests. And favour us with your commands, just as you do your own subordinates.'

Observing that grace had softened their hearts, the king told the yakshas: 'There is no need to worry. You have in fact helped, not troubled me. On attaining enlightenment how could I forget those who have assisted me thus on the path of dharma? You will indeed be the first to whom I distribute the nectar of dharma and salvation. But, if you wish to please me, you must renounce violence like poison, and also refrain from coveting others' property, speaking evil and the sin of drinking intoxicants.'

The yakshas promised to do so and, after saluting and circumambulating the king, they vanished. At the moment when that great man had decided to give away his flesh and blood,

> The earth trembled many times
> and shook the golden mountain,
> whose drums resounded

and trees shed flowers
which, carried by the wind,
spread through the sky
like a cloudy canopy,
like a flight of birds,
and, like a garland strung for him,
settled around the king.

The ocean, too, became turbulent, as if to restrain the monarch: the waters surged and roared like a host about to set forth. Shakra, the chief of the gods, was agitated and wondered what had happened. Fearing the king to be in some extremity, he came in haste to the palace where all the people were distracted by fear and grief. But, to his amazement, the king was serene, even in that condition. Shakra approached him joyfully, and praised his deed in an enchanting voice. 'You are an ocean of virtues! How great is your magnanimity and how tender your heart! The earth has indeed been granted a protector in you.'

With this eulogy, Shakra relieved the king of pain and, with special divine and human medications capable of healing his wounds immediately, restored his body to its former condition. Honoured by the king with courteous and respectful ceremonies, the chief of the gods thereafter returned to his own abode.

This history should be recounted to encourage donors, to explain compassion, to glorify the Tathagata, and to attract attention to the preaching of the dharma. When the Lord said, 'Monks, these five indeed did much,' it was with reference to this history. For they were the five yakshas at that time and, in accordance with his pledge, it was to them that the Lord first imparted the nectar of the dharma.[3]

9

Prince Vishvantara

IT IS NOT EASY FOR SMALL MINDS EVEN TO SYMPATHIZE WITH THE deeds of the Bodhisattva, much less to emulate them. Thus has it been heard:

Once there was a king of the Shibis named Sanjaya. He had mastered his passions and possessed an abundance of valour, prudence and discipline which had won him glorious victories. Regular attendance on the wise had gained him the essence of the three Vedas and all philosophy. His subjects were devoted to their respective duties, happy and at peace. Their affection for him gave proof of the excellence of his policies and administration.

On account of Sanjaya's merits, sovereign power dwelt with him like a devoted wife: other kings could no more think of usurping it than other animals the lion's den. But people who had devoted themselves to penance, learning or the arts could always approach the king, and receive ample honours on displaying their talents.

The Bodhisattva had been born as Sanjaya's son, Vishvantara, the crown prince. Next to the king in dignity, he was no less than him in reputation for merit. Though young, he had the graceful calm which comes with age. He was brilliant but patient, learned but free of conceit, fortunate but modest. His deeds were well known everywhere, and his fame so pervaded the three worlds that lesser reputations had no room or incentive to spread.

Vishvantara could not endure the spread of suffering in the world. He considered it an outrage, and fought it with the great bow of compassion, showering arrows of charity. Every day he would gladden seekers beyond their expectations with an unhesitating dispensation of his wealth, all the more pleasing because of the courtesy and kind words which accompanied it. On holidays he would inspect the alms halls he had established for supplicants all over the city. He did this after observing the Poshadha fast, when he would be tranquil, clad in white silk after a head bath, and mounted on an immense, scented elephant.[1] This animal was like a snow-covered mountain peak. Its face embellished with streaks of rut, it bore auspicious marks, and was well trained, swift and famous as an excellent mount.

Such tours would greatly please the prince. Wealth harboured at home never delights the charitable as much as that disbursed to supplicants. Once, when overjoyed recipients everywhere were proclaiming his charitable practices, the news reached the king of a neighbouring country. Considering that the prince's munificence could provide an opportunity to dupe him, the king sent some brahmins to steal his fine elephant.

The brahmins came and stood before Vishvantara while he was inspecting the alms halls, his countenance radiant with pleasure. As they raised their right hand and blessed him, he stopped his elephant and asked courteously what had brought them there. 'Command me,' he said, 'what do you want?'

'We have come here as supplicants,' the brahmins replied. 'It is on account of the merits of your elephant with the graceful gait, and your own heroic charity. Give us this beast which shines like the peak of Mount Kailasa and makes the world marvel.'

Thus addressed, Vishavantara was overjoyed. 'It is indeed after a long time that I see supplicants seeking such a grand gift,' he said to himself. 'But what will these brahmins do with this king of elephants? Obviously this is some wretched trick by a ruler whose mind is full of jealousy, greed and hatred. But if he is determined to ignore his own reputation and do me the favour of seeking my charity, his hopes should not be belied.'

Having taken this decision, the great-souled prince quickly dismounted from the elephant and faced the brahmins. Though he knew that in pursuit of material interests the science of government departs from the path of virtue, his devotion to the second was such that he did not fear to transgress the first. 'Please accept this gift,' he said to the brahmins, raising a gilded ewer to pour the ritual water,[2] and gave away the noble animal which, with its ornamental mesh of gold, looked like a mass of autumn clouds shot with lightning.

The prince was delighted to have gifted the elephant. But the citizens favoured prudence, and were deeply disturbed. Anger gripped the Shibis when they heard that the royal mount had been given away. Brahmin elders and ministers, warriors and city leaders went to King Sanjaya in a noisy demonstration, ignoring the restraint of decorum in their agitation and rage. 'What is this, Your Majesty?' they exclaimed. 'The kingdom's glory is being carried off, and you pay no attention! It does not behove Your Majesty to ignore the occurrence of such evils in your own realm!'

'What has happened?' the king asked uneasily.

'Does Your Majesty not know?' replied the Shibis. 'Vishvantara has given away the elephant which was the symbol of your victories. Its power subdued the strength and the influence of your adversaries, and laid their arrogance to rest. The rut flowing on its face maddened humming bees and scented the wind, humbling the pride of other elephants. And now it is being taken away to another land.'

'Cattle and gold, garments and comestibles are suitable gifts for brahmins,' the Shibis added, 'but to gift that noble elephant, which personifies victory and glory, goes beyond even heroic charity. How will sovereignty remain with this prince who goes against the dictates of prudence? It is not proper for Your Majesty to neglect something which may soon cause your neighbours to rejoice.'

The king, who loved his son, was not a little displeased to hear the Shibis' complaint. But his job required that he pacify them. 'I know that Vishvantara is generous to a fault and neglects the rules of prudent policy,' he said. 'Also, that this is not appropriate in someone entrusted with the affairs of the state. He has gifted his elephant, but that is now like vomit – who can take it back? Nevertheless, I will act to make him understand the limits of charity. So, do not be angry.'

'Great king, Vishvantara cannot be corrected merely by admonition in this affair,' the Shibis replied.

'What else can I do, then?' asked Sanjaya. 'My son has not committed a sin. He is only too generous. What price should he pay for gifting that elephant? Go to jail? Be put to death? So, do not get angry. I will control him.'

But the Shibis were not calmed. 'Who wants to put your son to death?' they cried. 'Or to imprison or chastize him? The fact Your Majesty is that he is a pious soul, and cannot bear the burden of the state because of his tenderness and compassion. Thrones should be occupied only by those of proven prowess who are adept in serving all the three human ends of virtue, wealth and pleasure. This prince is devoted to virtue but indifferent to politics. He is fit only to live in a hermitage.

'Bad policies of rulers indeed have consequences for their subjects,' they added. 'Such faults could be tolerated in the populace, but can never be accepted in kings, for that would undermine the state. What more is there to say? The Shibis cannot bear to see you ruined. This is their decision. Let the prince be sent away to Mount Vanka, abode of holy hermits, to practice penance.'

These people loved and trusted their king. They wished him well, and if they spoke to him harshly it was because they apprehended dangers in wrong policies. The king hung his head in shame at his subjects' anger, even as his heart was overwhelmed by the thought of separation from his son. 'If this is what you gentlemen insist upon,' he told the Shibis with a deep sigh, 'then give him at least a day and a night. Vishvantara will fulfil your wish in the morning at daybreak.'

The Shibis agreed to the king's request. He then told his chamberlain to go and apprise Vishvantara of what had happened. His face drenched with tears of grief, the functionary went to Vishvantara who was in his own palace. Once there, he was overwhelmed by sorrow and, weeping loudly, fell at the prince's feet.

'Is all well with the royal household?' Vishvantara asked anxiously. 'All is well,' replied the chamberlain in a strained and faltering voice. 'Then why are you so upset?' the prince asked. The old retainer replied slowly, his throat choked with emotion and his words interrupted with sighs. 'O prince,' he said, 'the hard-hearted Shibis are enraged. They have disregarded even the king's assurances and have ordered you to be banished from the country.'

'Why are the Shibis enraged and why are they exiling me?' asked Vishvantara. 'I do not see what wrong I have done. I do not stray from the path of discipline, and I abhor carelessness. So, why are they angry with me?'

'It is because of your excessive magnanimity,' said the chamberlain. 'When you gave away that best of elephants, your motivation was pure and unselfish, but the hearts of your supplicants were filled with greed. The Shibis' patience has now given way to anger. They are so upset with you that they insist that you go the way of hermits.'

'The Shibis are indeed fickle minded,' he said. 'It seems they do not understand my nature. I would give away even my organs what to say of things material. It is for the people's sake that I bear this body, not to speak of garments and vehicles. To think that someone ready to honour the requests of supplicants even with his own limbs would refrain from charity out of fear is both fickle and foolish. For sure, the Shibis can kill or exile me, but I will not give up charity. So I am all set to go to the hermitage.' Vishvantara's reply displayed both an affection for supplicants, which flowed from his practice of compassion, and an immense reserve of patience.

Thereafter Vishvantara spoke to his wife Madri who seemed startled by the bad news. 'Have you heard about the Shibis' decision, my lady?' he asked.

'I have, my lord,' she replied.

'Then take care of whatever money you have from me, fair one,' said Vishvantara, 'and also of that which you received from your parents.'

'How shall I take care of it, lord?' asked Madri.

'Always give alms to people of good character, and treat them with courtesy,' said Vishvantara. 'Money thus preserved is never lost and follows one after death. Also, be good to your parents-in-law, look after the children and be attentive to your duties. Do not grieve for me when I am gone.'

Though Madri's heart was on fire, she suppressed her grief and distress in order to bolster her husband's fortitude. 'Great king,' she said, 'it is not right that you go alone to the forest. O warrior, I too will go wherever you must. Even death will be a festival for me at your side. But living without you will be worse than death.

'Indeed, my lord,' Madri continued, 'living in the forest does not appear disagreeable to me. Penance groves are more pleasing than pleasure gardens. They are free of wily people. Their rivers and trees are unspoilt. They teem with animals and are full of the sounds of birds. The ground is covered with grass recalling the beauty of inlaid gemstones. When you see our two children decked out in garlands of wild flowers, playing around the forest bushes, you will think no more of this kingdom.

'Moreover, my lord, the changing beauties of the forest, its thickets and water-filled streams, will delight you with each season. The music of the forest, the varied mating calls of birds, the passionate dances of the peacocks, and the sweet hum of honeybees will fill your mind with joy.

'At night the rocks will be covered by a sheet of moonlight. A soft caressing breeze will waft the fragrance of flowering trees. The sound of water flowing over loose pebbles will be like the tinkling of the ornaments of river nymphs. All this will surely gladden your heart in the forest.'

Thus was Vishvantara reassured by his beloved wife. Eager to leave for the forest, yet concerned for his supplicants, he prepared to distribute gifts on a massive scale. Meanwhile the news of his banishment led to loud lamentations in the royal household. The seekers of charity, in particular, were virtually beside themselves with grief and distress which they expressed in myriad ways.

'It is clear that Mother Earth has lost all awareness,' they wailed, 'for she is not ashamed of those who raise their axes to cut down a shady tree which yields succulent fruit. The guardians of the quarters are so called in vain, or are mere names, or gone away, for there is no one to stop those who want to destroy a well of cool, pure and sweet water. Dharma is surely dead or asleep, and its opposite reigns, for the prince Vishvantara is banished from his own kingdom. Who is intent so cruelly on killing us innocent beggars? He must be an expert at causing calamities.'

The prince distributed his wealth suitably to all the supplicants. He gave away his treasury, full of jewels, gold and silver; his stores of goods and grain; his chariots and animals, garments and ornaments. Having bowed at the feet of his sorrowing mother and father, he then mounted a fine chariot with his spouse and two children, and left the capital to the sound of lamentation from a humungous crowd.

The people loved Vishvantara and many followed him, their faces wet with tears of grief. Turning them back with some effort, he took the chariot reins himself and proceeded towards Mount Vanka. His mind at ease, he went past the outskirts of the capital with their pleasing groves and gardens, and approached the forest. Gradually, the trees planted for shade became fewer, and human traffic ceased. Herds of deer could be seen at a distance and the sound of crickets resonated. Here the prince chanced upon some brahmins who begged him for the horses which drew his chariot.

The prince was on a long journey. He had no attendants and his wife was with him. Yet such was his joy in charity that, without any thought for the future, he gave away his four horses to the brahmins. As he girded himself to pull the chariot in person, four young yakshas[3] appeared in the guise of red deer and, like well-trained horses, took the chariot's yoke on their own shoulders.

Madri stared at the deer with delighted astonishment. 'These forests are blessed by being the abode of ascetics,' Vishvantara told her. 'Look at their great power. Hospitality towards visitors is manifested even by these excellent deer.'

'On my part,' she replied, 'I consider this to be due to your extraordinary power. The merits of virtue may be obvious, but their manifestation is not the same everywhere. If blooming night lilies surpass the splendour of stars reflected in water, it is because moonbeams search them out.'

As the couple went onwards, exchanging words of mutual affection, another brahmin approached the Bodhisattva and asked him for his fine chariot. And that dear friend of supplicants, who never cared for his own comfort, again complied. Getting down from the chariot with his family, he gladly gave it away to the brahmin. Then, taking his son Jalin in his arms, and followed by Madri calmly carrying their daughter Krishnajina, the prince continued his journey on foot.

> Trees bent their boughs before him,
> as if to bid him taste their fruit,
> and to greet him like good pupils.
> Lakes appeared, filled with lotus blooms,
> wherever he sought to drink.
> Clouds spread an awning above
> and a soft breeze sprang up below.
> Thus was his path eased by the yakshas
> who could not bear to see him toil.

As a result the prince felt nothing of the fatigue of travel. The journey with his wife and family became as pleasant as a promenade in a park. Eventually they beheld Mount Vanka and, following the path pointed out by a forest denizen, they arrived at a penance grove.

The place was full of many kinds of pleasing shady trees, laden with flowers, fruit and fresh new leaves. It echoed with the cheerful twitter of birds. Peacocks danced and herds of deer wandered around. The air was fragrant with floral pollen, and a stream of clear blue water circled the grove. Here stood a cottage thatched with leaves. Charming, secluded and comfortable in all seasons, it had been built on the orders of Shakra, the king of heaven, by the god of artisans, Vishvakarma, himself.

The prince and his family made that cottage their home. It was like living in a garden. Looked after by his dear wife, and listening to the sweet and artless talk of his children, he forgot all the cares of government and spent six months there in ascetic practice.

One day, when the princess had gone out in search of fruit and roots, and the prince had stayed behind to look after the two children, a brahmin appeared at their hermitage. His feet and legs were rough with the dust of travel, and his eyes and face sunken with toil. A water pot hung from the wooden staff on his shoulder. He had been sent by his wife with strict instructions to find some servants.

Vishvantara was delighted to see a mendicant after a long time. His face beamed with joy as he went out and welcomed the brahmin with kind words. After bringing him into the hermitage and offering him the hospitality due to a guest, he enquired about the purpose of his visit. The brahmin, on his part, was so besotted with his wife that he had lost all sense of shame and restraint. He was solely interested in getting a gift for her, and said so quite precisely. 'People do not go where the path is difficult, but only where it is even and well lit,' he said. 'This world is so dark with selfishness that others will not accept my request. The glorious fame of your charity has, however, spread everywhere. That is why I have endeavoured to importune you. Give me these two children to be my attendants.'

The prince was used to giving with joy. That great being had never learnt to say no. 'I will gladly give you my two dear children,' he bravely replied.

'Bless you!' said the brahmin. 'But then what are you waiting for?' he asked the great man. Meanwhile the children had heard that they were to be given away. As their eyes welled with tears of despair, a surge of affection for them rocked the prince's heart. 'I have already given them to you,' he told the brahmin, 'but their mother has gone to the forest to look for fruit and roots. She will return this evening. Stay here tonight, and let her see them with their garlands and kiss them goodbye. Tomorrow you can take them both away.'

'Do not insist on that, sir,' said the brahmin. 'If women are called charmers it is because of their nature. I would not like to stay here, for it may hinder your charity.'

'Do not worry about any hindrance,' Vishvantara replied. 'She is my wife and my partner in pious duty. Or, do as you please, sir. But, great brahmin, these children are young and delicate. They do not know the work of servants. What pleasure will you get from their service? On the other hand, when their grandfather, the king of the Shibis, sees them in this condition, he will certainly give you all the money you want in order to redeem them. So it is best that you take them to him. In this way you will gain both great wealth and merit.'

'I cannot go to the king with such an unpleasant offer,' said the brahmin. 'It would be like approaching a serpent. He will take these children away, and may also punish me. Therefore I will take them to my wife as servants.'

'As you please,' said the prince, and did not complete the sentence. Instead he spoke to his two children, teaching and persuading them to work as servants. He then tilted a water pot over the brahmin's hands,[4] outstretched to receive the gift in the ritual manner. It was an effort for him to pour out the water; tears flowed simultaneously from his reddened eyes.

The brahmin was overjoyed at his acquisition. Anxious to make a quick exit with the children, he uttered a brief blessing and harshly asked them to move as he commenced bundling them out of the hermitage. But they were overwhelmed by the sorrow of seperation. Saluting their father with tears in their eyes, they cried: 'Mother has gone out and you wish to give us away! Don't do that until we can see her.'

'The mother of these two may soon return,' thought the brahmin, 'or their father, who adores them, may have second thoughts.' Tying their little hands with a creeper, he then began to threaten and drag them away as they turned to look at their father. The girl Krishnajina wept aloud in a calamity she had never experienced before. 'This cruel brahmin is beating me with the creeper, father,' she cried out. 'It is obvious that he is not a brahmin, for they are pious. He is a yaksha disguised as a brahmin, and he is carrying us off to devour us. Father, why are you letting this ghoul take us away?'

The boy Jalin lamented for his mother. 'To be beaten by this brahmin,' he cried, 'does not hurt me as much as not seeing my mother today. That is what tears me apart. Long will she weep in this empty hermitage, distraught with grief like a chataka bird whose offspring have been killed. How else will she feel when she returns from the forest after gathering many roots and fruit for us, and finds the hermitage empty? Here are our toy horses, elephants and chariots, father. Give half of them to mother to lessen her grief. You must stop her in every way from feeling sad. Give her our salutations, father, for it may be difficult for us to see you both again.'

'Come, Krishna,' the boy then told his sister, 'let us go and die. What is the point of our living when father has given us away to this greedy brahmin?' And with these words the two departed.

Vishvantara's resolve was not shaken by the piteous cries of his children. 'One should not have regrets after making a gift,' he reflected. Even so, his heart was engulfed by the flames of an uncontrollable sorrow, and he remained where he was sitting, inert and insensible as if paralyzed by poison. Fanned and revived at last by a cool breeze, he saw around himself a silent hermitage devoid of his children, and his voice choked with tears. 'Children are one's very heart,' he said to himself. 'Fie on that shameless brahmin! How could he dare to strike them in front of my eyes? They are tender and cannot bear fatigue. How will they walk barefoot on the road as his servants? Who will give them rest when they are wayworn and exhausted, and to whom will they go when they are hungry and thirsty? Here am I, wanting to be strong, but when even I am suffering, what will be the condition of these children who have been brought up in comfort? Alas, seperation from them has set my mind on fire! Nevertheless, in view of the duty of good people, how can one give way to regret?'

Meanwhile Madri had been disquieted by various ill omens and portents of some accident. Though she had wanted to come back earlier after collecting the roots and fruit, she was

held up on the way by predatory animals, and returned to the
hermitage much later. Not seeing the children at the usual place
where they came to meet her, nor at the playground, she
became extremely uneasy. Concerned that something uncalled
for may have happened, she looked around anxiously and
called out to them repeatedly. Receiving no answer, her distress
increased and she began to lament. 'This grove earlier used to
resound with the prattle of children,' she cried, 'but today it
seems a desolate wilderness! Have these two been tired out by
their games and gone to sleep? Have they got lost in the dense
forest? Or, have they childishly hidden themselves because they
are annoyed with me for coming so late? But why are these
birds not chirping? Are they confused because they witnessed
some accident? Has this fast-flowing stream carried the two
away in its angry waves?

'May my suspicious prove false and baseless!' lamented
Madri. 'May the prince and the children be well. May the evil
of any portents fall on me. But why does my heart seem to be
sinking? Why have these omens emptied it of joy and shrouded
it in a dark sadness? My limbs seem to be failing. The quarters
seem in turmoil. This grove has turned gloomy and appears to
be in a whirl.'

After entering the hermitage, the princess placed the fruit
and roots on one side and hurriedly went to her husband.
'Where are the children?' she asked him. But Vishvantara kept
silent. He knew the tenderness of a mother's heart and how
distraught his wife would feel on hearing the bad news.

'It is obvious that something bad has happened to the
children,' Madri told herself. 'If he says nothing it is only
because he is sad and dejected.' She stared blankly all around
the hermitage and, seeing it empty, said tearfully, 'I do not see
the children and you do not speak to me. Evil is never

mentioned, but surely I am undone!' And, with these words, she collapsed, overwhelmed by grief, like a vine cut down from its root.

Vishvantara caught his wife as she fell. He laid her down on a straw pallet and sprinkled some cold water on her. When she had regained her senses, he comforted her, saying, 'Madri, I did not give you this bad news all of a sudden. To bear it would have been impossible for a heart tender with love. A brahmin had come to me. He was distressed with old age and poverty. I gave both the children to him. Compose yourself. Do not mourn. Look at me, Madri. Don't look for the children and grieve. Grief for them has already broken my heart. Don't hurt it any more. Wouldn't I give even my own life if it were begged for? Think of that, my love, and support me in this gift I have made of the children.'

Madri had feared that the children were dead. The news that they were not, eased her anguish somewhat, and she sought to bolster her husband's fortitude. Wiping the tears from her eyes, she looked at him in wonderment and said, 'It is a marvel! What more can I say! Even the gods are amazed that selfishness has no place in your heart. That is why all the quarters echo with the sound of divine drums, proclaiming your glory in the sky. The great mountains, the bosom of this earth, tremble as if in exultation. Golden flowers fall from the sky, making it gleam as if with lightning. There is no need for grief and dejection. Give and gladden the heart! Be like a well of water for the people, and give yet again!'

When the earth trembled, it shook Sumeru, the king of the mountains, who glitters with the glow of varied gemstones. 'What is this?' asked Shakra. On being told by the astonished guardians of the quarters that Vishvantara's gifting of his children had caused the earth to quake, Shakra was filled with wonder and joy. The next morning he went to the prince in the guise of a brahmin supplicant.

The prince greeted the visitor with due ceremony and invited him to make a request. Shakra then asked him for his wife. 'The good are like great lakes,' he said. 'The dutiful charity of the one and the waters of the other never go dry. That is why I ask you for your wife who is like a goddess. Give her to me as a gift.'

'Very well,' said Vishvantara. He remained calm as he made the commitment. Holding Madri with his left hand and the water pot in his right, he poured the ritual water over the mendicant's palm, even as he set Mara's[5] heart afire with anguish. As for Madri, she knew her husband's nature. She neither raged nor wept. She just stood and stared at him, still as a statue, such was the hurt of this fresh pain.

Shakra was wonderstruck. 'How vast is the difference between the conduct of the good and the wicked!' he exclaimed, praising Vishvantara. 'How can the self-indulgent even be capable of giving credence to such a deed! That dear children and wife should be given up in the spirit of detachment by one who loves them – can there be anything nobler? There can be no doubt that when your virtues are recounted by those who adore them, and your fame spreads in all directions, other brilliant reputations will be eclipsed just as lesser luminaries are dimmed by the splendour of sunlight. And now, this extraordinary deed of yours is approved and applauded by the yakshas, the gandharvas[6] and the celestial serpents, together with all the gods, including Shakra.'

After this paean, the king of heaven assumed his own effulgent form. 'I am Shakra,' he said, introducing himself. 'I return to you Madri, your wife, for moonlight cannot stay apart from the moon. Do not worry about your children or regret the loss of your kingdom. Your father will come here with both little ones, and restores you to your dignity and the kingdom to its protector.'

Shakra then disappeared. His power made the brahmin bring the prince's two children to the Shibi kingdom itself. The hearts of the Shibis melted when they heard about the prince's deed. They redeemed the children from the brahmin's hands, propitiated Vishvantara and re-established him in the kingdom.

The deeds of the Bodhisattva are indeed wondrous. This account should be narrated while describing the Tathagata and discoursing on the dharma.

10

The Sacrifice

ONE SHOULD STRIVE TO PURIFY THE HEART, FOR THE PURE-hearted will never succumb to the deception of wickedness. Thus has it been heard:

The Bodhisattva was once a king by hereditary succession. The power of his merits accumulated in previous lives had brought him to rule the earth, his sole sovereignty acknowledged by all the vassals. His kingdom was free of troubles and at peace, both at home and abroad.

The king had subdued his enemies – the passions. Exceptionable ends had no attraction for him. Given entirely to the welfare of his subjects, he was like a sage whose only purpose is the practice of virtue. Aware that it is the nature of people to emulate the conduct of their leaders, he devoted himself in particular to pious duties for the edification of the populace. He gave alms, followed moral precepts, practised forbearance and sought the good of the world. Mild in appearance and intent on the wellbeing of his subjects, he shone like virtue personified.

Though the country was protected by the king, once it was afflicted by a drought. There was much distress in some areas. The king concluded that this calamity was due to some transgression on his part, or by his subjects whose welfare was his constant concern. Unable to see them suffer, he consulted respected persons about how they could be given relief.

In this connection the king questioned experts in religion, leading priests, brahmin elders and learned ministers. All of them were of the view that abundant rainfall depended on the ritual of sacrifice as laid down in the Vedas. They gave an account of this terrible ritual which involved the slaughter of hundreds of creatures. The king's compassionate nature did not approve of the killings ordained for a sacrifice, but he was too polite to rebut his advisers with harsh words, and simply ignored what they said by turning to some other subjects.

The counsellors did not understand the king's deep underlying feelings. At the next opportunity for discussing religious matters, they urged him once more to undertake a sacrifice. 'You are always prompt in performing the royal duties prescribed for gaining and ruling a kingdom,' they said, 'and this is in keeping with religious precepts. You wield the sword for the benefit of your subjects, and are skilled in pursuing the threefold human ends of virtue, wealth and pleasure. Then why this inertia and inattention in respect of the rite of sacrifice, which is a bridge to heaven? Other kings obey your commands and carry them out like servants. O vanquisher of foes, the time has now come for you to earn further glory and merit by a sacrifice.

'Of course, your love of charity and respect for the ritual abstinences always keeps you in the pure state of an initiate,' they added. 'Even so, it would be appropriate for you to discharge your debt to the gods by the rite of sacrifice, which is celebrated in the Vedas. When it is performed properly and correctly, the gods are satisfied and in turn honour the people with rain. You should perform this glorious ritual for the benefit of your subjects as well as yourself.'

'These are meager minds,' the king reflected. 'They depend on others and do not think for themselves. They have no love for what is right, only blind belief. While people regard them with respect, they favour even violence in the name of virtue. One who follows the wrong path they enjoin will certainly come to a sorry pass.

'What indeed is the connection of virtue, of propitiating the gods and going to heaven, with the slaughter of animals?' the king said to himself. 'It is not true that the victim sacrificed with powerful incantations goes to heaven, and to kill it is therefore virtuous. Can one reap the fruit of something done by another? How can an animal, which has neither abjured evil actions nor been devoted to good ones, go to heaven without reference to its own deeds, simply because it has been the victim in a sacrifice? If being slaughtered in this way were to convey it to heaven, would not the brahmins themselves choose to be sacrificial victims? But, since this never happens, how can one accept the word of these advisers? As for the gods, would they spurn ambrosia of incomparable flavour, fragrance and potency, held out to them by beautiful heavenly nymphs, and take delight in the sacrifice of a poor animal for the sake of its marrow and other parts?'

Having decided that it was time to act in this matter, the king replied to his advisers as if agreeable to their counsel and eager to undertake a sacrifice. 'I am indeed in good hands,' he told them. 'I am gratified that you gentlemen are so devoted to my welfare. I would like to hold a thousand human sacrifices. Let the ministers assemble the requisites for this according to their respective responsibilities. Find a suitable place for erecting the sacrificial hall, and an appropriate time for the ceremony, its date, hour and planetary configurations.'

'Great king,' replied the head priest, 'to accomplish what you have in mind, it would be better to have separate ceremonies, ending each with the ritual final bath. The sacrifices can then take place one after the other. For, if a thousand human victims were to be collected at the same time, it is obvious that your subjects will get agitated and proceed to blame you.'

The other brahmins supported the priest. But the king told them: 'Do not worry about the wrath of the people, gentlemen. I will make such arrangements that my subjects do not get perturbed.' Therefore he assembled the townsmen and those from the countryside. 'I wish to perform a thousand human sacrifices,' he told them. 'But it is not my intention that any innocent person gets designated as the victim. What you should know is that from now I will have you all kept under observation by watchful spies of good character. Whoever is found to transgress the limits of morality or my orders – I will arrest that person and use him for the sacrifice.'

The leaders of the assembly replied with folded hands. 'All that Your Majesty does is for the benefit of the people,' they said. 'What would we gain by opposing your actions? They deserve support even by Brahma, the god of creation. You are a criterion of virtue, and our criterion also. Whatever pleases you must please us too, for you take pleasure in nothing apart from our comforts and welfare.'

His proposal accepted by the townsmen and country folk, the king dispatched trusted ministers to the cities and the rural regions for apprehending wicked persons. At every place he had the following proclamation made daily for public information:

'The king is the protector! He grants protection to all good persons of steadfast purity and character. But miscreants will be taken in thousands as human victims for the sacrifice he intends to perform for public benefit. The king's command is respected even by vassal kings. Whoever disregards it mischievously will, from today, qualify as a victim by his own actions, and will be bound to the sacrificial stake where people will see him shrivelling up with misery.'

This grim proclamation was repeated day after day. The people heard it, noticed the king's careful search for evil-doers to serve as sacrificial victims, and observed his officers going about everywhere, determined to catch such persons. As a result they gave up evil behaviour and adhered to moral conduct. Putting enmities behind them, they turned to mutual love and respect. Acrimony and conflict ceased. The advice of elders was followed. People became good at sharing with others, hospitable, courteous and modest.

It was as if the Golden Age had returned. People feared death and thought of the next world. They were proud of their families and concerned for their reputations. Purer feelings strengthened their sense of shame. Embellished by the purity of their conduct, even as they became more virtuous, the officers increased their efforts to look for evil-doers; therefore no one deviated from righteousness.

The king was very pleased to learn about these developments. He rewarded the spies who brought him this good news. 'My greatest wish is to protect the people,' he told the ministers. 'Now they are fit to receive the sacrificial gifts. It was for the sacrifice that I had set aside all this wealth, and I intend to use it accordingly. Wealth is a means to comfort. Let anyone who wants it come to me and take as much as he desires. The poverty which afflicts our country will be driven out in this way.'

In accordance with the royal command, the ministers had alms halls established in all the villages, towns and market places, as well as at resting posts on the roads. Here money was daily distributed and the supplicants satisfied as ordered by the king.

The people thus received much wealth from their ruler. Their poverty disappeared. They came out in colourful garments and ornaments, displaying the splendour of a festival. Praised by happy supplicants, the king's fame spread far and wide, like lotus pollen carried over a lake's expanse by its ripples. And, following his wise policies, the people applied themselves to good deeds, by the merit of which all the calamities totally disappeared.

The seasons assumed an agreeable regularity. Like kings newly installed, they behaved as they should. The monsoon winds kept pace with seasonal change. The planets moved along auspicious paths. The earth was laden with all kinds of grain, and the lakes with pure blue water filled with lotus flowers. Medicinal herbs became more efficacious than ever before. The people were virtuous, modest and disciplined. None were afflicted by incurable diseases. No danger threatened them from abroad or within, nor from the heavens.

It was a virtuous sacrifice that the king conducted in this manner. With it he put an end to the distress caused by the drought, and also to the sufferings of the indigent. Filled with happy people, the country became prosperous and delightful to see. The people blessed the king and spread his fame everywhere. 'It has indeed been well said,' exclaimed one of the leading ministers, 'that the ruler's mind moves at a higher level than that of others as he has to constantly scrutinize the deeds of the good, the bad and the average people. Your Majesty performed a virtuous sacrifice, untainted by the sin of animal slaughter. By it you assured the welfare of your subjects, both in this world and in the next. You also put an end to the distress occasioned by drought and the sufferings caused by poverty.

'What more is there to say?' the minister added. 'Your subjects are fortunate: you did not wrap yourself in a deerskin dark as the spots on the moon; you did not let your fine demeanour be affected by the painful exertions of sacrificial initiation; the splendour of the hair on your head remained as before.[1] Yet you surpassed by your largesse the glory of the great Shakra, the performer of a hundred sacrifices.

'The sacrifices performed by seekers of material gains generally involve violence, and are pitiable. Yours, O wise ruler, was in keeping with your faultless and delightful character. It has embellished your glory. Your subjects are indeed fortunate to have you as their protector.

'The rich give in charity with the hope of obtaining more wealth. Others observe morality because they seek approbation in this life or heaven in the next. But actions such as yours, impelled only by the wish to do good to others, can only come from the wise and the virtuous.'

Thus one should strive to purify the heart, for the pure-hearted will never succumb to the deception of wickedness. Also, it should be remembered that the practice of virtue brings prosperity to the people, and one who seeks the second should engage in the first.

The slaughter of animals can never lead to true prosperity. That comes from charity, restraint and discipline, and one who seeks prosperity must practise these virtues.

11

Shakra

NEITHER ADVERSITY NOR POWER AND PROSPERITY WILL DIMINISH the compassion that great souls have for all creatures. Thus has it been heard:

Having long performed good deeds, personified charity and self-discipline, restraint and compassion, and devoted his actions to the service of others, the Bodhisattva was once born as Shakra, the king of the gods.

Like moonlight on a palace freshly painted white, the glory of the celestial king appeared even more splendid on him. To attain it the demon race would have bared their breasts before the tusks of charging cosmic elephants. But though Shakra had gained it effortlessly by his fortune, it did not tarnish him with any arrogance.

As the king of the gods, Shakra guarded heaven and earth with distinction. His fame spread throughout the universe. The demons could not bear his prosperity and wonderful majesty. They set out to attack him with a vast army of elephants, chariots, cavalry and infantry. The tumult of his force was

awesome, like that of an angry sea, and it so blazed with all
kinds of weapons and missiles as to dazzle the eye.

Shakra was the soul of dharma. But the intransigence of his
adversaries and his own concern for the people's welfare, his
heroic nature and the path of proper policy impelled him to
face the turbulence of war. He mounted a fine chariot drawn
by a thousand choice horses, and went forth to meet the demon
army on the sea shore.

The chariot was made of gold, with a white woollen
upholstery. It glittered with inlaid gems and sharp, shining
weapons laid out on both its sides. Its tall standard was adorned
with a figure in the garb of an Arhat,[1] and it was surrounded
by the marvellous army of the gods with its elephants, horses,
chariots and foot soldiers.

Then there commenced a battle which terrified timid hearts.
The soldiers' armour was smashed, struck by each others'
weapons. The clamour was so deafening with the clash of arms
and the crash of drums, that it seemed the very sky would burst.

Tusker elephants charged at each other, maddened by the
smell of rut. They looked like great mountains in the grip of
tempests at the end of time. Chariots gathered like storm
clouds. Their rumbling was like claps of thunder, and their
banners fluttered and flashed like lightning. The warriors of both
sides cut down each others' flags and parasols, weapons, armour
and heads, with their sharp arrows. Eventually the army of the
gods was borne down by demon swords and missiles. It broke
ranks and fled in terror, while the king of the gods alone
remained in the fray, barring the enemy forces with his chariot.

Matali was the royal charioteer. He observed that the demon
forces, roaring with joy like lions, were about to fall upon them,
and their own army was intent on flight. Concluding that the
time had come to retreat, he turned round the chariot of the

god king. As it flew back, Shakra noticed en route the nests
of some eagles on a silk cotton tree which were likely to be hit.
As soon as he saw this, his heart filled with compassion. He
told Matali: 'The nests upon this silk cotton tree are filled with
chicks which have still to grow wings. Drive my chariot so that
I can save them.'

'But the demon hordes will be upon us, noble one!' Matali
pointed out. 'How does that matter?' replied Shakra. 'Protect
these eagles' nests properly.' However Matali persisted. 'O
lotus-eyed lord,' he said, 'having worsted the gods after many
attempts, the enemy force is now at our heels. Turning the
chariot back at this point will be disastrous.'

Moved by compassion, Shakra, the king of the gods, then
displayed his extraordinary goodness and firm determination.
'Turn back the chariot nevertheless!' he cried:

> 'Better it is to die, struck down
> by mighty blows of demon chiefs,
> than to live with the infamy
> of killing these poor frightened creatures.'

Driven by his master's fortitude, Matali turned back the
chariot drawn by a thousand horses. And then,

> His foes had seen his deeds in battle.
> Observing now his chariot turned,
> they stumbled and then fled in terror,
> like rainclouds scattered by the wind.

> For, when an army is repulsed,
> should a single man turn back
> and confront the enemy forces,

their arrogance can be contained
by his unexpected bravery.

And, when the demon army scattered,
the godly force returned to battle,
as its enemies fled in terror
with no spirit to turn and fight.

Shakra's handsome figure was radiant with the victor's glory as, hailed by the happy but embarrassed gods, he returned to his capital and his eager family. Thus was victory gained in that battle. It is said:

The base will sin because they're cruel,
the kindly middling when in trouble,
but the good, their lives at stake,
can no more sin than can the sea
roll across its natural boundary.[2]

In this way did the Lord protect creatures in the days of yore. Now too it is not proper to harm them, and one should be compassionate towards all living beings. Dharma protects one who practices it.

12

The Brahmin Student

It IS BECAUSE THEY WOULD BE ASHAMED OF THEMSELVES IN DOING so, that good people do not overstep the bounds of right behaviour. Thus has it been heard:

The Bodhisattva was once born in a brahmin family of impeccable lineage and character, famous for devotion to its duties, and esteemed for the modesty of its comportment. Having received the birth and other sacraments in due order, he went to stay with a learned, well-born and pious teacher for the purpose of studying the Vedas.

As a student the Bodhisattva was quick to grasp what he was taught and to commit it to memory. He was devoted to his studies, in keeping with the well-known tradition of his family. Calmness marked his temperament even though he was very young. All these qualities earned him his teacher's affection and favour. For virtues which are always consistent charm even those who are consumed by animosity, not to speak of healthy minds.

Now the teacher wished to test the moral character of his students. To this end he would continually speak to them about the hardships he was suffering on account of his poverty. He did so during the intervals of rest between their lessons. 'Poverty is a curse,' he would say. 'It makes even kinsmen indifferent, and festivals joyless. One lags in talk about charity, and is unable to fulfil any wish. Indigence means humiliation as well as toil. It deprives one of comfort and saps one's energy. It always causes grief, like a calamity. To be devoid of money is, in effect, a most terrible thing.'

The students loved their teacher. Like well-trained horses when they are spurred, they were moved by his words and began to collect richer food in alms for him. But he said: 'Gentlemen, do not trouble yourselves. No alms of food will ever put an end to anyone's poverty. If you cannot bear to see me suffer, it would be better if you were to devote the same effort to the acquisition of wealth. And why do I say this? Because just as food relieves hunger, water thirst, and spells or medicines illness, the wealth acquired by one's children relieves the pain of poverty.'

'O teacher, what can we do?' replied the students. 'It is our misfortune that to do anything more is beyond our capacity. If wealth were also obtainable like alms, by ritual begging, then we would never acquiesce in your being poor and put to hardship. But, for brahmins, the means of acquiring wealth are limited to the acceptance of gifts, and the people here are not charitable. That is why we are at a loss.'

'There are other methods of acquiring wealth foreseen in the scriptures,' said the teacher. 'However I am too old and feeble to make use of them.'

'But sir, our energies are undiminished by age,' the students protested. 'If you consider us capable of putting to use these other methods prescribed by the scriptures, please tell us, so that we may repay the debt we owe you for your labours in educating us.'

'These methods of earning wealth are not for the faint hearted, even if they are young men,' said the teacher. 'But if you gentlemen insist, I will tell you a good one. There is a dharma of what is lawful during calamities. A respected course for the twice-born is theft. Now poverty is certainly the ultimate calamity in the world. It is no sin for us to partake of the wealth of others: it all belongs to brahmins in any case.'

'People like you no doubt have the strength to seize wealth even by force,' the teacher added. 'But that will not be appropriate as you must also guard your reputations. So your efforts should be made when no one else is around.'

Thus did he loosen the bridle on his students. 'Very well,' they said, and accepted his words as proper even though they were not. That is, except for the Bodhisattva. Because of his innate goodness, he did not endorse them. Nor did he oppose brusquely what the others had agreed to as a duty. He merely hung his head in embarrassment, sighed softly and kept silent.

The teacher noticed that the Bodhisattva, whose qualities he respected, had neither welcomed nor denounced his suggestion. 'Why does he not agree to steal?' he wondered. 'Is it for lack of enterprise, or want of affection for me? Or is it because he considers it wrong.' He then tried to get the Bodhisattva to reveal his feelings. 'O great brahmin,' he said, 'these other twice-born students have opted for the brave man's method because they cannot bear to see me suffer. But you appear inactive and unenthused. Obviously you are not troubled by my distress, even thought it is evident. I have made it known in plain words and hidden nothing. How can you then sit quietly, unaffected and without any feeling?'

'Heaven forbid!' replied the Bodhisattva, saluting the teacher with respect. 'I am neither hard-hearted nor lacking in affection. Nor am I untroubled by the guru's suffering. But the course he has pointed out is impossible. No one can act sinfully without being observed. And why? Because there is no such thing as being alone.

> 'In this world, an evil-doer
> can never be alone.
> Beings whom we cannot see
> watch over every man,
> as do sages, pure of mind,
> endowed with sight divine.
> Not seeing them, it is the fool
> who gets into evil ways,
> thinking he is alone.

'For my part,' the Bodhisattva added, 'I do not see any place at all where I can be alone. Even though there may be no one else in that place, my own self ensures that it is not empty. One's evil actions may be witnessed by someone else or by oneself. In the latter case they are perceptible more clearly. Another person may not notice one's actions because he is concerned with his own. But one who commits a sin with his mind wholly involved in it knows what he is doing. It is for this reason that I keep to myself.

'My mind, sir,' he continued, 'cannot accept the conclusion that even you could misguide us in this way, merely for the sake of money. For, knowing the difference between the good and the bad, who indeed would be prepared to give up the former for the pursuit of wealth? As for my intent, let me explain:

> 'Better take a begging bowl,
> put on the cloak of mendicants,
> and gaze upon the opulence

of the mansions of one's foes,
than abandon shame,
and think of murdering virtue,
even for the sake of
the sovereignty of heaven.'

The teacher was amazed and delighted. 'Well said! Well said, my boy!' he exclaimed, as he got up from his seat and embraced his pupil. 'Well spoken, great brahmin! This is in keeping with your intellect, embellished as it is with calmness. The foolish may forsake the path of their duties for any reason whatsoever. But the virtuous, whose wealth lies in penance, learning and wisdom, will not go astray even in circumstances of the greatest distress. You are an adornment for your family, just as the rising autumnal moon is for the sky. Your conduct proves that your studies have been successful, and their success has made my labours both pleasing and fruitful.'

Thus it is that because they would be ashamed of themselves that good people do not overstep the bounds of right behaviour. The noble should have a sense of shame. It is a barrier which protects the noble devotee so that he can abjure the noxious and foster the wholesome.

13

The Enchantress

EVEN THOUGH THEY ARE IN GREAT PAIN, BECAUSE OF THEIR fortitude and determination, the good will abjure a path which is base. Thus has it been heard:

Once the Bodhisattva was the king of the Shibis. He strove for the people's good with honesty and generosity, with calmness and wisdom, together with his other surpassing merits. He was, in effect, an embodiment of virtue and discipline, as he devoted himself like a father to the welfare of his subjects.

The people rejoiced in both worlds as the king restrained them from wicked actions and inculcated noble qualities in them like a parent does with his children. His dispensation of justice was righteous and equal, both for his compatriots as well as others. Perceiving that public welfare lay in the pursuit of virtue, he applied himself to this single goal with all his heart, never permitting its transgression by others.

Now, a leading citizen of the royal capital had an extremely good-looking daughter. Endowed with the beauty and the charms of a heavenly nymph, she was like Shri, the goddess of good fortune, or Rati, the love god's consort – a veritable pearl of womankind. Except for those who are past passion, all who saw her would be so smitten by her looks that they could not turn their gaze away from her. Because of this her kinsmen called her Unmadayanti, the enchantress who turns men mad.

The girl's father informed the king about her. 'Sire,' he said, 'there is a jewel among women in your kingdom. It is for Your Majesty to decide if you will accept her or not.' The king sent for some brahmins learned in the bodily marks of women. 'Go and see, gentlemen,' he ordered them, 'whether she is suitable for me or not.'

Unmadayanti's father led the brahmins to his house. 'My dear,' he said to his daughter, 'you must serve food to these people yourself.' 'Very well,' she replied, and duly did so. But they were so struck by her beauty that they just stared at her face in wonderment, their eyes and even their minds out of control, and their composure so destroyed by the god of love that they appeared as insensate as if they were drunk. How could they eat in this condition? The father was impelled to withdraw his daughter from their presence and serve them food himself before letting them go.

Eventually the brahmins regained their senses. 'This lovely girl's looks are indeed magical,' they said to each other. 'It is not suitable for the king even to see her, much less to make her his wife. The splendour of her beauty will definitely enchant him and dull his enthusiasm for religious and political duties. The work of the state will then be delayed, and the people's welfare impeded, leading to dire consequences. The mere sight of this girl could obstruct even the attainment of sages. Who knows what may happen to the king, who is young and used to comforts, if he looks at her with ardour?'

Having thus made up their minds, they went to the king. 'We have seen that maiden, great king,' they told him. 'She is beautiful and attractive, but no more. Adverse marks make her beauty inauspicious. It is not suitable for Your Majesty even to see her, much less to make her your wife. A censurable wife clouds the glory and the prosperity of both families, just as an overcast night obscures the moon, as well as the glory of both heaven and earth.'

On learning that the girl had unlucky marks and would not be suitable for his family, the king abandoned any desire to have her. And, knowing of the monarch's disinterest, the girl's father married her to a royal minister named Abbhiparaga.

In due course it was time for the Kaumudi festival.[1] Eager to see the celebrations in his capital, the king mounted a fine chariot and drove through the city. Its streets and squares had been washed and cleaned; colourful flags and banners fluttered above; and the white ground was strewn with flower petals. Everywhere there was dancing and singing, gaiety and laughter, and the sound of music. The fragrance of flowers and incense, powders and perfumes, garlands, wine and unguents filled the air. All manners of goods were on display for sale, and the main roads were thronged with happy townsmen and villagers in their brightest dresses.

Now Unmadayanti was angry with the king. 'He has spurned and humiliated me as having inauspicious marks,' she felt. Feigning curiosity to see him, she stood on the roof of her house in all her loveliness, radiant as a streak of lightning on the crest of a cloud. 'Let us now see if he is able to keep his calm and hold his mind steady on seeing this inauspicious person,' she said to herself. And it so happened that, as the king looked around, curious to see the festive capital, his gaze suddenly came to rest upon the girl who stood on the roof in front of him.

The king was pious and endeavoured to subdue his senses. He had tremendous composure. In the harem he had seen the wanton charms of beautiful women whenever he wished, but had always remained unexcited. He was, moreover, bashful by nature and shy to look at strange young women. Even so, at the sight of Unmadayanti, he was filled with the wonder of love. For a long time he could not take his eyes off her. 'Is this the lady Kaumudi[2] in person,' he said to himself, 'or is she the goddess of this house? Perhaps she is a celestial nymph or a demon damsel, for this is not a human form.' He could not look long enough at her as his chariot moved on, against his will.

The king returned to his palace, thinking of nothing but the woman he had seen. His calm had been shattered by Manmatha, the god of love, and his heart felt a deep void. At home he took Sunanda the charioteer aside. 'Do you know,' he asked when they were alone, 'whose house that was, surrounded by the white wall, and who was the woman there, who shone like lightning in a white cloud?'

'That was the house of Abhiparaga, one of Your Majesty's ministers, and that woman is his wife. She is the daughter of Kiritavatsa, and her name is Unmadayanti,' replied the charioteer.

On learning that she was the wife of another man, the king's heart was overcome with dismay and his eyes misted with sadness. 'O the soft and lovely name she bears is indeed apposite,' he said to himself slowly with a deep sigh, his mind still fixed on her. 'The sweet smile of Unmadayanti seems to have enchanted me:

'I wish I could forget her
but I see her in my mind,
my thoughts are fixed upon her
or they are in her thrall.

'And all this, my infirmity,
for another's wife!
I am today enchanted,
bereft of shame and sleep.

'My heart is smitten, as it dwells
on her lovely smiles and glances;
and the bell which calls me rudely
to duty's ways infuriates me.'

Thus was the king's composure shaken by the love god's power. Though he tried to calm himself, his pale and gaunt appearance, and his absent-minded sighs and yawns made it obvious that he was in love. Despite his great efforts to conceal them, his feelings were soon evident from his brooding face, moist eyes and wan appearance.

Abhiparaga the minister knew how to infer meanings from outward gestures. He loved the king and, having learnt of his condition and its cause, and aware of the love god's power, he became apprehensive that his master may die. So he sought an audience and met the king in secret. After taking leave to speak, he said, 'O lotus-eyed lord, today when I was praying to the gods, a yaksha came to me and asked if I did not know that the king's heart had been lost to Unmadayanti. With these words, it suddenly disappeared. I have come here, thinking about this. If this is so, why is Your Majesty angry and does not speak to me? For the sake of doing me a favour, sire, please accept her.'

The king hung his head in shame at the minister's declaration. But though he was in the love god's grip, such was his rectitude that his firmness did not falter. 'This cannot be,' he said, refusing the offer resolutely. 'And why? Because I am not immortal, and my store of merit will deplete. People will know that I have committed a sin. And the anguish of separation from her will consume your heart just as fire incinerates dry straw. It is only the foolish who indulge in deeds which have evil consequences both in this and the next world; the wise abjure them for the very same reason.'

'Your Majesty should not worry that there will be any transgression of dharma in this,' replied Abhiparaga. 'Dharma lies in facilitating the giving of a gift. In fact, to hinder it by not accepting a gift from me will be a transgression. Moreover I do not see any danger in this to Your Majesty's reputation. For who will know about it apart from the two of us? Therefore you should not fear any public disapproval. Besides, you will be doing me a favour, not causing me pain. There is no room for pain in a heart content to serve one's master. Do not be concerned for me on that count, sire. Fulfil your desire.'

'Heaven forbid!' said the king. 'It is obvious that your affection for me is so great that you overlook that dharma does not lie in facilitating every gift. A friend who does not care even for his own life out of love for me is more to me than a brother. And the wife of such a comrade is also my comrade. So, it is not proper to entice me into something sinful. And will it cease to be a sin if no one else knows about it? To sin in secret is like drinking poison and expecting to stay healthy. The gods and the pure-eyed sages are always witness to the acts of mankind. Furthermore, who will believe that you do not love your wife and will not suffer if you give her up?'

'You are my master and my god,' said Abhiparaga. 'I am your servant, together with my wife and children. How will Your Majesty transgress dharma by taking this maidservant? And even if Your Majesty thinks that I love her, what does it matter? Indeed, I do love her, sire, and that is why I wish to give her to you. It is only by giving up something one loves that one obtains another still more lovely in the next world. Therefore accept her.'

'No,' replied the king. 'Do not speak thus. It is not proper. And why? I may fall upon a sharp sword, or into a flaming fire, but I cannot yet again strike a blow at dharma, through which I have attained my sovereignty.'

Abhiparaga then said: 'If Your Majesty does not wish to accept her because she is my wife, I will order her to become a harlot who is accessible to all. Then Your Majesty can take her.'

'Are you mad!' exclaimed the king. 'If you abandon a woman who is innocent, the people will condemn you, I will punish you, and you will come to grief both in this as well as the next world. So, do not insist on what should not be done. Consider propriety.'

'I will accept the consequences with all my heart,' said Abhiparaga, 'though they may be breach of dharma, public censure, or the loss of my own happiness. Whatever gives you pleasure will make me glad. There is no one in the world, great monarch, whom I revere more than you. You are like a presiding priest at a sacred rite for the enhancement of my store of merit. Accept Unmadayanti as your ritual fee.'

'There is no doubt that because of your great affection for me, you are trying to help me without considering your own interests,' said the king. 'It is particularly for this reason that I cannot ignore what you do. One should not be indifferent to public censure. The people will never trust someone who pays no heed to their disapproval and disregards dharma and its consequences in the next world; nor, for certain, will he have glory in this one. That is why I say to you: may you never want to transgress dharma for the sake of this life; there is no doubt that it is a great sin, and every doubt that it gives any benefit.

Furthermore, the virtuous will never wish others to suffer censure and suchlike for the sake of their own pleasures. Therefore I will stand by dharma and do my duty by myself without hurting anyone else.'

'If I act out of devotion to my lord,' Abhiparaga responded, 'or if he accepts her whom I offer, where is the possibility of any infringement of dharma? Let the Shibis, both town dwellers and country folk, say if there is any infringement. Therefore Your Majesty should accept her.'

'I agree that you want to help me,' said the king. 'But you must also consider who knows dharma best: is it the Shibi populace, or you, or is it me?'

'Your Majesty has laboured long in learning from the wise,' Abhiparaga hastened to reply. 'You have an acute intellect and are a master of the scriptures. If anyone fully understands the science of the three pursuits,[3] it is you, apart from Brihaspati, the preceptor of the gods.'

'Then you cannot dupe me in this matter,' said the king. 'The people's loss or gain depends on the conduct of their rulers. And, bearing in mind the people's devotion to me, I will follow the righteous path which alone leads to glory. Just as the cows which follow the bull trail him without hesitation, whether he takes a good or a bad road, so do the people emulate the actions of their king.'

'You should also consider,' the king added, 'if I lack the ability to rule myself, what will happen to the people who seek my protection? I am the bull of this herd. I cannot go just where I please, for I must look to the people's welfare, to my own duty and to the purity of my reputation.'

The king's steadfastness gladdened the heart of Abhiparaga. Saluting the monarch with folded hands, he said:

'It is the people's great fortune,
O King, to have you as protector:
love for dharma, which spurns comfort,
is rare even in hermitages.

'On you alone the appellation
"great king" is an ornament:
to speak of merit, for those without it,
is but a word of harsh contempt.

'You are a treasure trove of merits,
as the ocean is of gems;
how could this great act of yours
astonish or trouble me?'

Thus it is that even though they are in great pain, because
of their fortitude and determination, the good will abjure a path
which is base.

14

Suparaga the Navigator

DHARMA SHOULD BE FOLLOWED. BASED ON IT, EVEN A SINGLE
word truly spoken can avert a calamity. What more can be said
of the results of abiding by dharma? Thus has it been heard:
  As a Bodhisattva, the great one was once an extremely
skilled navigator of ships. Owing to their innate intelligence,
it is in the nature of the Bodhisattvas to be the best in
whatever science or art they wish to know. Accordingly, that
great soul understood the movements of the stars, and was
never at a loss about the directions. Familiar with the signs
of approaching turbulences, he was adept at judging good and
bad times for a voyage. He could also recognize regions of
the sea by the colour of the waters, the fish and the birds, the
types of earth and rocks, and similar features. He was,
moreover, vigilant, impervious to sloth and sleep, and able to
endure the excesses of cold, heat and rain. Alert and steadfast,
he knew how to avoid dangers and follow favourable routes
in taking traders to the destinations of their choice. Because
of his accomplishments in navigation, he was named
Suparaga, and the town where he lived came to be

famous under the same appellation. It is now known as Sooparaga.

Even in his old age, Suparaga would be approached by seafaring merchants who wished to ensure a successful voyage. They considered him lucky, and would entreat him with great respect to accompany them. Once some merchants of Suvarnabhumi,[1] coming from Bharukachha and anxious for a good journey back, came to Suparaga's town and requested the great man to embark with them. 'What help do you expect from me?' he replied. 'Old age has dimmed my eyesight. The stress of labour has affected my memory. I have no strength, even for the functions I should perform myself.'

'We are aware of your physical condition,' saïd the merchants. 'We know that you can no longer support the strains of exertion, and do not wish to trouble you with any such task. What we seek is simply that our ship be blessed by the touch of your feet, so that it may sail safely through this vast and perilous sea. It is for this reason, sir, that we have come to you.'

Though he was feeble with age, Suparaga boarded the ship out of compassion for the merchants. They were delighted and convinced that their voyage would be successful. In due course the vessel entered the limitless waters of the ocean, which reached down to the nether world, the home of serpents and demon armies. Many species of fish inhabited these waters, whose restless murmuring surface, coloured by the glow of precious stones in the sea bed and flecked with garlands of foam above, was forever whipped into waves by the wind.

They found themselves in the middle of a deep sea, with no shore visible on any side. The water was a sapphire blue. It seemed as if the sky, heated by the sun's rays, had melted into it. Towards the afternoon, the sunlight mellowed and there appeared fearful portents of a great storm. A fierce howling gale arose, tossing the waves and scattering the foam. The waters convulsed as the sea suddenly assumed a terrifying form. It looked like the final deluge, when the earth quakes with its mountains, as immense masses of water were whirled around by the storm wind. Many-headed dark clouds, flashing tongues of lightning amidst terrible thunderclaps, spread over the sun's orb like a multitude of serpents, obscuring its light. It was the end of the day, and the sun set gradually while darkness merged with the clouds.

It then began to pour. Its waves pierced by arrows of rain, the sea arose, as if in anger, and the ship began to tremble, as if with fear. The merchants' dismay accentuated their individual propensities. Some were beside themselves with terror, others mute with dejection. Some were brave but confused about what to do, and others were busy praying to their gods. Meanwhile the ship was driven on, caught in fast currents built up by a mighty wind.

For many days the merchants saw neither land nor any favourable signs on the sea. This unprecedented situation heightened their despair, and they were distraught with fear and gloom. Suparaga comforted them. 'It is no surprise,' he said, 'that those at sea should suffer the tribulations of a storm. But you gentlemen should not despair. Calamities cannot be overcome by dejection. There is not point in being miserable. Difficulties are surmounted only by the steadfastness of those who know what to do. Therefore you should shake off this despondency and apply yourself to opportune work. For an intelligent man, the power generated by his perseverance is the best method of achieving success. So, let everyone be alert to his responsibilities.'

Thus were the merchants reassured by that great soul. Eager for sight of land, they gazed at the sea and saw seemingly human figures in silver armour, rising from and disappearing into the water. Amazed by this spectacle, they carefully noted the shapes and other characteristics of the figures, and told Suparaga: 'This is indeed something never seen before. These creatures with fierce looks and ugly hoof-like mouths seem like demon warriors in silver armour. They leap and dive as if they are playing in the water.'

'They are neither human nor supernatural,' Suparaga commented. 'They are fish, and there is no need to fear them. But we have been swept far beyond the two ports. This is the Khuramali sea, and we should try to get back.'

However, the ship was caught in a swift-flowing current and the wind was adverse. The merchants could not turn it back. As they advanced further, they saw another sea, gleaming like silver with masses of white foam. 'What great sea is this?' they asked Suparaga as they marvelled at the sight. 'It is covered with its own foam, as if with white silk, or with liquid moonlight. Spreading in all directions, it seems to mock at us.'

'Alas, we have come too far,' said Suparaga. 'This is the Dadhimali, the sea of milk. If we can turn back, we should not go any further.'

'The ship is being swept along too swiftly,' replied the merchants. 'The wind is against us. We cannot even slow the vessel down, much less turn it back.'

Having also crossed this sea, the merchants beheld another, the waters of which were flame coloured and its waves tinged with a golden glow. 'What is this sea?' they asked Suparaga with amazement and curiosity. 'Its high, bright billows have the colour of the rising sun, and it glows like a great blazing fire.'

'This sea is well known as the Agnimali,' said Suparaga. 'It would indeed be good to turn back from here,' he added, having mentioned, farsightedly, only the name of the sea and not the reason for its changed colour. Meanwhile they had crossed it also, and were faced with yet another, whose water had the colour of ripe kusha grass and the radiance of topazes and sapphires. 'What sea is this?' they asked curiously. 'Its water has the colour of old kusha leaves, and its foam-tipped waves, raised by the wind, seem to strew it with flowers.'

'Try to turn back, O merchants!' said Suparaga. 'It is not prudent to go any further. This is the Kushamali sea. Its currents are irresistible, like an elephant out of control. They will sweep us away by force, unless we turn back.'

But the merchants could not change course, despite all their efforts. They were swept forward and saw yet another sea whose green water had the glow of beryl and jade. 'What sea is this?' they asked Suparaga once again. 'It looks like a fresh meadow with its emerald-green water, sprinkled as it were with flowers of foam.' The mariner's heart was heavy, for the merchants were now on the verge of disaster. Heaving a deep sigh, he said slowly, 'You have come too far. It will be hard to return from here. This is the Nalamali sea. It is practically at the end of the world.'

The merchants were deeply dismayed. Their enthusiasm evaporated and they sat down dejectedly as the ship passed through that sea also. In the evening, as the sun's rays faded and it seemed about to sink into the water, they heard a sound from the sea. It was a horrendous roar, reverberating like claps of thunder or like bamboo clusters exploding in a forest fire. The sea seemed to be in commotion.

The merchants were terrified. Jumping up in consternation, they looked about on all sides and beheld a gigantic torrent hurtling down, as if over a precipice into a chasm. Overwhelmed with fear and perturbation, they went to Suparaga and said, 'This deafening noise, which can be heard from afar, has thrown our minds into a whirl. The ocean sounds enraged. All its water is crashing down into this great abyss. What sea is this, sir, and what do you think we ought to do?'

'Alas!' cried the great soul, as he looked agitatedly at the sea. 'Alas! You are at the dreadful Mouth of the Mare. It is like the gateway to death, a portal from which no one returns.'

Realizing that they were at the Mare's Mouth, the merchants gave up all hope of survival. Overcome with the fear of death, some wept aloud, lamented and screamed. Others were petrified or frightened out of their wits. Some prayed ardently to the king of the gods, or to other deities such as the Adityas, the Maruts, the Vasus,[2] and even to Sagara, the spirit of the sea. Some told their beads and muttered incantations, and some made obeisance to the goddess Devi.

Some others approached Suparaga, gesticulating and wailing piteously. 'You have always been compassionate to others,' they cried, 'and have freed from fear those who were caught in calamities. The time has come for you to use your extraordinary power. This furious sea wishes to swallow us into the Mare's Mouth. Stricken and helpless, we seek your sanctuary, O steadfast one. It is for you to save us, who face disaster surrounded by the sea. It cannot disobey your command, and you should pacify it.'

The great soul was filled with compassion. Assuring the merchants, he said, 'It seems that there is still a way to meet this situation, and I will attempt it. Meanwhile you should keep patient for some time.' Thus reassured, the merchants became quiet.

Suparaga then placed his cloak on one shoulder and, kneeling on the ship with his right knee bent, paid earnest homage to the Tathagatas.[3] Addressing the merchants, he said:

'Listen you respected traders, and you distinguished gods who abide in the sea and the sky,

> 'When I look back upon myself
> from the time I gained awareness,
> I cannot recall, despite deep thought,
> ever harming any creature.

> 'With the power of this truth,
> and of my store of past good deeds,
> may this ship turn safely back
> and escape the Mouth of the Mare.'

Miraculously, by the power of his veracity and his merits, the current changed and the wind altered. The ship was turned back. The astonished and delighted merchants informed Suparaga of this development with respectful salutations. 'Be calm, gentlemen,' he replied, 'and quickly hoist your sail.' They carried out his order with joy, for their energy and enthusiasm had now been fully restored.

> The white sail spread, like stately wings,
> the ship was filled with joyous laughter
> as it sped back through the sea,
> as splendid as a swan in flight
> across a cloudless sky.

The ship sailed back with favouable winds and currents, moving as easily as an aerial vehicle flies through the sky. The colours of dusk had not yet faded and the sun's glow still lingered on the horizon, but darkness was spreading and the stars had begun to appear. As night descended upon them, Suparaga told the merchants, 'O traders, load the vessel with as much sand and stones as it can take from the Nalamali and the other seas you have seen. This will make its sides stable, even in a violent storm. Moreover these sands and stones are auspicious, and you will certainly profit from them.'

The merchants did as he suggested. The gods showed them places from which they loaded the ship with beryl and other gems, thinking that these were sand and stones. During that very night they reached the port of Bharukaccha, and in the morning they found themselves on the shores of their homeland with a full shipload of silver and gold, beryl and sapphires.

What more can be said of the results of abiding by dharma? Based on it, even a single word truly spoken can avert a calamity. Thus, dharma should be followed. While discoursing on the sanctuary which the auspicious friend[4] provides, it should be stated that those who seek such refuge attain all happiness.

15

The Fish

THE GOOD INTENTIONS OF PEOPLE OF CHARACTER WILL BE accomplished in this world itself, not to speak of the next. Therefore one should strive for purity of character. Thus has it been heard:

The Bodhisattva was once the chief of the fishes in a certain lake. It was a small sweet-water lake, blooming with pink, white and blue lotuses and lilies. Its surface was strewn with flowers from the trees on the shore, and pairing swans, ducks and geese made it a splendid sight. The Bodhisattva devoted himself there, as always, to securing the welfare of others, for the constant practice of this virtue in his many previous lives had made it a part of his nature.

> Deeds good or wicked, by dint of practice,
> become a part of the nature of men;
> so that in future lives they do them
> as effortlessly as in a dream.

The Bodhisattva showered affection on the other fishes as if they were his own children. With skilful efforts he made them forget the cruel propensities of fish, fostering in them love for each other and restraining their inclinations to mutual violence. Nurtured and protected by him, the fish of the lake flourished and prospered, just as a city freed of troubles does under a just king.

One year, the rainfall was insufficient. In the absence of adequate rain, the lake could not fill with fresh water as it did in the past. With the advent of summer, its water, pale with the pollen of kadamba blossoms, was soaked up daily by the sun's strong and relentless rays, by the earth they heated, and by a searing, dry wind. In due course the lake became a mere pond.

> The sun is aflame in the summer,
> the wind seems to emit gusts of fire,
> the earth is hot, as if with a fever:
> it soaks up water, in a burning rage.

The fish were reduced to misery and despair. They could do no more than writhe and gasp as hosts of crows and other birds on the lakeshore eyed them hungrily. Their chief felt a deep pity for their condition. 'What a calamity has befallen the fish!' he said to himself. 'The water decreases every day, as if it is racing against their lives, and the rains still appear to be far away. There is no way of escaping, and none to take us elsewhere. Our adversity has attracted our enemies who are drawing near. There is no doubt that, once the remaining water dries up, they will devour these writhing fish before my eyes.'

'What should be done now?' the great soul wondered. He saw that the sole refuge of those who suffer is in the power of truth. His heart filled with compassion, he looked up at the sky and said with a deep sigh:

'Despite much thought, I cannot recall
that, even while in great distress,
I ever injured any creature.
By the power of this truth,
may the king of gods bring down
rain, and fill all lakes with water.'

And, by virtue of his accumulated merits, by the power of
his veracity, and by the grace of the gods unseasonal dark
clouds gathered in the sky. Their deep thunder was like sweet
music. Heavy with rain, they hung low, their huge blue heads
gleaming with streaks of lightning, as they seemed to stretch
out and embrace each other.

It was a splendid spectacle:
the clouds were like mountains
reflected in the mirror of the sky;
their peaks cast long shadows
as if to measure the horizon;
the laughter of their thunder
set peacocks adancing
and calling out in joy.
Finally, streams of rain
fell from them like pearl drops,
the dust subsided, and the earth
exhaled a gentle fragrance, which
was carried and spread by the wind.

The strong summer sun was obscured by the clouds.
Foaming torrents now raced down from the hills. Lightning
danced to the drumbeats of thunder, illuminating the distance
with its golden glow. The lake began to fill up with pale

currents of water flowing in from all sides. The crows and the other birds were driven away by the rain, and the fish rejoiced, their hope of life restored.

The chief of the fishes was delighted. But, concerned that the rain may cease he called out to the clouds, again and again. 'Thunder loud and long, O clouds,' he cried, 'and rain down water glittering like jewels amidst the lightning flashes. Dispel the glee of the crows.'

This was heard by Shakra, the lord of the gods. Marvelling greatly, he went to the chief and praised him. 'O great lord of fishes,' he said, 'it is only because of the vast power of your truthfulness that these lovely thundering clouds pour out their waters like pitchers tilted downwards. I was exceedingly careless, sir, and erred in not assisting the endeavours of someone like you who is totally devoted to the benefit of all. But do not worry on this account for the future. I am bound to help in the work of the virtuous. And, because of your merits, this land will never again be afflicted in this way.'

After praising the chief of the fishes with these pleasant words, Shakra disappeared. Meanwhile the lake was brimful with water.

Thus, the good intentions of people of character will be accomplished in this world itself, not to speak of the next. Therefore, one should strive for purity of character.

16

The Fledgling Quail

ONE SHOULD APPLY ONESELF TO SPEAKING THE TRUTH. WORDS purified by truth cannot be contravened even by fire. Thus has it been heard:

Once the Bodhisattva was a fledgling quail in a certain forest. It was only a few days earlier that he had merged from the egg. His young wings were still sprouting, and his other limbs were as yet too tender to have assumed full shape. He lived with his many brothers in a nest his parents had built among the vines of a thicket and concealed with grass.

Even at that stage of his life, the Bodhisattva had retained awareness of what is right. He did not want to eat the creatures his mother and father brought as food, but subsisted on the grass, seeds and banyan berries they gathered. Because of this coarse and inadequate diet his body did not strengthen, nor did his wings develop properly. The other baby quails fed on everything given to them, became strong and grew wings.

This situation is quite normal: one who is unconcerned about what is right, and consumes everything, lives at ease, but one who seeks a livelihood and food in accordance with dharma will suffer. The Lord has also said:[1]

'The shameless and impudent crow,
who lives by base and dirty deeds,
has an easy livelihood;
though such a life is full of sin.

'But a modest, scrupulous person,
who always strives for purity
and seeks a life of righteousness,
will have a hard time here.'

While the fledgling quails were living thus, a great forest fire broke out not too far away. It fumed and crackled fiercely, spewing sparks from widening rings of flame. A disaster for the vegetation of the forest, it terrified the animals which dwelt there. Their courage vanished before its spreading fiery arms and its swirling, dishevelled hair of smoke, as it advanced in a strange, leaping dance propelled by the wind. The forest grass was ignited by glittering sparks and blown about by gusts of air. The birds fled, terror stricken, and so did the beasts as they ran helter-skelter. Covered by a pall of smoke and filled with the sounds of the conflagration, the forest itself seemed to scream in agony.

Driven by a violent wind in its search for more grass and plants, the fire finally came near the nest of the quails. The fledglings shrieked with fear and agitation and suddenly flew away without any thought for each other. The Bodhisattva alone made no effort to fly, for he was as yet too weak and his wings were still sprouting. Yet he was aware of his power, and remained calm. Addressing the fast-approaching fire, he said humbly:

> 'My feet cannot be called as such,
> my wings have yet to grow;
> scared by you, my parents have
> already flown away.
> For a guest like you, O Fire,
> there's nothing fit to offer here;
> it is therefore right that you
> turn back and make retreat.'

As soon as these words purified by truth had been uttered by the Bodhisattva, the fire suddenly abated. Though driven by the wind and raging amidst dry wood and dense grass, its progress came to a halt as if it had reached a river in flood. Even today, when a forest fire whipped by the wind into soaring flames reaches that famous spot in the Himalayas, its blaze slackens and subsides, like a many-headed serpent spellbound by some incantation.

It might be deduced that even fire cannot transgress the commands of truthful souls, just as the sea with its crests of waves cannot overflow its natural bounds, and a truth-loving person disobey the discipline ordained by the Lord of the sages.

17

The Pitcher

DRINKING LIQUOR IS ATTENDED BY MANY EVILS, AND IS altogether bad. God people will restrain even others from this habit, not to speak of themselves. Thus has it been heard:

The Bodhisattva was once Shakra, the king of the gods. His thoughts suffused with compassion, he was always intent on securing the welfare of others. Charity, restraint and discipline marked his many merits. Even though the most exquisite sensual pleasures of paradise were available to him at will, such was his compassion that he never slackened his resolve to work for the benefit of the world.

The wine of prosperity makes people lose awareness even of their own interests. But Shakra remained unaffected by the riches which come with celestial sovereignty. He was ever watchful of others' interests, and felt for those who suffered as if they were his brothers. Steadfast and cognizant of his own nature, he never forgot to work for others.

Once Shakra happened to look down at the mortal world, his large eyes soft and tender with friendliness and sympathy. He observed that a king named Sarvamitra had fallen into bad company and taken to tippling together with his town and country folk. Noticing that the king was blind to the evils of drinking intoxicants, he was moved by a deep pity. 'Alas!' he said to himself. 'What a calamity has befallen these people! They are unable to see the demerits of drinking, though it is pleasant enough to begin with. But it is like a charming path which leads one astray.'

'The king needs to be cured,' the great soul reflected, 'for it is the constant nature of people to emulate their leaders. Whatever happens to them, good or bad, will depend on him.'

Having come to this conclusion, Shakra assumed the form of a majestic brahmin. His complexion was the colour of burnished gold, and his long hair was twisted in a coil. Dressed in a deerskin and garments of bark, he carried in his left hand a small pitcher of wine. In this garb he appeared in the air before King Sarvamitra.

The king was seated in his assembly where the talk had already turned to wines and spirits, to ales, grogs and honeyed liquors. On seeing Shakra the astonished assemblage stood up respectfully and greeted him with folded hands. He addressed them in a deep voice, resonant like the thunder of a cloud heavy with rain. 'Who will buy this splendid pitcher?' he cried. 'A garland of flowers smiles around its neck, and it is full to its brim. Who among you wishes to purchase it with its floral wreath trembling in the breeze?'

The king's amazement turned to curiosity. Gazing at Shakra with great respect and folded hands, he said, 'Like the newly risen sun is your lustre and like the moon your grace. From your appearance it seems that you are one of the holy sages. Tell us who you are, for we cannot make you out.'

'Who I am, you will know in due course,' replied Shakra. 'Meanwhile apply yourself to buying this pitcher – if you are not afraid of sufferings in the next world or painful addictions in this one.'

'Sir,' said the king, 'your style of selling is really unprecedented. It is well known that people wishing to vend something extol its merits and conceal its defects. But your method befits only the likes of you, who fear to speak falsely. The virtuous will of course not resile from the truth even if they are in trouble. So, tell us what this pitcher contains and what a person like Your Honour expects in return.'

'Listen, great king,' Shakra replied. 'This pitcher does not contain water fresh from a cloud or drawn from some sacred river. It is filled neither with excellent ghee nor with honey as fragrant as the flowers from which it is made. Nor is it full of milk, bright as the moonbeams which awaken water lilies on a cloudless night. Inside it is something wicked, the power of which you must hear.

'One who drinks it gets intoxicated and loses control over his functions. He slips and stumbles even on plain ground. His memory fades: he eats everything, unable to tell between what is forbidden and what is not. That is what this worst of pitchers contains. Buy it, for it is now on sale!

'It hijacks the mind. A man loses self-control and goes about like a stupid beast, the object of ridicule by his enemies. He dances in the middle of an assembly, drumming on his cheeks. That is the wretched thing inside this pitcher, which deserves your purchase!

'On drinking it, a man also loses all sense of propriety and shame. He becomes like the naked Nirgranthas, unburdened by the trouble and the discipline of wearing clothes. In that state he walks boldly on crowded roads. That is what is offered for sale in this pitcher.

'On drinking it, men lie senseless on the royal roads while dogs boldly lick their mouths for the food they have vomited. That is the lovely merchandise on sale inside this pitcher.

'Partaking of it, a woman may get so drunk that she may even tie her parents to a tree and disregard her husband, rich though he may be. That is the thing in this pitcher.

'On drinking it, the Vrishnis and the Andhakas[1] so lost their senses that they forgot they were kinsmen and obliterated each other with their clubs. Thus is the maddening beverage in this pot.

'Addiction to it destroyed many illustrious and eminent clans. That ruin of rich families is up for sale in this pot.

'When the mind is stricken with the beverage inside this pot, one weeps and laughs, sits and stands without self-control, the eyes dull and heavy, as if possessed by a demon. One becomes, for certain, an object of contempt.

'The thing vended in this pot befuddles even mature people, so that they speak excessively without thinking and are too confused to do what is in their own interest.

'Drunk on it, the gods of old were deprived of their splendour by the king of heaven and sought protection by diving into the ocean. Take this pitcher filled with it.

'Under its influence man confuses right with wrong. He utters falsehoods as confidently as if they were true, and does what is prohibited as joyously as if it were prescribed. The thing in this pitcher is indeed a curse personified.

'Buy this deep darkness of the mind. To know it, is to go mad. It is the home of trouble and the embodiment of misfortune. The mother of evils, it is the single road to sin.

'Buy and take it, O king. It can rob a man of his senses so that he will even kill his innocent father or mother or a holy hermit without any care for his own future happiness.

'Such is this intoxicant drink, O glorious king. It is known in the world as wine. Let someone who is not partial to virtue make an effort and purchase it.

'But can anyone think even of looking at it? People get addicted to evil actions when they imbibe it. They then go to frightful hells or are born again as animals or as suffering spectres.

'The least result of consuming liquor is that it destroys moral discrimination in those who have been born as human beings. They then go to the fearful firey hell Avichi, or to the world of phantoms, or are born again as lowly animals.

'Drinking liquor kills character and annihilates reputation. It does away with shame, besmirches the mind and puts an end to every merit. Does it still deserve to be drunk by you, O king?'

These persuasive and purposeful words convinced the king of the evils of drinking. 'Whatever you have stated is meant for my welfare,' he told Shakra, his craving gone. 'You spoke like a loving father, like a teacher responding to a pupil's devotion and humility, or like a sage who knows right from wrong. I will try to honour your words by my deeds.

'Meanwhile these well-said words deserve respectful reciprocation,' the king added. 'Accept, sir, these five excellent villages, a hundred maidservants, five hundred cows and ten chariots drawn by fine horses, which I give to you as my teacher who speaks for my good. Or, if there is anything else that I should do, please favour me by commanding it.'

'I have no need for these excellent villages and the other gifts,' Shakra replied. 'Know me as the king of the gods. The only way to honour a well-wisher is to act on his words. This is the way to fame and prosperity in this world, and to every happiness in the next. So, give up drinking and take refuge in dharma. Thus will you attain my kingdom in heaven.'

With these words, Shakra disappeared. As for the king, together with his town and country folk, he gave up drinking intoxicants.

18

The Renunciant

THE HOUSEHOLDER'S LIFE IMPEDES A MORAL AND TRANQUIL existence. As such it does not please seekers of spiritual betterment. Thus has it been heard:

The Bodhisattva was once born in an affluent family, admired for its conduct and character and much sought after by people of good birth. This family was like a well of plenty for both shramans[1] and brahmins. Its treasuries and stores were open to friends and relations and always accessible to poor mendicants. Endowed with great wealth, patron of craftsmen and recipient of royal honours and favours, it was a family held in high popular esteem.

In course of time the Bodhisattva grew up. He laboured at studying the established sciences and applied himself equally to the various arts. With his pleasing personality, and his understanding of conduct in consonance with the sacred law, he soon won a place in the hearts of the people.

Now the great soul was familiar with the renunciant's life. He understood the happiness of the hermitage, and knew that the life of the householder impedes the pursuit of righteousness and causes the pains which come with cravings. Domestic pleasures did not therefore appeal to him. Much affected when his parents died, he duly distributed his estate worth many millions among his friends and relations, the poor, the shramans and the brahmins, and abandoned his home. After that he wandered successively through villages, hamlets and towns, through kingdoms and their capitals, and eventually made a forest his abode.

The practice of meditation had given a natural calmness to the Bodhisattva's senses. His words were pleasing both to hear and to understand. They revealed his learning, but were free of conceit and of the wretched baseness which accompanies the hope of some gain. His speech was courteous but powerful, marked by elegance in treating everyone with due respect, and skilled in discriminating between right and wrong. His conduct accorded with that of a renunciant approved by good people. And when the curious populace learned that he had renounced a high family, it honoured him all the more.

> Virtue, supplemented
> by beauty and birth,
> turns more attractive;
> as moonbeams do
> when they illumine
> some handsome object.

A friend of the Bodhisattva's father came to know of his new abode, and paid him a visit to enquire about his welfare. He had great respect for the Bodhisattva's virtues and, after telling him about the paternal friendship, said affectionately, 'Your Holiness has surely been impetuous in assuming the renunciant's life at this age, without regard to your family and lineage. The virtuous can live rightly at home just as well as in the forest. Why did you choose to give up a prosperous household and live in a jungle?

'Here you live on alms, depending on the mercy of others,' the paternal friend continued. 'People may consider you a charlatan. You wear rags and are stuck in this wilderness, devoid of your friends and relations. It is poverty personified, which you seem to have embraced. How can you suffer so? Even your enemies would weep to see you in this condition.

'You should therefore return to your paternal home,' the visitor added. 'Its riches are surely known to you. Living there you can fulfil your desire, both to live righteously and to have a virtuous son. One's home is a source of comfort even for a hired labourer, will yours not be more so when it is well provided and near at hand?'

The Bodhisattva's mind was suffused, and his heart filled with the nectar which is the bliss of detachment. He knew the difference between living at home and in the forest, and an invitation to partake of worldly pleasures did not tempt him at all. 'It is obvious that you have spoken out of affection,' he replied, 'so, what you said does not trouble me much. But you must not use the word 'comfort' to describe the householder's life. It is in fact extremely stressful for the rich as well as the poor. One is troubled by guarding his wealth, and the other by labouring to acquire it. That being the case for both, the illusion that it gives pleasure can only be due to one's past misdeeds.

'It is true that a householder too can live righteously,' the Bodhisattva continued. 'But that seems exceedingly difficult to me. The householder's life is replete with impediments to virtue and full of toil. It is not for one who has no desires, does not lie, abjures violence and does not hurt others. A person addicted to domestic comforts will always search for methods of securing them. Household life requires effort, while the road to righteous living is marked by tranquillity. So, if one seeks to live rightly, he cannot have domesticity, and if one looks for the latter, there is no room for the former.

'The defect of the householder's life is its contradiction with what is right. Which soul can accept it? There is no certainty of comfort if righteousness is discarded in its pursuit. This only leads to disrepute, remorse and trouble. That is why the wise will never accept such paths to pleasure as are opposed to virtue.

'It seems to me, moreover, that it is just a belief that the householder's life gives pleasure. What is certain is that it causes pain – the pain of acquiring and guarding wealth, of fearing murder, imprisonment and other calamities. Even a king is no more satisfied with the wealth he has than the ocean is with a shower of rain. So, how can the householder have pleasure unless he chooses to imagine it? In fact, sensual attachments give only an illusion of pleasure, the same as one gets from scratching at a sore.

'Indeed, I would say that, as a rule, in the householder's life prosperity often leads to vainglory, lineage to pride, and power to arrogance. Sufferings cause anger and adversities dejection in that life. There is no room in it for tranquillity. I would as such submit to you, sir, that it is a nest of serpents – of vanity, pride and delusion. It ruins the comfort of calmness and confronts one with disaster. Would anyone wish to dwell in this abode of tribulations?

'In the forest, on the other hand,' the Bodhisattva concluded, 'one has the happiness of detachment. It is the place for those who are content. The bliss that it provides cannot be had even in heaven. That is why I am happy to be here, clad though I may be in rags and living on the charity of others. For

I have no desire for comforts tainted with what is not right, just as a prudent person has none for food laced with poison.'

With these profound words did the Bodhisattva convince his father's friend about the merits of detachment.

19

The Lotus Stalks

LIKE DECEPTION AND VIOLENCE, SENSUAL ENJOYMENTS ARE anathema to those who know the pleasure of detachment. Thus has it been heard:

The Bodhisattva was once born in a noble brahmin family of impeccable standing, well known for its merits. He had six younger brothers and a sister, who shared his virtues and followed his example out of affection and esteem.

The Bodhisattva studied the Vedas together with the Upavedas and the Vedangas.[1] He became famous for his erudition and much respected by the people. Wise and modest, he looked after his parents with utmost devotion and guided his brothers into the world of learning like a teacher or a father.

His parents died in the course of time, and the Bodhisattva was deeply affected. He performed their funeral rites and, after some days spent in mourning, assembled his brothers and told them: 'This is the inevitable and tragic way of the world. Death separates us, no matter how long we live together. Therefore I wish to renounce all this, and take the blessed road to salvation, before death strikes me down like an enemy while I am still enjoying a householder's life.

'For this reason,' said the Bodhisattva, 'I would like to inform all of you that the lawfully obtained wealth in this brahmin household will be adequate for your needs. You should live here properly, with mutual love and respect. Never slacken your regard for character and conduct. Devote yourself to studying the Vedas; attend to your friends, guests and kinsfolk; and observe the rules of righteousness. Adhere well to the householder's life, always courteous, delighting in charity and intent on your studies. In this way your fame will increase together with your virtue and your wealth. Even your afterlife will be secured. So, take care as you live here.'

The Bodhisattva's brothers were greatly agitated by his talk of renunciation. Bowing to him with tears in their eyes, they said: 'Grief at the loss of our father has pierced us like an arrow. The wound it caused is not yet healed. It does not behove you, brother, to rub the salt of yet another sorrow into it. Please give up this idea. Alternatively, if you consider domestic attachments to be inappropriate and the bliss of forest life the way to salvation, why do you wish to go away by yourself, leaving us bereft in this house? Your chosen path is equally ours. We will also renounce the world.'

'Those who have not practised detachment are usually motivated by worldly desires,' the Bodhisattva replied. 'They generally consider renunciation to be like falling off a cliff. That is why I desisted from asking you to take to forest life, even though I know fully well the difference between that and a householder's existence. But, if it pleases you, we can all renounce the world.'

Thus, all seven brothers and their sister gave up their estate and valuable properties, their sorrowing friends and relations, and took to the life of homeless ascetics. With them went three others: a companion, an attendant and a maidservant.

Eventually the renunciants came to a vast forest. In it was a large lake whose pure, blue water seemed ablaze with blooming lotuses in the day and shimmering with lovely lilies at night. By the side of this lake, frequented by honeybees, they built themselves separate huts of leaves under shady trees, at some distance from each other to provide pleasant solitude. Here they lived, observing all the vows and rules and absorbing their minds in meditation. Every fifth day they would go to the Bodhisattva to listen to his pious discourses on the joys of tranquillity. His inspiring words exhorted them to meditate and avoid the pitfalls of worldly desires. Dwelling at length on the peace of mind which comes with detachment, he also condemned idleness, hypocritical talk and other vices.

Their maidservant, who loved and respected them deeply, continued to look after them as before. Every day she would pull out lotus stalks from the lake and place them in equal portions on large lotus leaves at a clean spot on the shore. After that she would announce the meal time by striking a piece of wood against another, and withdraw. Having performed their daily prayers, the hermits would then come out one by one in the order of their age and, taking their portion of the stalks, return to their respective huts. There, they would take their meal in the prescribed manner and pass the remaining time in meditation. In this way they avoided seeing each other except at the time of the discourses.

The hermits' fame spread far and wide on account of their faultless character and conduct, love of detachment and contemplative life. Shakra, the king of the gods, also heard about it and came down to test them. His respect for their virtues increased on observing that they were given to meditation, averse to wrongdoing and always calm and serene:

> One free of desires,
> who lives in the forest
> devoted to peace,
> instils in the hearts
> of all good people
> respect for his virtues.

But Shakra became all the more keen to put them to a test. On the following day the maidservant gathered lotus stalks for the sages as usual. She washed the stems, white and tender as the tusklets of an elephant calf, and placed them in equal portions, decorated with lotus petals and stamens, on emerald-green leaves of the plant. After that she struck together two pieces of wood to announce the meal, and withdrew. At that moment Shakra, the lord of the gods, decided to test the Bodhisattva by causing the first portion of the lotus stalks to disappear.

The extent of a good man's patience can be seen as it grows when troubles occur and comforts vanish. When the Bodhisattva came to the place where the first portion of the lotus stalks used to be kept, he noticed that the decorations were in disarray and there were no stalks on the lotus leaf. 'Someone has taken away my share,' he concluded without any agitation or anger, and returned to his hut where he resumed his meditation. To avoid upsetting the other sages, he did not inform them about this; they in turn assumed he would have taken his share as they took theirs before returning to their huts to eat and meditate.

On the following day Shakra again concealed the Bodhisattva's share of lotus stalks, and repeated this test on the third, fourth and fifth days. As for the great one, he remained calm and content as always:

> For good people, the mind's turmoil
> is more deadly than death itself;
> the wise will not get agitated
> though their lives are put on stake.

On the afternoon of the fifty day, when the other sages came as usual to the Bodhisattva's hut to hear his discourse, they found him looking gaunt, with sunken eyes and hollow cheeks, his face wan and his voice weak. But, though emaciated, he was as delightful to look at as the crescent moon, for his fortitude and tranquillity were unaffected.

The Bodhisattva's brothers were worried. Approaching him politely, they enquired why he had become so thin. When he told them what had happened, they could not imagine that any of them would do such a thing. 'Alas! Alas!' they cried, distraught at his suffering, and stood before him, their heads hanging in shame.

The power of Shakra had clouded the brothers' judgement, and they could not figure out how the lotus stalks had disappeared. At last the eldest brother uttered an extraordinary imprecation to display both his emotion and his innocence. 'O brahmin!' he cried, 'may he who stole your lotus stalks find fulfilment with a charming wife, children and grandchildren, and a house embellished with all the signs of prosperity!'

'O chief of brahmins!' exclaimed the next brother, 'may he who stole your lotus stalks indulge in exquisite worldly pleasures, flaunting garlands and sandalwood paste, fine garments and ornaments which his children have touched for good luck.'

'May he who stole your stalks even once,' said the third brother, 'enjoy himself at home without worrying about the passage of time; and may he make money from farming, live with his family and delight in the prattle of his children.'

'May he who stole your lotus stalks out of greed rule the entire earth,' said the fourth brother. 'May other kings pay him homage, humbly like servants, the plumes quivering on their bowed heads.'

'May he be a royal priest, that person who stole your lotus stalks,' said the fifth brother. 'May he know the auspicious incantations and receive honours from the king.'

'May he who sought your lotus stalks and not your virtues be a teacher well versed in the Vedas,' said the youngest brother. 'May people come and honour him with the reverence due to ascetics.'

'May the person who could not subdue his greed for your lotus stalks receive four hundred fine and prosperous villages for his enjoyment from the king,' said the companion, 'and may he die before his passions fade.'

'May he who harmed his own interest for the sake of the lotus stalks become a village chief,' said the attendant. 'May he enjoy himself with his friends amidst the singing and dancing of women, and never be troubled by the king.'

Then spoke the sister. 'May the person who stole the lotus stalks of even someone such as you have a figure of radiant beauty,' she said, 'and may the king make her his wife, the first among a thousand women.'

'And may she who saw your lotus stalks and not your righteousness, look past good people,' said the maidservant. 'May she amuse herself eating all alone the tasty morsels she receives as gifts.'

Now some denizens of the forest – a yaksha,[2] an elephant and an ape had also come to listen to the Bodhisattva's discourse. They too were disturbed and ashamed to hear what had happened. The yaksha pronounced a curse to demonstrate his innocence. 'May he who betrayed even you for the sake of the lotus stalks live in the great monastery of Kachangala,' he cried, 'and be an artisan making windows every day.'

The elephant followed suit. 'O best of sages,' he said, 'may he who stole your lotus stalks be exiled from the delightful forest into human habitation, there to be bound in six hundred strong fetters and suffer the pain of the sharp elephant goad.'

The ape spoke next. 'May he who was so greedy as to steal your lotus stalks wear a floral garland and a tin collar to chafe his neck,' he said. 'And may he be beaten with sticks, made to confront serpents and be kept in the snake-charmer's house, tied to a harness.'

The Bodhisattva replied to all of them in persuasive words full of courtesy, which displayed his profound calmness. 'Someone stated that the stalks have vanished when actually they have not,' he said. 'Or someone suspects you all of having done this. May he obtain all the pleasures he desires and live out his life as a householder.'

Shakra, the king of the gods, marvelled at the extraordinary imprecations which had been uttered. They indicated an abhorrence of indulgence in pleasures which roused his respect. Revealing himself in his radiant form, he approached the sages and said, as if in anger, 'You must not speak like this! Why do you run down worldly pleasures? People are so anxious to obtain them that they cannot sleep; they are prepared even to undergo the travails of penance for their sake.'

'Sensual enjoyments, sir, mean endless sufferings,' the Bodhisattva replied. 'Listen in brief to what these are. It is because of them that sages have no praise for such pleasures.

People suffer imprisonment and death while seeking them. They are afflicted by grief and fear, by fatigue and all kinds of misery. It is only for the sake of pleasure that kings oppress virtue and go to hell when they die.

'It is due to the pursuit of pleasure,' the Bodhisattva added, 'that friendships fade suddenly. People tread the dirty paths of political chicanery, lose their reputations and suffer in the afterlife. Pleasures are destructive, of both this and the next world, for all kinds of people, the worst, the middling as well as the best. That is why, O Shakra, they are avoided like angry snakes by sages who seek spiritual betterment.'

The king of the gods welcomed these words. Pleased at the sages' nobility of mind, he admitted his own misdemeanour. 'Respect for merits comes when they are tested,' he said. 'It was in order to test you all that I hid the lotus stalks. They now testify to the firmness of your character. The world is fortunate to have sages like you whose fame is based on facts.'

With these words Shakra presented the lotus stalks to the Bodhisattva. But the latter rebuked him for his discourtesy and audacity. 'We are not your kinsmen or companions,' he said forcefully, 'nor are we performers or buffoons. On what basis did you then come here, O king of the gods, to play such a game with sages?'

Thus addressed, Shakra hastily took off the earrings which lit up his face, and his crown, in a gesture of penitence, and, bowing to the Bodhisattva with the utmost respect, asked for forgiveness. 'You have no selfish thoughts,' he said. 'I have explained why I acted so rashly. You must pardon me, sir, like a father and a teacher. Some people are blind to wisdom, and it is natural for them to give offence even to the virtuous. But for those who are self-contained it is equally natural to forgive. So, do not be angry with me.'

Having sought forgiveness, Shakra disappeared straightaway. Thus it is that sensual enjoyments are anathema, like deception and violence, to those who know the pleasures of detachment.

The Lord thus explained this birth story. 'I – the son of Sharadvati – Maudgalayana, Kashyapa, Purna, Aniruddha and Ananda were then the brothers. Utpalavarna was the sister, Kubjottara the maidservant, and the householder chitra, the attendant. Satagiri was the yaksha, Parileya the elephant and madhudata the ape. Kalodayi was Shakra. Thus should this birth story be remembered.[3]

20

The King's Banker

PRAISE FOR A MERIT THEY DO NOT POSSESS ACTS LIKE A SPUR UPON good people. The acquisition of merit is something one should always strive for. Thus has it been heard:

The Bodhisattva was once a king's banker of noble lineage. His learning was as great as his modesty, and his mind as lofty as it was sharp. Honest work gave him pleasure. His speech was marked by the elegance which comes with the study of many sciences. A compassionate nature allowed his wealth and prosperity to flow in all directions. With his munificent charities and immense resources, he was esteemed as a jewel among the householders.

> He was, above all others,
> respected by the people
> as adorned by learning
> and every other merit,
> the soul of truth and virtue
> by his very nature.

Once, while the banker had gone to the royal palace for some business, his mother-in-law came to his house to see her daughter. After the welcoming ceremony, when the lady was alone with her child, she enquired about her welfare. 'My dear, I hope your husband does not treat you with disrespect,' she asked. 'I hope he understands the virtue of being considerate, and does not hurt you by any misconduct.'

The daughter looked down bashfully, and said in a whisper: 'Good character and virtuous conduct such as his will be hard to find even in a renunciant. There is none to equal him.' But the mother's hearing and comprehension had been affected by old age, and she could not quite grasp her daughter's words, constrained as they were by some embarrassment. The mention of 'renunciant' brought her to the conclusion that her son-in-law had renounced the world, and she burst into tears, grieving for her daughter with loud lamentations.

'What kind of character and conduct is this, that he renounces the world and abandons his own dear ones?' the old woman wailed. 'And what will he get from this renunciation?' He is young and handsome, fastidious and used to comforts. The king is fond of him. How could his mind turn to living in the forest? How could he leave an affluent home so suddenly, without any provocation? He had not become old or ugly. His family had not crossed him. How could he treat them so cruelly and casually, specially when he is wise and courteous, pious and caring of others?

'He always respected the shramans and the brahmins, his friends, dependents and family, as well as all those in distress,' she continued. 'Purity and character, he considered to be the real wealth. What could he not find in the householder's life that he must look for it in the forest?' He is so attached to dharma, but does he not see that he has transgressed it in abandoning an innocent and devoted woman who is his wedded wife? What luck, that in forsaking their families people feel not a shred of pity or gain even a grain of merit.'

In keeping with the ways of women, the banker's wife was deeply moved by her mother's mournful and spontaneous lamentation. She was also confused. Overcome with distress, and assailed by grief and anguish, she forgot the wider subject and context of their conversation. 'My husband has renounced the world,' she decided, 'and on getting this sad news my mother has come here to console me.' Weeping and wailing loudly, she then fell into a faint.

On learning what had happened, the other members of the family and the servants also began to sob and cry in sorrow. Hearing the commotion, neighbours and friends, kinsmen, relations and dependents, brahmins and other householders, in fact almost all the citizens, gathered at the house of the royal banker, to whom they were greatly attached. For he generally treated other people's joys and sorrows as his own and they did the same to him, as if learning from his example.

In due course the banker returned from the royal palace. As he neared his home he heard the sounds of lamentation and noticed the large crowds assembled there. He then ordered one of his men to find out what had happened. After gathering information, the man came back. 'Noble sir,' he said, 'the people have heard from somewhere that you have forsaken this great house and taken to a renunciant's life. Their affection for you has reduced them to this condition.'

Pure-hearted by nature, the banker was embarrassed to hear these words which sounded to him like a reproof. 'Indeed, the people hold me in high esteem,' he said to himself. 'Having earned their admiration for my merits, what will be my worth if I just continue to stay a householder? This will be seen as an unfeeling disregard of virtue on my part, and a devotion to wrongdoing which will debase me in the eyes of good people. Would I want even to live in that condition? Therefore I must honour the people's respect for me by deeds of due merit. I must give up the wicked and painful life of the householder for one in the hermitage.'

His mind made up, the banker promptly turned back. He had it conveyed to the king that he wished to see His Majesty once again and, on being permitted, went up to the monarch with the usual ceremony. 'What is it?' the ruler asked. 'I wish to renounce the world,' he replied, 'and beg Your Majesty to grant me permission.'

The king was mystified. 'What troubles you,' he asked affectionately, 'that you want to retire to the forest while a friend and a well-wisher like myself is here? What is the problem which cannot be solved by my power or my wealth, my policies or my forces? If you need money, take it from me. If you have some vexation, I will relieve it. What have you found in the forest that you wish to go there, despite my request and that of your family?'

The banker replied in conciliatory words to the king's friendly enquiry. 'How can anyone under your protection be vexed or suffer from want of money?' he said. 'It is not because of any trouble that I go to the forest. There is another reason which I would like you to understand. It is being said that I have taken the vows of renunciation. The people are weeping and mourning. It is because they believe me capable of such virtue, sire, that I want to leave for the solitude of the forest.'

'You cannot leave us merely because of some public perception,' said the king. 'The merits of people such as you, sir, do not depend on the cultivation of public opinion, nor are they lost by ignoring it. Rumours are sparked by imagination, and their spread cannot be controlled. It is ridiculous to take them to heart, and more so to act upon them.'

'No, great king,' the banker replied. 'A favourable public opinion must not be ignored. Your Majesty, when a good man comes to be respected as a person of high virtue he must live up to that reputation, even if out of shame. His glory will be greater if he is seen to act in keeping with his esteemed virtues; otherwise he will be no better than a waterless well. When favourable opinions grow without any basis in fact, and are later disproved as a result of scrutiny, it destroys a man's good name which is then hard to revive.

'Possessions, sire, are the root cause of strife,' the banker added. 'They should be avoided like angry black snakes. It is not right that you stop me from renouncing them. Your affection for your servants and your recognition of their loyalty is indeed most appropriate. But what will I, a renunciant, do with money and the pain it causes?'

Thus did the great soul persuade the king and obtain his permission, after which he set out straightaway for the forest. His friends, relations and dependents came to him with eyes full of tears, clasping his feet and seeking to stop him. Some blocked his way, standing there with folded hands. Others sought to lead him homewards with embraces and entreaties. Yet others spoke to him harshly because of their affection. Some said he should have pity and concern for his friends and kinsfolk. Some tried to convince him by citing the scriptures and arguing that the householder's life was the best. Others endeavoured in a variety of ways to have him turn back. They magnified the hardships of penance and forest life; urged him to fulfil his remaining worldly responsibilities; or expressed doubts about the existence of any rewards in the next world.

It is obvious that on seeing that his friends, their faces wet with tears, were opposed to his renouncing the world and determined to prevent his going to the forest, the banker was plunged into thought. 'When a friend has gone astray,' he reflected, 'those who claim to be his well-wishers should tell him what is right and in his interest, even if it be a harsh thing to say. If it is pleasant as well as beneficial, so much the better. But this is the accepted and proper way for all good people.

'But how have they formed the impression that worldly life is superior to that in the forest?' the banker wondered. 'They have balanced minds, and yet they boldly oppose my taking to forest life as if it were a sin. One may weep for a man who is dead or about to die, or who has fallen from the path of virtue, but by what logic do they mourn for me, simply because I wish to live in the forest?

'If they grieve because I am leaving them, why don't they come with me to the forest? And if I am less dear to them than their homes, why this flow of tears? If love for their families does not allow them to become ascetics, why did it not prevent them from going into battlefields?

'Their tears testify to their friendship, acts of which I have already seen in times of trouble. Yet it now seems make-believe, for they do not follow my example. They sob, shed tears and shake their heads reverentially to stop me from going, because they respect me. The same sentiment should induce them to give up this charade, which shames good people, and follow me in renouncing the world.

'The fact is that even a worthless person will have at least two or three friends to be with him in times of trouble,' the banker thought further. 'But for a man of virtue it is hard to find even a single comrade for the forest life. Those who marched before me in battlefields full of rutting elephants will not follow me today into the forest. Are they and I still the same? I cannot recall that I ever harmed them so that their love for me could diminish. Perhaps this attitude of my friends is due to their concern for my welfare. Perhaps it is due to my demerits that they will not come with me, for a heart attracted by virtues could never turn contrary.

'If they cannot perceive the obvious evils of the householder's life and the virtues of the renunciant's life, they are simply blind to wisdom. What else can I think about them? They cannot renounce sensual pleasures which are the cause of sufferings in this world as well as the next. On the contrary, today they renounce me and the forest. Alas for their delusions! But, with the goodly power that I earn in the forest, I will destroy those very evils, deluded by which my friends, and the whole world, cannot attain peace.'

Thus did the Bodhisattva ponder and make up his mind. Turning down with sweet, conciliatory but plain words the affectionate entreaties of his friends, he then went away to the forest as a renunciant.

Thus it is that praise for a merit they do not possess acts like a spur upon good people. A good person, esteemed for the virtues of a monk or a lay devotee, will endeavour to attain them and improve himself. Another conclusion to be drawn is that companions are hard to find for seeking refuge in dharma.

21

A Question of Anger

BY CONTROLLING HIS ANGER A MAN PACIFIES HIS ENEMIES. Otherwise he merely incites them. Thus has it been heard:

That great being, the Bodhisattva, was once born in a noble brahmin family, famous for its practice of virtue – prosperous, honoured by the king and favoured by the gods. In course of time he grew up, received the various sacraments and, with his study of the Vedas, soon became well known in learned assemblies.

> The fame of the learned
> spreads in temples of learning
> like that of gems among jewellers
> and of heroes in the battlefield.

The Bodhisattva had adhered to dharma in his previous births. His mind had been cleansed by wisdom, and he was familiar with the renunciant way. He did not, therefore, enjoy the life of a householder. So he gave it up, just as a person conscious of his health will shun poisoned food. He shaved off his handsome hair and whiskers, and, forsaking the householder's splendid garb for a discoloured ochre robe, embraced the rules and discipline of the renunciant.

The Bodhisattva's wife loved him very much. She too cut off her hair, divested herself of external ornamentation, and followed him into the renunciant life, adorned only with her natural beauty and virtues, her body covered with just an ochre garment. The Bodhisattva understood her intention, but he knew that a delicate woman is unsuited to life in a hermitage. 'My dear, you have demonstrated your love for me,' he told her. 'But do not persist in following me. It is better for you to stay where other renunciant women live. To make a home in the forest is hard. It is only the homeless ascetics who live in jungles full of snakes and wild beasts, though the sun also sets over them in cemeteries, deserted houses and hilltops. They endeavour to meditate, prefer solitude and are averse even to looking at women. So you should think of going back, for what will you gain from such wandering?'

But she had made up her mind to follow him. 'Going with you is a joy,' she replied, her eyes brimming with tears. 'If I considered it a labour, why would I take this trouble and do something disagreeable to you? You must forgive me for disobeying your order, for I cannot bear to live without you.'

When she would not turn back despite being told several times, the Bodhisattva ceased to pursue the matter. And, as they wandered through villages, towns and markets, she followed him as the wild goose follows her mate.

One day they found themselves in a lonely wooded region. It was clean, beautiful, and full of groves of shady trees. It was afternoon. The Bodhisattva had just risen from his meditation after a meal, and was mending some rags. His wife sat not far away under a tree, adorning it like a goddess with her radiant beauty. She too was engaged in meditation as he had taught her.

The king of the country came there at that time. He had been touring the groves and gardens of the region. At this period they shone with the new foliage of spring and were filled with the hum of honeybees and the ecstatic calls of koels. Their lovely lakes were embellished with lotuses and lilies. A pleasing breeze laden with the fragrance of different flowers wafted through them:

Forests in their springtime glory
are a sight to gladden hearts:
they are bright with banks of flowers;
koels, peacocks, humming bees,
fill them with their merry sound;
the lakes are full of lotus blooms;
the earth is covered with soft grass;
in that season they become
the playgrounds of the god of love.

The king approached the Bodhisattva courteously and, after an exchange of compliments, sat down on one side. He then saw the beautiful renunciant woman and was smitten by her straightaway. 'She must be his companion in religious duties,' he concluded. But, being capricious by nature, he nevertheless began to think of ways and means by which he could carry her off.

Though unsettled by the god of love, the king however did nothing rash to cause offence. He had heard of the power of ascetics' curses, which rose like flames from the fire of their wrath. 'One must first ascertain the power of his penance,' he said to himself. 'It is only then that one may act as appropriate.

His penance will obviously have no power if he harbours a passion for her in his mind. If he does not, on the other hand, or if he is indifferent, it is then possible that it may be very potent.'

The king then addressed the Bodhisattva like a well-wisher. 'O renunciant,' he said, 'in a world full of rogues and desperados it is not proper for Your Holiness to go about in desolate forests with such a charming companion in religious duties. If someone were to misbehave with her, we too will be blamed.

'Sir,' continued the king, 'this is a lonely place and you have been weakened by penance. If someone were to disregard both you and righteous conduct, and carry her off by force, what could you do but grieve? For anger serves only to agitate the mind and destroy a virtuous reputation. She ought to live where there are other people. Moreover, what is the need of female company for hermits?'

'You speak well, great king,' the Bodhisattva replied. 'But listen to what I would do in such a situation. If anyone were so arrogant or unwise as to act against me here, it is obvious that he will never escape me while I live, just as dust cannot the raincloud.'

'He desires her much,' thought the king, 'so he must lack the power of penance.' Confident that he would come to no harm, he then gave way to his lusts and, disregarding the Bodhisattva, he ordered the attendants of his harem to take the woman away.

Like a wild doe in the grip of a predatory beast, the Bodhisattva's wife was overcome with fear and distress on hearing the king's command. Her eyes filled with tears, and she began to lament piteously in a voice choked with sobs. 'The king is the only refuge of suffering people,' she cried. 'He is like a father. If he himself acts improperly, whom will the people look to?

'The guardian gods have lost their authority,' she lamented. 'Indeed they never existed or have died, for they do nothing to save those who suffer. I think that even dharma is no more than a name. But what is the point of reproaching divinities? My lord himself is silent at my fate. Even a stranger deserves protection, when harassed by the wicked.

'His curse could obliterate a mountain,' she wept. 'His one word, "perish," would be like a thunderbolt. But he stays silent, even when I am in such straits, and I, the unfortunate, still live. Is it not the rule of ascetics to have compassion for the suffering? Or, perhaps, I am a sinner unworthy of pity in my troubles. For I did not go back when I was asked to, and this still rankles in his mind. I sought what I wanted, even though it was unpleasant for him. Is this, alas, the result?'

While she wept and lamented, the officers ordered by the king put her in a chariot and took her away to the harem before the Bodhisattva's eyes. But he deliberately repressed his anger and continued to mend his rags, as calm and unagitated as before.

The king addressed him again. 'You made a great commotion with angry and indignant words,' he said. 'But now you sit silent, even after your wife has been abducted before your eyes. You are miserable because you can do nothing. Demonstrate your anger with your arms or by the power of your penance. One who swears in vain does not make a good impression.'

'Do not think that I swore in vain, great king,' relied the Bodhisattva. 'The one who acted against me here has not escaped me, despite his efforts. I put him down by force. I have kept my promise.'

The Bodhisattva's calm, indicative of an extraordinary forbearance, raised in the king's mind the possibility of his possessing ascetic virtues. 'This brahmin implied something else by his words,' the king wondered, 'without understanding which I have perhaps acted rashly.' Turning to the Bodhisattva, he then asked, 'Who was it that acted against you? Who could not escape you despite his efforts? Who did you put down as the cloud does the rising dust?'

'Listen, great king,' the Bodhisattva replied. 'There is something which causes harm wherever it finds refuge – anger. When it happens, men cease to see. It delights one's enemies and ill-wishers. It happened to me, but I did not let it escape. I put down anger which blinds men, O king, so that they can do nothing good when it rises.

'Anger is a demon, fierce and hideous,' the Bodhisattva continued. 'When it rises, a man spurns his own welfare, and loses even that which he already has. But I put it down while it was still stirring within me.'

'Anger rises from a man's false conceptions,' he added. 'It destroys him just as fire, ignited by rubbing pieces of wood, burns up the very log from which it springs. Anger's fire heats up his mind. The man who cannot calm it is held to be of little worth. His reputation fades like moonlight at dawn. In contrast is the man who ignores the insults of others and sees anger as his real adversary. His fame grows daily, like the light of the new moon.

'There are the other great evils in anger,' said the Bodhisattva. 'A man looks ugly when he is angry, even though he is decked with ornaments. The fire of rage deprives him of his glory. Anger's barb rankles in his heart, so that he cannot sleep at ease even in the best of beds. He forgets his own interests and gets into bad ways. He falls over the precipice of folly, despite his friends stropping him, and cannot tell what is good or bad for him. Often he is stupid enough to pick quarrels. Anger leads him to commit sins which will make him suffer for centuries. What more can even the most ill-disposed enemies do?

'Anger is the enemy within,' the Bodhisattva concluded. 'I know this. Which man will tolerate its insolent spread? So, when it stirred in my mind, I did not let it escape. For who can ignore a foe capable of such mischief?'

The king's mind was purified by the Bodhisattva's marvellously calm and persuasive words. 'Your words are in keeping with your serenity,' he exclaimed. 'What more can I say? Those who have not beheld you are truly deprived.' And he fell at the great man's feet, praising him and admitting his own misdeed. He also sought forgiveness from the renunciant's wife and, sending her back, dedicated himself as a servant of the Bodhisattva.

Thus it is that by controlling his anger a man pacifies his enemies. Otherwise he merely incites them. One should endeavour to control one's anger. Animosities are pacified by amity. Hostility is staunched by self restraint. One who refrains from anger thus benefits both parties.

22

The Two Swans

THE CONDUCT OF THE VIRTUOUS, EVEN WHEN THEY ARE IN trouble, is such that the wicked cannot emulate it. Much less can they emulate how the virtuous behave when they are in comfortable circumstances. Thus has it been heard:

Once the Bodhisattva was a king of the swans. His name was Dhritarashtra, and he was the lord of an immense flock, comprising hundreds of thousands of swans, who lived at the great lake Manasa.

The commander of the king's army was a swan named Sumukha. He had a politic mind and a good grasp of strategy. He was also endowed with talent, courtesy and modesty. Steadfast and pure in conduct and character, he was moreover brave, inexhaustible, vigilant, loyal and skilled in various forms of war. It was the noble elder Ananda in that birth.[1]

The capabilities of the king and the commander were reinforced by their mutual affection. As a teacher and his chief disciple do with other students, or a father and his eldest son with the remaining children, so did they initiate their flock into all that would benefit it in both worlds. The two swans were entirely occupied with the betterment of the flock, just as the two wings of a bird are occupied in keeping it aloft in the sky.

The sages and other celestial beings marvelled at the extraordinary merits of the two swans. 'Their bodies have the lustre of burnished gold,' they proclaimed. 'Their speech is clear. Their modest demeanour and conduct are based on virtue. We do not know who they are – they only bear the shape of swans.' The two swans' fame gained credence in the councils of kings where its accounts were passed around like gifts.

At that time there was a king named Brahmadatta in Varanasi. He often heard trustworthy ministers and brahmin elders talk in the assembly about the remarkable qualities of the two swans, and this made him increasingly curious to see them. 'O men of skill,' he said to his clever courtiers who had studied many sciences, 'think of some method whereby we may at least get a glimpse of these two noble birds.'

The ministers considered various possibilities, each according to his experience. 'Sire,' they replied, 'the prospect of pleasure attracts people from far and near. The news of something excellent which they can enjoy may therefore bring the swans here. Your Majesty should have a lake built in some wooded region, even more splendid than the one where these beautiful birds are reported to live. Then make it known by daily proclamation that you have granted safe passage to all birds at this lake. Such news should certainly excite their curiosity and draw them here. Look, sire:

'Pleasures often turn insipid
once they have been enjoyed,
and people do not care for them.
But one lauded by hearsay

will always charm the mind
since it is as yet unknown.'

The king agreed. Within a short time he had a great lake constructed not too far from the city park. Its magnificence rivalled that of the lake Manasa. Its pure and lovely water was full of various kinds of lotuses and lilies,

Trees covered with flowers,
their foliage glinting in the light,
stood around its periphery,
as if to view the lake.
Rocking in its gentle ripples,
lotus blossoms seemed to smile,
by which enchanted honeybees
hovered all around.
The water-lilies bloomed at night,
dappling, as it were, the lake
with specks of moonlight
filtering through the shade.
The lake's wave fingers
spread lotus pollen
like strings of gold
to grace its shores,
and lotus petals
flecked with pollen
seemed like gifts
as if of splendour.

The lake was adorned by schools of fish whose varied shapes were as clearly visible in its calm transparent waters as if they were flitting through the sky. At some places elephants blew sprays of water which scattered like pearls as they struck the rocks. At others the lake was fragrant with the lotions of bathing nymphs, the rut of elephants and the pollen of its own flowers. It was overall a mirror for the stars, and full of the merry sound of birds.

After the lake had been constructed and dedicated to the unrestricted ease and enjoyment of all birds, the grant of safe passage for them was assured through a daily proclamation. 'The king is pleased to give this lake and its water full of lilies and lotuses to the birds,' it was proclaimed. 'He also grants them safe passage here.'

The season changed in due course. The dark curtain of clouds was lifted and the sky sparkled with the glow of autumn. The lakes looked lovely with lotuses blooming in their limpid waters. The moon shone with renewed brilliance, the earth was embellished with various rich crops, and young swans became active. At this time, a pair of swans came out from the flock on lake Manasa and, cruising through the clear autumn sky, arrived in King Brahmadatta's country.

The swans saw the new lake. It was full of the sound of birds and honeybees. A pleasant breeze blowing over its waters spread everywhere the perfume of the lotuses and the lilies with which the lake was ablaze. 'How wonderful it would be if our entire flock were to come there,' thought the couple, even though they were accustomed to their own lake Manasa. And they stayed at the new lake for a long time, enjoying themselves at will.

The seasons changed and once more it was time for the rains. The swan couple returned to lake Manasa at this time. They went to their king Dhritarashtra and told him about the lake they had seen. 'Sire,' they said, 'in Varanasi, to the south of the Himalayas, there is a king called Brahmadatta. He has built a great lake of marvellous beauty and indescribable loveliness for the free enjoyment of all birds. Safe passage is proclaimed there every day and the birds enjoy themselves at that lake as freely and fearlessly as they would in their own home. Your Majesty should also visit it after the rains are over.'

All the swans became curious to see the new lake on hearing about it. The Bodhisattva looked quizzically at Sumukha the general. 'What is your view?' he asked. 'I think that it will be unsuitable for Your Majesty to go there,' replied Sumukha with a salute. 'These charming and attractive pictures are an enticement, really. But we lack nothing here. The hearts of men are often villainous, and their contrived courtesies and kind words frequently conceal a cruel wickedness.

'Consider, my lord,' Sumukha added. 'Birds and beasts generally say what is in their hearts. Man alone is adept in doing the contrary. His words can certainly be sweet, well meaning and helpful, but, as with merchants, expense is always incurred in the hope of making a profit. So it is not good to give credence to mere words. That is a dangerous and mistaken policy which will not succeed in attaining the end desired. However, if it is essential to go there and savour the beauties of that lake, one should do so for a short while, and not decide to live there. This is my view.'

But the other swans were most eager to see the lake at Varanasi and, on their repeated requests, the Bodhisattva agreed. On a clear autumn night adorned by the moon and the stars, he set out, surrounded by a multitude of swans led by Sumukha, and duly reached this destination.

The beauty of the lake delighted and amazed the swans. Though they had a variety of tastes, they were united in wanting to stay there. And they did so for a long time, enjoying themselves in a place which so surpassed Manasa by its many merits, that it soon replaced the latter in their hearts. Their pleasure was further enhanced on hearing the proclamation of safe passage and seeing the free movement of the other birds.

The officers responsible for the lake informed King Brahmadatta about the arrival of the swans. 'Sire,' they added, 'we have heard of two excellent swans. This brace has enhanced the beauty of Your Majesty's lake. Their wings shine like gold, and their beaks and feet are even brighter. Large and well built, they are here with hundreds of thousands of others.'

The king selected a fowler famous for his skill in snaring birds and formally ordered him to catch the two swans. The fowler swore that he would do so, ascertained the places frequented by the two, and set up strong, concealed traps there. Thus, while the swans went about credulously, suspecting no trouble and intent on pleasure, the foot of their king was caught in the trap.

> Credulity always causes
> carelessness and imprudence;
> and, in its subtle course,
> fears of danger are ignored;
> trusting only leads to harm.

Dhritarashtra was concerned that a similar calamity should not befall some other swan, and he signalled the dangers at the lake through a special cry. The swans were distressed to find their king ensnared. They flew away screaming with fear and confusion. General Sumukha alone stayed by the side of his king. Loving hearts do not care if their lives are at risk: for them the sufferings of a friend are even more painful.

'Fly, Sumukha, fly,' Dhritarashtra urged him. 'It is not good to linger there. You cannot help me in my present condition.'

'I will not die just because I stay here,' said Sumukha. 'Nor will I escape old age and death if I go away. I have served you in good times, my lord. How can I leave you at the time of trouble? O king of birds, if I were to abandon you merely for the sake of saving my life, how will I save myself from the shower of reproaches which would follow? To leave you in this adversity would not be right, great king, and I will be pleased to share your fate, whatever it may be.'

'What else can be the fate of a bird caught in a snare, except the cooking pot?' asked Dhritarashtra. 'How can that please you, who are free and sane? What good will it do to you or to me or to the rest of our flock if we both perish? What will you gain, Sumukha, by giving up your life? Its benefit is as hard to see as the evenness of the ground in dark.'

'O best of birds,' replied Sumukha, 'why do you not look at the benefit of doing right? Righteous action, well performed, gives the greatest of benefits. For these reasons, my lord, and also because of my devotion to you, I do not care for my life.'

'This is the way of the virtuous,' said Dhritarashtra. 'Bearing in mind what is right, a friend will not abandon a comrade in distress, even at the cost of his life. You have done this and also demonstrated your devotion to me. Now accept my final request, and leave. You have my permission to do so. You are wise and must fill the gap which will be caused among our friends by my loss in these circumstances.'

The hunter appeared while the two birds were thus conversing affectionately. They saw him descending upon them like death personified, and fell silent. The hunter observed that the flock had flown away and concluded that some bird must definitely have been caught. He searched for the places where the snares had been set and beheld the two excellent swans. Marvelling at their splendid looks, and thinking that both had been caught, he shook the two nearby snares and was astonished to find that though one bird was indeed trapped the other was free but remained there as if attending on the first.

The hunter approached Sumukha and said, 'This other bird is caught in a mighty trap. He is powerless and cannot fly away even when I come close. But you are free and healthy, strong and equipped with wings. Why did you not take to the sky when I came here?'

'There is a reason why I did not leave,' Sumukha replied in a powerful tone, in keeping with his steadfast nature. 'This bird has suffered entrapment. You have caught his foot in a great snare. But I am caught in the even stronger snare of his virtues.'

The hunter's hair stood on end in wonder. 'The other swans left him and flew away,' he said. 'They were afraid of me. What is he to you, that you do not leave him?'

'He is my king and my comrade, dear to me as my life,' replied Sumukha. 'He brings me joy and stands by me in adversity. That is why I cannot desert him, even to save myself.' And, seeing that the hunter was pleased as well as wonderstruck by his words, the bird added: 'Friend, may our conversation have a happy end. May you obtain the glory of virtuous conduct by letting both of us go.'

'I do not wish to harm you,' said the hunter, 'nor have I caught you. So you can go where you wish, see your kin and gladden them.'

'If you do not wish to harm me,' replied Smukha, 'then do what I request. If you are pleased to have one bird, then let him go and take me instead. We both are of the same age. Our sizes are comparable. Consider me his ransom and your profit will not diminish. Think of this, sir. I am sure you will like me. You can tie me up first and only then free this king of birds. In this way your profit will remain the same, but my request will have been fulfilled and you will have pleased and gained the friendship of our flock of swans. May they rejoice to see their king, released by you and adorning the clear sky, just as they do on seeing the moon freed by the demon of eclipse.'

The hunter's heart had been hardened by his cruel work. Even so, it melted on hearing Sumukha's words, full of devotion and gratitude to his master and heedless of himself. 'Well spoken! Well spoken, noble one!' he said to the swan, his hands clasped together with wonder and respect. 'The virtue which you have demonstrated by your readiness to sacrifice yourself for your master would be hard to find even among gods and men. So, I release your king with all honour. Who could harm him when you love him so?' And, disregarding his own king's orders, he respectfully released the king of the swans from the snare.

General Sumukha was overjoyed. 'O delighter of friends,' he said to the hunter with an affectionate look, 'just as you have gladdened me today by releasing our king, so may you rejoice with your friends and kinsmen, for a thousand years. But your labour should not go fruitless. Take us both, free and unbound, in your basket and show us to your king in his private suite. There is no doubt that he will be pleased to see the lord of the swans with an attendant, and reward you with more wealth than you can imagine.'

'The king must certainly see this extraordinary pair of swans,' thought the hunter and, agreeing with Sumukha's suggestion, he took the two birds, free and unbound, to his king.

'My lord,' he said, 'look at this wonderful present. I have brought to you the king of the swans with his general.'

The king was delighted and amazed to see the two great swans who glowed with the splendour of a mass of gold. 'Tell me in detail how these free and unbound birds came to be in your hands,' he said to the hunter.

'I placed many a cruel snare where the birds played about in the lake,' the hunter replied with a salute. 'This excellent swan suspected nothing. He was trustful and his foot was caught in a hidden trap. The other swan was not caught, but stayed by the side of the first and begged me for his life, offering himself in ransom. He spoke in human language, with words sweet and clear, and the offer of his own life gave power to his plea. I was so taken by the gentleness of his speech and the steadfastness of his efforts on behalf of his master that I released the latter, freeing myself at the same time from my cruel ways. He was delighted at his king's release and said many kind things to me. He also urged me to come to you so that my labour may not go waste.

'Though he has the appearance of a fine bird, he is a very holy being,' the hunter added. 'Within moments he softened even my heart. Grateful for the release of his king, if he has come here with him by his own volition, it is for my sake.'

The amazed and delighted ruler of Varanasi ordered a golden seat fit for kings for the lord of the swans. It was spread with a handsome rich cover and its feet glowed with gems. It was also equipped with comfortable cushions and a footstool. For Sumukha he ordered a seat of cane appropriate for a chief minister. Considering that the time had now come for words in reciprocation, Dhritarashtra then addressed the king in a voice as sweet as the sound of an ankle bell.

'You deserve the best, O king,' said Dhritarashtra. 'I hope that your glorious person is in good health, and your spiritual body too is well with the breath of charity and pious discourse.'

'You are dedicated to the protection of your people. Do you enhance their welfare and affection for you, as well as your own glory, by the timely dispensation of rewards and punishments?

'I hope you monitor the people's wellbeing through honest and unprejudiced, dedicated and efficient ministers, and not merely through hearsay.

'Vassal kings have been humbled by your policies and prowess. When they appeal to you, I hope you resort to the light of compassion, but not to the heedless slumber of credulity.

'I hope, O hero, that your lawful pursuit of virtue, wealth and pleasure is applauded by all good men who spread your fame in every direction. I hope too that your enemies can react to it only with sighs.'

The king's glad reply reflected his inner satisfaction. 'O swan,' he said, 'all will now be well with me in every way, for I have today secured this long-awaited meeting with a holy personage. I hope that this hunter did not hurt you with his staff out of exuberance when you were caught in his snare. For these villains do get boisterous and commit such acts when birds are entrapped.'

'Even in that adversity I was all right, great king,' Dhritarashtra replied. 'In no way did he behave with us like an enemy. He spoke kindly to Sumukha whom he was surprised and curious to see there even though he was free. Sumukha's true and gentle words softened his heart and he released me most respectfully from the snare. Sumukha then thought of his welfare and so we have come here. May this help him also.'

'You are welcome here, sir,' said the king. 'I was hoping that you both would come. To see you is a pleasure and I am overjoyed. This hunter will get a big reward today, for he deserves it after treating you both so kindly.'

Having honoured the hunter with a rich gift, the king of Varanasi then addressed the lord of the swans once again. 'You are here in your own house,' he said. 'Do not be formal with me, but tell me what you need. All my wealth is at your service. To ask a friend for something is to do him a great favour. A friend asking freely gives greater satisfaction to a man than all his own wealth.'

The king was also curious to talk to Sumukha. Looking at the general with wonder, he said: 'Obviously one will not speak candidly to a new acquaintance in whose heart one has yet to find a place. But one will still talk with courtesy and kindness. So, speak to me, sir, to give me joy and to fulfil my wish for your friendship.'

General Sumukha saluted the king respectfully. 'You are like great Indra, the king of the gods,' he said. 'To speak with you is a pleasure. Whose desires would not be more than satisfied by this demonstration of your friendship? But, when a prince of men and a prince of the swans are engaged in friendly conversation, it would be inappropriate and an insolence for a servant to intervene. How could I knowingly commit such a discourtesy? That is why I have kept silent, great king. Pardon me, if I deserve it.'

The king praised Sumukha with wonder and joy. 'Justly, sir, are people pleased with the catalogue of your merits,' he said. 'Justly has the lord of the swans made you his friend. None but the self-possessed have such humility and skill in conduct. Trust me, so that our newborn friendship grows further. Between good people it can indeed never decay.'

Dhritarashtra observed that the king was eager for friendship and keen to demonstrate affection. Praising him, he said, 'Though ours is a new acquaintance, you have been magnanimous and treated us as you would the closest friend. Who, great king, would not be won over by the kind of honours you have accorded us?

'Could friendship with me indeed have any ulterior purpose, my lord?' he added. 'You love and practise virtue, and your hospitality, it is certain, flows only from that. It is not strange in you, a person who has subdued his senses, assumed royal duties for the benefit of the people, and observes the austerities of a hermit. You are by nature a repository of virtues.

'Virtues are admirable. They conduce to happiness. None of this is to be found in the strongholds of wickedness. Knowing the difference between the two, which intelligent person would act against his own interests? The status that a king may attain without labour and expense by following the path of virtue, he will never achieve through prowess, wealth or politics. Even the sovereignty of the king of heaven depends upon virtue. So does humility. Glory comes from virtue, as does power and greatness. Virtue is lovelier than moonlight. It cleanses the minds even of enemies which may be full of anger and arrogance, hostility and jealousy.

'Therefore, O king,' the Bodhisattva concluded, 'awaken your people to the love of virtue. The proud rulers of this earth have bowed before your might. Protect the land with your ever-glorious virtues. The welfare of the people is the first duty of the king. To follow that path gives happiness in both this and the next world. And this will come to pass if the king loves righteousness, for the people will emulate him. May you therefore rule the earth in accordance with righteousness, and may the king of heaven protect you. Though we are glad to be with you, the sorrow of my flock now draws me away.'

The king applauded Dhritarashtra's words. He and his councillors then bade a kind and respectful farewell to the two excellent swans. The swans flew away into the clear autumn sky, which was blue like the clean blade of a sword. The flock was delighted to see them back. In course of time the compassionate swan again paid a visit with his flock to the king of Varanasi and, received by the monarch with reverence and courtesy, discoursed him on the virtuous path.

Thus are friendly words beneficial to both the speaker and the listener. This should be mentioned while lauding friendliness in speech, and also while describing good friends. It should also be recounted to show that the noble elder Ananda was the lord's companion in previous lives.

23

Mahabodhi the Renunciant

SUCH IS THEIR GRATITUDE AND READINESS TO FORGIVE THAT THE compassion of good people for their past benefactors does not diminish even when the latter treat them badly. Thus has it been heard:

While still a Bodhisattva, the Lord was once a renunciant named Mahabodhi. As a householder he had already studied the established sciences in due order and also such arts that roused his curiosity. After taking to a renunciant's life he worked for the benefit of people and applied himself in particular to the study of the sacred laws in which he obtained the rank of professor. Because of his good deeds and great wisdom, his worldly knowledge and apt demeanour, he was respected and sought after wherever he went: by learned men and the kings who patronized them, by brahmins and householders, as well as by renunciants of other persuasions.

> Virtues shine through deeds of merit,
> apt behaviour makes people love them;
> even foes will show them respect
> to protect their own reputations.

Wandering through villages and towns, markets, districts and capital cities in order to benefit the people, Mahabodhi once arrived in the realm of a certain king. The ruler was very pleased, for he had already heard of the renunciant's many virtues. Having received the news of his arrival in advance, he built a place for his stay in one of his own beautiful parks. Welcoming him into the kingdom with due ceremony, he honoured and waited on him as a disciple does his preceptor.

Mahabodi favoured the king daily with pious and uplifting discourses on spiritual betterment. For, those who love the righteous path are compassionate to others. They wish everyone well, even whose devotion is unknown, not to speak of the pure and zealous seekers.

The honours accorded to Mahabodhi for his great merits increased every day. The king's ministers and councillors could not tolerate this. They were respected as men of learning and shown all courtesies, yet their minds were overcome with jealousy.

The ministers were unable to defeat Mahabodhi in a debate on the scriptures. Nor could they bear the king's increasing attachment to the righteous path. Therefore they tried to alienate him from Mahabodhi. 'Your Majesty should not place any trust in the renunciant Bodhi,' they said. 'It is obvious that, having learnt of your love of merit and liking for the righteous path, some rival king has sent him here as a spy. He has been assigned to collect information and to entice you with sweet but wicked words into committing errors.

'He pretends to be a pious soul,' the ministers added, 'and preaches to Your Majesty only the practice of compassion based on some miserable feeling of shame. Such piety is incompatible with the lawful pursuit of virtue, wealth and pleasure, opposed to royal duties, and fraught with the dangers of misgovernance. He praises you lavishly while advocating what you should do, but he also likes to maintain contact with other foreign ambassadors, and he is far from being unfamiliar with the science of politics. That is why our hearts are full of apprehensions about him.'

The king was told this repeatedly by many people, ostensibly in his interest, but actually to create dissension. Soon suspicion entered his mind, his respect and affection for Mahabodhi dwindled, and his disposition changed. With the king's loss of confidence, his kind courtesies diminished and he no longer honoured the great man as before.

The pure-natured Mahabodhi felt that the king was busy with other duties and at first gave no thought to this change of heart. But from the slackened attention of the royal confidants he came to realize that the king had become indifferent. He then collected his triple staff, water pot and other belongings befitting a renunciant, and prepared to go away.

On hearing of his preparations, the king came to the great soul, for whom he still had some affection. Polite and courteous, he paid his respects and made out as if he wished to retain the renunciant. 'Why have you decided suddenly to leave us?' he asked. 'Has there been any carelessness on our part which has given you a false impression?'

'My plan to leave is not sudden,' replied the Bodhisattva, 'nor is it due to anger at some discourtesy. I am leaving because of your duplicity and divergence from the righteous path.'

The king's pet dog appeared at this moment, barking furiously, its jaws agape and slavering. 'Here is an animal to bear witness, great king,' said Mahabodhi, pointing to the dog. 'Previously it followed your example and showed me great affection. But now it betrays your feelings by its barks, for it does not know how to conceal them. Your devotion to me having ended, it must certainly have heard some harsh words from you about me. It is obvious that it is now acting them out to please you – this is what servants do.'

The king hung his head in shame at this reproof. Struck by Mahabodhi's acute reasoning which he could not match, he concluded that this was no time for circumlocution. 'Some officious members in our assembly had indeed talked about you,' he said with a bow. 'But I did not pay attention to them. You must forgive me and stay here. Do not go away.'

'It is not because of any disrespect or resentment that I am going away, great king,' replied Mahabodhi. 'I go because this is no more the time to stay.

'Consider, sir,' he continued. 'Because of indifference the hospitality here has lost its charm. Despite this, if I were not to leave voluntarily because of my attachment, apathy or some other weakness, I could be caught by the scruff of the neck and thrown out. Therefore I am leaving because I feel that is better, and not because I am displeased. Good people do not forget past kindnesses simply because of one affront. However, to seek patronage from someone no longer well disposed serves little purpose. It is like a dried-up pond for a man in need of water. Even if something is obtained after much effort, it is meagre and musty. The patron should be like a great lake in autumn, its water clear and pure. This is well known to all those who seek peaceful comfort and dislike trouble. Of course there are those who turn away from one who is devoted, abase themselves before another who does not care, and are slow to remember past favours. Such people may bear a human shape, but their decisions are doubtful.

'Friendship is destroyed both by inattention and by excessive attention,' Mahabodhi concluded, 'as it also is by persistent requests. I would like to safeguard whatever remains of our affection from the dangers of staying here. That is why I am going away.'

'If you have made up your mind to go, sir,' said the king, 'then you must favour us by coming here again. We must guard our friendship against inattention also.'

'Great king,' Mahabodhi replied, 'living in this world is fraught with obstacles and problems. I cannot therefore promise that I will come back. But if there is some pressing reason for my return I will certainly see Your Majesty again.'

Having thus conciliated the king and secured his courteous consent, the great soul departed from the kingdom. His mind had been troubled by dealing with householders, and he took to living in a forest. There he devoted himself to meditation and before long attained mastery over concentration and clairvoyance.

While he savoured the bliss of tranquillity, the Bodhisattva's compassion led him to remember the king. Concerned about that monarch's condition, he saw with his clairvoyant vision that the ministers were enticing him towards the various doctrines they professed.

One minister endeavoured to attract the king towards the doctrine of non-causality. He would cite examples where it was difficult to establish causality. 'Who or what is the cause,' he would say, 'of the shape and colour, the configuration and softness, of the stem, petals, pollen and stamens of a lotus flower? Who makes the wings of birds so varied? It is obvious that everything in this world is just natural. What makes thorns sharp, or birds and beasts diverse?[1] All this happens naturally. Effort has no role in it.'

Another reasoned that Ishwara, the supreme being, was the primal cause. 'All this could not have come into being suddenly on its own,' he said. 'Above everything there is one who is eternal. He creates this varied world in accordance with his own design, and later dissolves it also.'

'All this, good and bad, is the result of past actions,' argued yet another. 'Effort is incapable of changing it. How could anyone create countless things with so many different properties all at the same time? They are all the results of previous actions. For even one who knows how to be comfortable can end up in adversity.'

Another tempted the king towards the enjoyment of sensual pleasures by citing the doctrine of annihilation. 'Pieces of wood of different colours, qualities and shapes do not exist because of past deeds,' he would say. 'But they exist nevertheless, and once destroyed they do not materialize again. That is also the way of the world, and one should therefore devote oneself to pleasure.'

Another preached the doctrine of statecraft. To practise it was the duty of a king, even though it may be devious, blemished by cruelty and contrary to righteousness. 'Men are like shade-giving trees under which one may take shelter,' he said. 'For the sake of one's reputation they should be treated with gratitude, but only as long as they serve one's purpose. They should be used like victims in a sacrificial ceremony.'

Thus did the ministers try to mislead the monarch, each in a wrong direction of his preference. Mahabodhi observed that the king was in bad company, inclined to let himself be guided by those he trusted, and poised as it were on the precipice of adopting false doctrines. Moved by compassion, he considered how the ruler may be saved.

The practice of virtue makes people remember the good done to them; the memory of any injury slips away from their minds like water from a lotus leaf. Deciding that the time was ripe, Mahabodhi created a large monkey at his hermitage by his supernatural powers, and stripped off its skin, making the rest of the body disappear. He then put on the monkey skin and went to the gate of the king's palace where, he was duly admitted to the royal assembly.

Chamberlains with swords and staves stood at the entrance of the assembly hall. Men-at-arms guarded its perimeter. It was crowded with ministers, brahmins, warriors, envoys and city elders in fine garb. The king sat upon his throne in this solemn assembly. He received Mahabodhi with ceremonies due to an honoured guest and, after the customary exchange of compliments, seated him with all respect. Curious about the monkey skin, he then asked how it had been obtained. 'Who has done himself the great honour,' he enquired, 'of presenting this monkey skin to you, sir?'

'I got this myself, great king,' Mahabodhi replied. 'No one gave it to me. Sitting or sleeping on hard ground covered only with straw and grass is painful for the body. Religious observances cannot then be performed comfortably. I saw this big monkey in my hermitage and thought that its skin would be useful for facilitating my devotions. Sitting or sleeping on its skin, I would be able to carry out my religious duties without caring even for a royal couch spread with a precious coverlet. So I killed the monkey and took its hide.'

The king was too polite and courteous to say anything to Mahabodhi on hearing this account. But he was embarrassed and lowered his gaze. However the ministers, who already bore grudges against the great one, now got an opportunity to have their say. Their faces beamed as they looked at the king and pointed to Mahabodhi: 'What single-minded devotion to virtue does this lord have!' they cried. 'What steadfastness! What capability to do good works! He is thin and worn out with

austerities, yet he killed a big monkey all by himself as soon
as it entered the hermitage. It is a marvel! It can only be due
to the power of his penance!'

Mahabodhi was not ruffled. 'Your Honours must not
criticize me without regard to the glory of your own doctrines,'
he replied. 'This is not the way to gain a reputation for learning.
Consider, gentlemen, to run down another in words which hurt
your own doctrine is like committing suicide to defame
someone else.'

Having thus reproached the ministers in general,
Mahabodhi addressed the protagonist of non-causality: 'You
say that everything is natural,' he observed. 'If that is so, then
why blame me? What is my fault if the monkey died naturally?
Therefore it was rightly killed. If, on the other hand, it was my
fault, then it proves that its death was due to a cause. So you
should discard non-causality unless you want to speak against
reason. For, if the occurrence of a lotus and its parts were
without a cause, these would be found everywhere and always.
But they are caused by water, seeds and so forth: where these
exist, they occur, and not otherwise.

'Consider this also, my dear sir,' Mahabodhi added. 'One
who says that there is no causality says so for a reason, and thus
undermines his own contention. How can he contend at all, if
he has no reason for doing so? He then gets angry on realizing
the fundamental nature of causality, and tries to contradict it
by invective; for, without noticing it in one case, he has claimed
that it is absent everywhere. How can you insist that a cause
does not exist simply because you cannot see it? Another cause
may prevent your seeing it even though it is there, as with the
pureness of the solar orb at sunset.

'Moreover, sir, if you pursue the objects you desire rather
than those which you don't, it is for your own happiness. It is

for that alone that you serve the king. Nevertheless, you maintain that there is no causality. In that case the monkey's death had no cause, and you should not blame me for it!

After demolishing the proponent of non-causality with clear arguments, the great soul turned to the believer in Ishwara, the supreme being. 'You too cannot blame me, my dear sir,' he said. 'Your contention is that Ishwara is the cause of everything. If he does all, then he surely killed the monkey also. How then can you be so unfriendly as to blame me for the fault of another? And if Ishwara was compassionate enough not to slay the brave simian, how can you proclaim so loudly that he is the cause of this whole universe?

'Moreover, friend,' Mahabodhi continued, 'considering that Ishwara does everything, how can you hope to please him by praises, obeisances and the like, if he himself orders those actions of yours? If you perform a sacrifice, you cannot still say that he is not the doer, for he acts out of his own power. Further, if Ishwara performs all the sinful actions also, on the basis of what virtue does he become the object of your devotion? However, if he does not perform such acts because he fears to sin, it is then inappropriate to say that everything is his doing.

'The sovereign power of Ishwara,' Mahabodhi added, 'must be in accordance with righteousness or something else. If the former, he could not have preceded it. If something else, he must be subservient to it. Thus anything can be called sovereignty. Despite all this, if you still contend out of devotion and against reason that Ishwara is the cause and the lord of the entire universe, you cannot then hold me responsible for that great monkey's death, for he ordained it.'

Thus did Mahabodhi silence, with impeccable reasoning, the proponent of Ishwara. He then addressed skilfully the expounder of the doctrine of past actions. 'It does not behove you either to censure me, sir,' he said. 'It is your conceit that everything is due to previous actions. If that were so, I slew the monkey rightly. What fault was it of mine if he was destroyed in the fire of his past actions, and why should you blame me? But if I have sinned in killing him, then I, and not his deeds, constitute the cause of his death. Besides, if actions are the cause of fresh actions, no one will ever attain salvation.

'If happiness resulted from a painful situation and suffering from a comfortable one,' he continued, 'one could infer that both were due to past actions. But such situations are never seen, and earlier deeds cannot be their sole cause. Further, should there be no new actions, what would be the result of old ones? Even so, if you still hold that all is due to past actions, how can you think that it was I who killed the ape?'

After these irrefutable arguments, the great soul addressed the exponent of the doctrine of annihilation. 'Dear sir,' he said with a smile, 'if you believe in this ideology, why are you so anxious to blame me? If there is no world after this one, why should we shun evil and be so deluded as to esteem the good? The clever person would be one who does what pleases him and, that being the case, the monkey was rightly killed.

'If one takes the path of virtue and eschews that of evil, merely out of the fear of public opinion, he will not actually be able to escape the latter. His words and deeds will be in contradiction. Fearful of what people may say, he will not be able to enjoy even the happiness, which comes his way. This is a fruitless doctrine, and one deluded by it is just a simpleton.

'As for your statement that this world's condition is like pieces of wood with different colours and shapes, which exist without a cause and cannot recur once destroyed, is there any logic in this at all? But if you still profess the doctrine of annihilation, how can you censure someone who kills a monkey, or even a man?'

Having silenced the nihilist with clear and elegant words, Mahabodhi turned to the minister skilled in statecraft. 'Why do you also blame me, sir,' he asked, 'if you consider the policy propounded in the science of politics to be the correct one? According to it everything, good or bad, is worth doing for material gain. With it even virtuous ends can be secured if one looks after oneself.

'Therefore, I say to you,' Mahabodhi continued, 'if I killed that monkey for the sake of its skin, how can that be censured in the light of your science? It says that, depending on the occasion, one should disregard even the kindnesses of loving kinsmen. But if a deed is deplorable on account of its cruelty, and is bound to have evil consequences, how can you propagate a system which does not acknowledge this? If this is the essence of your policy, there is no room for confusion. It is an insolence, alas, to look down upon the people and lead them into wickedness in the name of science. Even so, if the false view specified in your science is what you maintain, I cannot then be blamed for the monkey's death, for I merely followed the policy you profess.'

Thus were the king's proud, eloquent and influential ministers worsted totally by Mahabodhi. He then addressed the monarch. 'In fact, great king,' he said, 'I did not kill a living monkey. It was merely an illusion. I took this skin off an ape I had conjured up just as an occasion for this discussion. Do not judge me otherwise.' And with these words he dissolved the illusory skin by his magic power.

'Which person who sees that everything proceeds from some cause,' he asked, 'which rightly thinking, compassionate person who believes in free will and the next world, will kill a living creature?'

'Consider, great king,' he continued, 'how can a proponent of reason do something which neither the believers in non-causality nor in external dependence, neither the materialists nor the followers of statecraft, would do for the sake of a meagre glory?

'A person's viewpoint, O best of men, whether good or bad, is the cause of the actions which follow from it. The words and the deeds of people manifest their points of view. One should adopt the right one and abjure that which is wrong and leads to disaster. This is achieved by keeping company with the virtuous and staying away from the wicked. Some of the latter go about in the garb of self-restraint. They are really demons dressed as monks. They ruin simple folk with their false creeds just as snakes do with their poisonous gaze.

'The contradictory words of the exponents of non-causality and the rest, like the howls of jackals, show the way they think. Wise people should shun them and look to their own interests while they can. Even the great do not make friends with an unfit person, no matter what the interest involved. Even the moon loses its lustre in conjunction with an overcast winter sky.

'Therefore avoid those who have no virtue, and cultivate those who foster it. Enhance your glory by turning your people away from wickedness and towards virtuous conduct. You have to protect them, and that is also your effort. So, take to the righteous path, lit by the rules of its discipline. When you follow it, the people in general will turn to it also, and will be set on the road to heaven.

'Purify your character. Earn the fame of giving in charity. Be friendly to people, consider them as your own kin. Rule the earth long, rightly and heedfully. Thus will you attain happiness and glory, as well as heaven.

'The people engaged in agriculture and husbandry, the taxpayers, are like trees laden with fruit and flowers. A king who does not protect them forfeits the bounties of the earth. One who does not protect those who depend on buying and selling various goods, the merchants and townsmen who favour him with the payment of cesses, forfeits the wealth in his treasury. The monarch who ignores and fails to honour a skilled and disciplined army, which has shown its valour in war, will certainly forfeit victory in battle. Similarly, the ruler who takes the base path of disrespect towards sadhus whose character, learning and yogic skill are well known denies himself the happiness of heaven.

'One who plucks an unripe fruit from a tree destroys the seed but gets no juice. Similarly, a king who levies unrighteous taxes ruins the country without getting any joy from it. But a tree of good quality gives fruit in due course; and a country well protected by its ruler enables him to attain virtue as well as wealth and pleasure.

'You have clever and insightful ministers who promote your interests,' Mahabodhi concluded. 'You have true friends and your own kin. Bind them to yourself with kind words and honourable gifts. Dedicate yourself to the betterment of the people. Let righteousness be your goal. Protect the people with a policy free of partiality or hostility, and secure the next world for yourself.'

Thus did the great soul turn the king away from the wrong path of false belief, and establish him and his councillors on the road to virtue. He then returned to the forest while the people honoured him with reverential salutations.

It follows that the compassion of good people for their past benefactors does not diminish, even when the latter treat them badly. One should not, therefore, forget past favours merely because of some discourtesy. Also, while discoursing on the enlightened one, it should be mentioned that, even before enlightenment, the Lord refuted other doctrines and provided discipline to all creatures.

24

The Great Ape

GOOD PEOPLE ARE PAINED NOT SO MUCH BY THEIR OWN afflictions as by the harm done to those who injure them. Thus has it been heard:

The Bodhisattva was once an ape of great size in a beautiful land by the side of the Himalayas. Even in that state he was intensely aware of what is right. Compassion was his second nature.

It was a land where the demigods sported. Its ground was tinted with the charming hues of various ores. Its dense and rich foliage seemed to enfold it in a dark silken mantle. Its slopes and valleys were adorned with shapes and colours so picturesque that they seemed almost contrived. There were numerous waterfalls and deep caverns through which mountain streams gushed. An enchanting breeze rustled through trees laden with all kinds of flowers and fruit. The great ape lived in those woods like a hermit, subsisting only on wild leaves and fruit, and showing compassion to all the creatures who crossed his path.

One day a man came into that land, searching for a cow which had gone astray. He had wandered all over, lost his way, and no longer knew where he was. Exhausted by hunger, fatigue and heat, his mind aflame with the fire of melancholy, he sat down under a tree as if weighed down by his distress. There he saw some red-brown tinduki[1] fruit, which had ripened and dropped to the ground.

Such was the man's hunger that he found the fruit most tasteful and looked around to see where it came from. He then beheld a tinduki tree growing on the slope of a waterfall, the tips of its branches bent low with the ripe red-brown fruit. Wishing to get them, he climbed up the slope and on to the tree, to the very end of a fruiting branch which hung over the cascading water. But it was too thin and his weight was more than it could bear. With a sudden sound it broke and fell, as if cut down with an axe.

The man fell with the branch into the cavernous pit of the waterfall. It was like a well enclosed by walls of rock. Piles of leaves and deep water ensured that he broke no bones but when he surfaced and looked around, he could see no way of getting out. 'I can do nothing,' he said to himself, 'and soon I will die.' Despairing for his life, his face wet with tears, he then began to lament, his heart distraught and distressed.

'I have fallen into an inaccessible place in this desolate forest,' he wept. 'Who except death will ever find me here? I am trapped like a beast in a pit. Who will pull me out? There are no friends or kinsmen here, only mosquitoes to drink my blood. This hole is pitch dark. It is like a moonless night here. For me, alas, it blots out the world with its gardens and forests, its arbours and streams, and its star-spangled sky.

The man passed some days in that pit, lamenting and subsisting on water and the fruit which had fallen with him.

One day the great ape came there. He had been wandering about in search of food, and the upper branches of the tinduki tree had seemed to beckon him as they swayed in the breeze. He climbed up the tree and, looking down the waterfall, beheld the woebegone man below, his eyes sunken and face gaunt with hunger, his body pale and emaciated.

The great ape was moved to pity at the man's miserable condition. Abandoning his own search for food, he looked intently at the man and addressed him: 'You are under a precipice which a man cannot reach easily,' he said. 'Tell me clearly who you are and how did you get to be here.'

The man looked plaintively at the great ape. 'I am a human, sir,' he said with folded hands. 'I got lost while roaming in the forest, and was seeking fruit from the tree when I met with this accident. It is a great calamity, for I have no friends or kindred here. You must protect me, O chief of apes.'

These words filled the great soul with a deep compassion. 'Do not worry,' he said, 'that you are in a pit, weak and without your kin. Whatever is their duty, I will do it. Have no fear.'

Having reassured the man and given him some tinduki and other fruit, the ape then went aside and practised the rescue with a rock of a man's weight. Satisfying himself that he was strong enough to bring the man out of the waterfall, he then descended into it and again spoke to him kindly. 'Come, climb on my back,' he said, 'and hold fast onto it while I take you out and also fulfil the purpose of my own body. For the only purpose of this worthless frame, as good people know, is that men of intelligence should use it for helping others.'

'Very well,' said the man, and with a respectful bow he got on the ape's back. Though the weight was great, yet with a supreme effort the ape brought the man out. Overjoyed at having done so, he was also exhausted. Walking slowly to a rock dark as a raincloud, he lay down upon it to rest.

The ape was pure-hearted by nature and did not suspect any danger from the man. 'I am extremely tired,' he told him trustingly, 'and I want sleep for a while. But this forest is easily accessible and exposed to predatory beasts. One of them could suddenly kill me while I am tired and asleep, and also harm itself. You must therefore keep watch, sir, and guard me as well as yourself.'

The man promised to do so. 'Sleep as long as you like, sir,' he said, 'and wake up refreshed. I am here to keep guard.' But when the ape had fallen asleep, the man began to entertain wicked thoughts. 'My body is worn out,' he said to himself. 'How will it even survive, much less find nourishment here? It needs great effort to find roots, and wild fruit can be had only by chance. I have become very weak. How will I be able to get through this impassable forest? Perhaps the flesh of this ape will suffice for that purpose. Even through he has helped me, he is a permissible prey by his nature. That indeed is the righteous course in a time of distress, and therefore I must feed on him. But I can kill him only when he is trustfully and comfortably asleep. In open combat he could defeat even a lion. So there is no time to lose.'

The man's mind was overcome with greed. His sense of gratitude and awareness of what is right were destroyed. His feelings of pity and kindliness disappeared. Even though he had become weak the desire to do the vile deed was strong. He picked up a large stone and hurled it at the great ape's head. But weakness had made him unsteady on his feet. Intended to put the ape to sleep forever, the misdirected stone did not strike him with its full force, but merely bruised his head with the edge before falling to the ground with a crash like thunder.

Injured by the blow, the ape jumped up in haste. 'Who hit me?' he cried, and saw none other but the man, now looking shamefaced. Pale with confusion, dismayed and distraught, his throat dry with fear, and his body covered with perspiration, he was unable even to look up.

'This is his doing,' the great ape concluded. Unmindful of the pain of his own injury, he then felt a great pity for the person who had committed a terrible deed regardless of what was good for him. He was not angry or agitated, but his eyes filled with tears, as he grieved for that man. 'My friend, you are a man,' he said, 'and yet you did such a deed! How could you think of it, and how could you carry it out? You should rather have bravely stopped any enemy out to hurt me!

'I felt proud at having performed a difficult deed,' the ape continued. 'But you have made my pride disappear by doing something even more difficult. You were rescued, as it were, from the other world, from the very mouth of death. Yet, coming out of one abyss, you have fallen into another.

'You have cast yourself into a calamity and me into the fire of grief,' he added. 'You have spoilt your reputation and gone against the love of virtue. You have destroyed trustworthiness and made yourself an object of reproach. What did you hope to gain by acting in this manner?

'I am the occasion for your sin,' he added further. 'Yet I am unable to cleanse it. This pains me even more than the injury I suffered. Now follow me so that I may take you out of this fearful forest and set you on the road to some village. But, since you cannot be trusted anymore, stay by my side and within my sight, lest someone make my labour fruitless by hurting you if you wander alone in the forest, worn out and ignorant of the way.'

Thus did the great soul grieve for that man as he brought him to an inhabited area and set him on the road. 'Here ends the forest, my friend,' he said. 'You are now in settled country. Go safely, putting the fear of the wilderness behind you. And try to avoid evil actions for they will yield a painful harvest.' After instructing him kindly, as he would a disciple, the great ape then returned to the forest.

As for the man, even as he burned with remorse for the sin he had committed, he was soon struck by the dreadful disease of leprosy. His appearance was transformed. Ulcers drenched his body with their discharge and pervaded it with the foulest of smells. So hideous and twisted did he become that wherever he went, the people could not believe that he was human. His voice too had changed and become a whine. People thought him evil personified and drove him away with harsh words of abuse and stones and sticks.

Once a king out on a hunt saw him wandering in the forest like a ghost. His dirty clothes were in tatters – even his genitals were not fully covered. Seeing him in that wretched condition, the king was curious as well as afraid. 'Your body is disfigured by leprosy,' he said. 'You are covered with ulcers, pale, emaciated and miserable. Your hair is full of dust. Are you a ghost or a ghoul, a witch or a devil? Or are you afflicted with some other ailment?'

'I am human, great king,' the man replied sadly with a bow. 'I am not a spirit.' And, when asked how he came to be in that condition, he recounted his misdeed to the king. 'This is only the blossom of my treachery to a friend,' he said, 'the fruit is bound to be even more painful. I am a living example of what happens to those who behave like enemies towards their friends, their minds sullied with greed and other vices. From this it can be inferred what will happen to them in the next world. But one who loves his friends, and earns their trust and help, gains courtesy, glory and joy. Enemies cannot harm him and he finally goes to heaven. These are the consequences of good or bad conduct towards friends, O king. Knowing them, one should follow the path shown by the virtuous. That is the way to happiness.'

Thus it is that good people are pained by the harm done to the wellbeing of those who injure them. This should be recounted during discussions on faithfulness to friends and on the consequences of evil deeds.

25

The Sharabha Antelope

THOSE WHOSE COMPASSION IS TRULY GREAT WILL SYMPATHIZE IN the distress of even one who has tried to harm them: they will not turn away from him. Thus has it been heard:

The Bodhisattva was once a sharabha[1] antelope in a forest. It was a place far removed from the presence and the sounds of men. No footprints of travellers or tracks of their vehicles marked its borders or its rugged terrain of watercourses, anthills and deep pits. A home to many kinds of animals, it was full of bushes, and trees whose roots were embedded in the dense grass.

The sharabha was strong, vigorous and swift. His compact body was distinguished by its beautiful colour. The practice of compassion had freed his mind of hostility towards other creatures. Subsisting on grass, leaves and water, he lived contentedly in the forest. He adorned it like a yogi who seeks solitude. Though his body was that of an animal, his mind was steadfast like a man's, and his sympathy for all creatures like a sage's.

Once a king came upon that place. He was mounted on a fine horse, with a bow and arrows in his hands, and he wished to try his skill at arms upon the animals. He chased them with such enthusiasm and speed that his mount, a horse of surpassing swiftness, soon left the royal retinue of elephants and chariots, cavalry and infantry, far behind.

The king saw the sharabha from afar and immediately decided to kill him. Drawing a sharp arrow on his bow, he urged his excellent mount towards the antelope. The latter perceived the king bearing down on him with horse and weapon. Pursued by the monarch, he fled swiftly, leaping over a great pit on the way as if it were no more than a puddle. But the horse, coming fast behind him, hesitated to jump and came to a sudden halt, unseating its royal rider who fell down with his weapons into that chasm like a demon warrior into the sea.

> His gaze was fixed on the sharabha,
> he did not pay heed to the chasm,
> he fell when the horse stopped suddenly,
> but the fault was his carelessness
> which made him lose his seat.

The sound of the horse's hoofs ceased. 'Has the king turned back?' the antelope wondered, and looking back he saw the horse standing near the pit without its rider. 'It is certain that the king has fallen down the precipice,' he said to himself. 'There is no place for resting here, no shady tree, no lake of pure water, blue as a lotus petal, where one may bathe. It is not possible that anyone would leave a fine horse in a forest frequented by predatory animals in order to rest or hunt. Nor are there any thickets in which the king may be hiding. It is obvious therefore that he must have fallen into the pit.'

Having come to this conclusion, the great soul felt a surge of compassion for the king even though the latter had tried to kill him. 'It was but today that this man enjoyed regal pleasures,' he said to himself. 'Hordes of people revered him with folded hands as if he were a king of the gods. He marched to the strains of musical instruments, with an army of chariots and horses, footmen and elephants, glittering with weapons and armour and flaunting colourful banners. He was a splendid sight with the lovely royal parasol and waving fly-whisks. And now he is at the bottom of a precipice, his limbs injured by the force of his fall, unconscious or plunged in gloom. Alas, he is in deep trouble! Common people are used to suffering. It does not pain them as much as it does delicate patricians who have never seen it. He will not be able to come out by himself, and it will not be proper to ignore him in case he is still alive.'

Thinking thus, the sharabha went to the edge of the chasm, his heart filled with pity. There he beheld the king stirring below, his armour bespattered with dust, his diadem and dress in disarray. The shock of the fall had both hurt and dismayed him. Seeing him in that condition brought tears to the antelope's eyes. Compassion made him forget that this was an enemy, and he felt a pain similar to the king's.

In keeping with his kindly nature, the sharabha addressed the monarch with courtesy and civility: 'Great king,' he said, 'I hope you are not too badly hurt after falling into this hellish hole. I hope your limbs are unharmed and your pains have abated. I am not human, O best of men, but just an animal of your realm, brought up on your grass and water. You should trust me. Do not be despondent, for I can pull you out. If you believe me, just give me permission and I will come to you straightaway.'

The king marvelled at the antelope's wonderful words. He also felt a definite embarrassment as he said to himself: 'How indeed can he pity me when he has seen me behave like an enemy? How could I act so wickedly towards an innocent creature? How sweetly has he rebuked me for my cruel deed? It is I who am a brute animal; he is an exalted soul in the shape of a sharabha. I should therefore honour him and accept his kind offer.'

Making up his mind, the king then replied to the sharabha. 'My limbs are covered with armour and were not much injured,' he said. 'The crushing pain I felt is bearable. In any case, it does not hurt me as much as having transgressed against a kind-hearted being like you. I did not understand your nature and, on the basis of your appearance, took you for an animal. Please do not be angry with me.'

Hearing the king's friendly words the antelope practised bringing him out with a rock of a man's weight and, having estimated his own strength, went down into the pit for the purpose. Approaching the king, he said respectfully, 'Forgive me if I touch your body for a moment. It is out of necessity. If I bring you joy it will be for my own benefit. Climb upon my back, great king, and hold fast onto me.'

'Very well,' said the king, and mounted the sharabha as he would a horse. The antelope raised his forelegs like an elephant carved on an arch, and climbed up with great strength and speed. Delighted at bringing the ruler out of that inaccessible place, he then told him the way to his capital and himself turned to go back to the forest.

Full of gratitude for the kind and courteous service he had received, the king embraced the animal. 'My life is at your disposal, O sharabha,' he said, 'and, it goes without saying, so is all that I control. Please come and see my city and live there if you so desire. It will not be fitting for me to go back by myself and leave you in a fearsome forest full of hunters and exposed to the onslaughts of heat, cold and rain. So let us go together.'

The antelope praised the king in sweet and humble words. 'O best of men,' he replied, 'this attitude is entirely appropriate for upholders of virtue like you. Virtue becomes by practice a part of good men's nature. But desist from wishing to favour me, a forest dweller, by having me live in your home. The pleasures of men and animals are of different kinds. If you want to please me, O hero, then give up the practice of hunting. Animals are dull-witted by birth. The poor creatures deserve to be pitied. You should know that all beings feel the same in respect of the pursuit of happiness and the removal of pain. It is not proper to do to others what will not please oneself. Know that sin causes suffering, censure and loss of reputation. It should be extirpated like an enemy. It is not good to ignore it any more than you would an illness.

'It is by the merit of your good deeds,' the sharabha added, 'that you have obtained kingship, an abode of prosperity and an object of people's respect. Enhance that merit. It is your benefactor and should not be left to diminish. It is the means to happiness and glory. Accumulate it by ample, timely and courteous charity, by moral conduct determined in the company of good people, and by wishing all creatures well as you would yourself.'

Thus did the great soul favour the king with words of advice about the next world. The king accepted them and, as he looked on respectfully, the sharabha returned to the forest. This should be recounted during discourses on compassion and on the glory of the Tathagata. It should be emphasized while explaining how hostilities can be mitigated. It shows how, despite being born as animals, great souls are compassionate towards their killers. How then can anyone born as a human join glory by being cowl to others?

26

The Ruru Deer

IT IS THE PAIN OF OTHERS WHICH AFFECTS GOOD PEOPLE: IT IS THAT, and not their own pain, which they cannot bear. Thus has it been heard:

The Bodhisattva was once a ruru deer in a great forest. It was a thickly wooded region, full of sal, bakul and other trees, and of vidula and nichula reeds growing in clumps. Dense with thickets of shami and palash, bamboo and cane, it also abounded in kadamba, arjuna, khadira and other flora, the branches of many trees covered with canopies of different kinds of creepers.[1]

Many animals lived in this forest, which was far removed from the haunts of men. There were deer of the ruru, prishat, srimara and chamara varieties; antelopes of the type harina and nyanku;[2] elephants and boars; buffaloes and wild oxen; panthers and tigers; hyenas and wolves; lions, bears and various others. Among them the ruru deer stood out by his surpassing beauty.

His colour was as bright as burnished gold. His velvet skin was dappled with spots of lovely tints, which gleamed like rubies and sapphires, emeralds and beryls. His blue eyes were large and tender. His horns and hoofs and a soft glow, as if they were fashioned out of gemstones, he was, as it were, a moving treasury of jewels.

The ruru deer was aware of the great desirability of his body and the pitiless nature of men. He went about, therefore, in the depths of the forest unfrequented by humans. He had a quick mind, and took care to avoid the traps set by hunters with snares, nets and pits, poisoned twigs, seeds and other bait. He also brought these to the notice of the other animals who followed him, guiding them like a teacher or a parent:

> When beauty and wisdom
> are joined in good action,
> which seeker of comforts
> will fail to respect it?

Once, when the great soul was deep within the forest, he heard the cries of a man being swept away in the strong current of a nearby river, in spate due to the recent rains. 'Save me, kind people!' the man cried. 'I have been caught in the rapid flow of this swollen stream. My arms are tired and I cannot find a foothold. Come quickly, for there is no time to lose.'

These piteous cries struck at the very heart of the ruru deer. 'Do not be afraid! Do not be afraid!' he exclaimed, loud and clear, as he rushed out of the dense forest. These were the words he had been accustomed to use in hundreds of previous births to drive away fear, misery and dejection. Reaching the riverside in no time at all, he looked at the man from afar, like a precious gift being carried in the river's current.

Regardless of any risk to his own life, the deer plunged into the fast-flowing river like a warrior attacking an enemy force. 'Hold on to me!' he cried as he blocked the flow with his own body. And the man, who was beside himself with fear as well as overcome with fatigue, instantly climbed upon his back. Despite being buffeted by the powerful current, the strength of the deer's willpower sustained his great energy, and he safely reached the river bank.

Having thus rescued him, the deer dispelled the man's weariness and pain with his own enthusiasm. He warmed his cold limbs with the heat of his own body, and then showed him the way out of the forest. As for the man, he was overwhelmed by the deer's wonderful kindness, which would have been hard to find even among loving kinsmen and friends. He also admired and marvelled at the splendid beauty of his benefactor. Saluting him, he spoke to him most lovingly:

'What you have done for me, no dear friend from childhood or kinsman could ever do,' said the man. 'My life is therefore at your disposal. If it can be of even the slightest use to you, I would deem it an honour. So favour me, sir, and command me to do whatever you consider me fit for.'

The deer praised the man in his reply. 'Gratitude is no surprise in a good man,' he said. 'It is but a part of his nature. But, looking at the faults of which the world is full, even gratitude must now be counted as a merit. For this reason, sir, I must say to you that, on account of grateful remembrance, you should not tell anyone that you were rescued by such a creature in particular. My appearance makes me a highly desirable catch, and the hearts of men are often hard and wilful because of their greed. So guard your merits as well as mine. Betrayal of a friend can never lead to happiness.

'Do not be angry at what I say,' the ruru deer added. 'We are but animals, unused to the guileful ways of men. Those experts in false courtesy are adept in tricking others. They can do such things that even naturally polite people come to be looked upon with suspicion. So, this is what will please me, sir, and this is what I would like you to do.' The man promised to comply with the deer's request and, having saluted and circumambulated the great soul, set out for his home.

Now, at that time there was a king whose queen's dream always came true. Whatever dream she had, no matter how extraordinary, would come to pass. Once, when she was asleep, she dreamt at dawn of a ruru deer, blazing with splendour like a horde of jewels of every kind, seated upon a throne. Surrounded by the king and his assembly, he was preaching dharma to them in a human voice with distinct words and articulation.

The queen woke up to the sound of drums beaten for her husband's reveille. Her heart was filled with wonder. At an appropriate time she went to the king who received her with affection and due honour. Wide-eyed with astonishment, her cheeks atremble with joy, she then presented to the king an account of that marvellous dream. 'Your Majesty,' she said respectfully, 'it will be good to make an effort to get hold of that animal. That jewel of a deer will light up your inner apartments like the deer constellation[3] does the sky.'

The king had known her dreams to come true. He accepted her request as he wished to please her, and also because he himself coveted the jewel-deer. Ordering all his hunters to search for that animal, he had a proclamation made in the capital every day:

There is a deer of golden hue,
its body dappled as it were
with many hundred shining gems;
in the scriptures it is mentioned
and some have seen it actually.
To the one who shows this deer to him,

the king will give a village rich,
and of charming women, ten.

The proclamation was heard repeatedly by the man who had
been rescued by the ruru deer. He remembered the immense
help he had received, but also felt depressed at the thought of
the poverty he suffered. Gratitude and greed pulled him in
different directions as his heart swung to and fro. 'What should
I do?' he asked himself. 'Should I look to virtue, or to wealth?
Attend to the needs of thankfulness, or of my family? Think
of the next world, or this one? Follow the goodly path, or one
which is worldly? Pursue material wealth, or the inner wealth
dear to good people? See to the present, or to the future?'

Eventually he was swayed by cupidity. 'Apart from enjoying
myself in this world,' he considered, 'I will be able to take care
of the next world also if I have great wealth and prosperity
wherewith to entertain kinsmen, friends, guests and
supplicants.'

Having come to this conclusion, he went to the king. 'Your
Majesty,' he said, 'I know that excellent deer and where he
lives. Command me as to whom I should show that animal.'
The king was delighted. 'Show him to me, my friend,' he
replied and, dressing himself for the hunt, he set out from the
city, surrounded by a large force.

Following the path indicated by the man, they reached the
banks of the river. There the king encircled the forest with his
entire force and, accompanied by some resolute and trusted
men, himself entered its depths, bow in hand. The man guided
them forward till he saw the ruru deer, standing free of any
suspicion. 'There is that excellent animal, Your Majesty,' he
told the king. 'Look at him, sire, and take your aim.'

As he raised his arm to point
to the deer, his hand broke off
at the wrist and hurtled down,
as if severed by a sword.
For actions which are aimed against
those by merit purified
will recoil immediately:
no good deeds can balance them.

The king was meanwhile looking in the direction pointed out to him, curious to see the ruru. The forest was dark, like a fresh raincloud. Within it, like a flash of lightning, he saw the magnificent deer, his body glowing with the lustre of a horde of jewels. Charmed by his beauty, and eager to catch him, the king fixed an arrow on his bow string and advanced, intent on shooting him down.

The ruru heard the shouts of men everywhere. 'It is obvious that I am surrounded from all sides,' he said to himself, as he beheld the king approaching to strike him. 'There is no time to flee.' He then addressed the king in a human voice: 'Wait for a moment, great king,' he said. 'Do not strike me, O hero, till you have satisfied my curiosity. I live in a dense and desolate wilderness. Who told you that such a deer was here?'

The king was much affected by this wonderfully human reaction. 'This is the person who showed us this marvel,' he replied, pointing to the man with the tip of his arrow. The deer recognized him. 'This is sad!' the ruru said. 'There is truth in the adage that it is better to take a log out of water than a man with no gratitude. This is his response to my exertions on his behalf. How could he not see that it harms even his own interest?'

'What is he deploring?' the king wondered. His curiosity aroused, he asked the ruru eagerly: 'Your censure is deep, but your words are obscure. My heart trembles on hearing them without understanding their object. Tell me, wonderful deer, to whom do you refer? Is it a man or a spirit, a bird or a beast?'

'It was a blameworthy deed, O king, ' the deer replied. 'I spoke harsh words, not because of any wish to blame him, but in order to see that he does not do it again. To speak harshly to someone who has made a mistake is like sprinkling salt on a wound. Who would like to do it? But if there is an illness, it must be treated at the very root. This man was being swept away in the current, and I rescued him from the river out of pity. Yet it is because of him, O best of men, that I am now in danger. Indeed nothing good comes out of wicked company.'

The king looked sternly at the man. 'Is it true,' he asked in a tone harsh and menacing, 'that you were rescued by this deer in the past when you were in trouble?' The man broke into a sweat and turned pale with fear and distress.

'It is true,' he said slowly, looking ashamed.

'Fie on you!' the king rebuked him. 'This will not do!' And placing an arrow on his bow he added: 'What is the point of this basest of men continuing to live! He is a blot on his fellow beings. Even all this effort did not soften his heart!'

With these words, as the king clenched his fist and drew the bow to kill the man, the deer placed himself between the two. 'Stop! Great king! Stop!' he cried, his heart choking with compassion. 'Do not slay one who is already slain. As soon as he yielded to the vile seduction of his enemy – greed – he was dead, both to this world because his reputation was ruined, and to the next by the destruction of his virtue. This is how men meet with disaster when their minds are affected by unbearable suffering. They are enticed by hopes of rich profit like foolish moths by the light of the lamp. Therefore this is a time for pity, not anger. Whatever he hoped to get thereby, let not his rash action be fruitless. I bow my head to your command.'

The king rejoiced and marvelled at one who was compassionate even towards a person who had harmed him, and wished only to help in return. 'Well said! Well said, good sir!' he exclaimed, looking at the noble ruru with respect. 'Such compassion for one whose offence is so terrible shows your truly humane virtues. We are human only in shape. Since you are kind to this villain, and he has enabled me to meet a paragon of virtue, I give him the wealth he desires. To you I give the freedom to go wherever you please in this kingdom.'

'I accept this meaningful gift from the great king,' the ruru replied. 'Command me if, as a result of our meeting, I can be of any use to you.' The king then had the ruru mount a fine chariot and took him with all the respect due to a guru to his capital. There he honoured him as a guest and placed him on a great throne. Surrounded by his ladies and ministers, he encouraged the ruru and, looking at him kindly with affection and reverence, questioned him about the righteous path. 'Men have many opinions about dharma,' he said. 'Please tell us what is your judgement on this.'

The ruru then addressed the king and his assembly. His words were clear, sweet and elegant: 'Dharma has many elements and actions like non-violence and abstinence from theft,' he said. 'But, in brief, O king, I consider it as compassion for creatures.

'Consider, great monarch,' the ruru continued. 'If one had the same compassion for others, kinsmen and strangers, as one has for oneself, who indeed would be vitiated by love for unrighteousness? But, in the absence of compassion, a man's thoughts, words and actions with respect to others, and even to his own kin, get distorted. Therefore, one who seeks dharma should never give up compassion. It engenders other virtues and yields the fruit desired just as good rains make crops grow.

'A heart full of compassion becomes free of malice. The words of such a person are pure and his actions uncorrupted. His wish to help others increases. It gives birth to other virtues like charity and forbearance, and leads to happiness and glory.

'The compassionate man does not cause harm to others, because he is calm. He is trusted by people like a brother. A heart steadied by kindliness is impervious to the turbulence of passions. Nor can the fire of anger rage within a mind cooled by the waters of compassion.

'In brief, compassion is dharma. Thus do the wise firmly believe. What virtue dear to good people does not come in the wake of compassion? Therefore treat your people with great compassion, O king, as you would your son or yourself, and win all hearts with virtuous conduct as you exalt your sovereignty.'

Praising the words of the ruru deer, the king and his subjects then devoted themselves to the righteous path. The monarch also granted full protection to all birds and beasts. This should be recounted in discourses on compassion, on glorifying the virtuous, and on censuring the wicked.

27

The Great Monkey

THOSE WHO FOLLOW THE PATH OF VIRTUE CAN WIN THE hearts even of their enemies. Thus has it been heard:

There was a rich and beautiful region in the heart of the Himalayas. The ground there was covered with numerous medicinal herbs with different qualities of flavour, potency and efficacy. It was also full of hundreds of trees with various types of flowers and fruit. There were streams of crystal clear water, and the sound of birds resonated everywhere.

The Bodhisattva was once the chief of a troop of monkeys in that region. Even in that state he practised renunciation and compassion. As a result jealousy, malice and cruelty stayed far from him. It was as if they were opposed to the good qualities he cultivated.

The monkey chief lived on a great banyan tree which stood out against the sky like a mountain peak. The thick foliage on its branches was like a mass of clouds. The branches bowed under the weight of its excellent fruit, which was of a lovely hue and fragrance. Extremely tasty, this fruit was larger in size than even those of the palmyra tree.

One branch of the banyan tree bent over a stream flowing nearby. 'Till all the fruit from this branch has been picked,' the farsighted monkey chief ordered his troop, 'none of you should eat from the other branches.'

The monkeys did not see any fruit on that branch. It was young and not very big, and was covered by a pocket of leaves made by ants. In course of time this fruit matured, gained colour, scent and juice, and turned soft. Fully ripe, its stalk became loose, and it dropped into the stream where it was carried away by the current.

Eventually the fruit was caught in the side of a cane mesh let down into a river where the king and the women of his harem were engaged in water sports. Its lovely fragrance surpassed that of the garlands the ladies wore and the wine they drank as they bathed and hugged each other. For a moment they were intoxicated by its scent as they inhaled it deeply with half-shut eyes. But then they became curious and, looking all around, saw this banyan fruit stuck to the side of the netting. It was bigger in size than a ripe palmyra fruit, and they could not take their eyes off it as they wondered what it was.

The king had the fruit brought out and, after it had been examined by physicians, tasted it himself. He was wonder-struck by its marvellous flavour. Its unique colour and scent were remarkable enough, but its taste was heavenly. Though the king was used to delicacies, he was so taken up by it that he thought:

'One who can't such fruit obtain,
what royal fruit does he then gain?
Who has this fruit is truly king
without the toil that kingships bring.'

The king made up his mind to find out the origin of the fruit. 'It is obvious,' he said to himself, 'that the excellent tree from which it comes must be on the river bank and not too far from here. This fruit could not have been long in water, for its colour, smell and taste are unaffected, and it is neither damaged nor gone bad. So it should be possible to reach its source.'

Having come to this conclusion, the king terminated the water sports and, accompanied by a large force equipped for travel, proceeded up the river. In the course of this he cleared the dense forest of ferocious beasts, frightening off wild elephants and other animals with the beating of drums. At last he came to the tree in a place which was difficult for men to approach.

The king saw the lordly tree from afar. It was like a mass of rain-clouds hanging low or like a majestic hill. Its lovely fragrance was even more enticing than that of ripe mangoes and, as it wafted towards them, the king became sure that it was the tree he was looking for. Coming closer, he saw that its branches were full of hundreds of monkeys busy eating its fruit.

The king was enraged to see the monkeys plundering what he longed for. 'Strike! Hit them!' he ordered his men harshly. 'Finish them off! Destroy all these wicked simians!' And the king's men advanced on the tree, some with their bows and arrows at the ready, others with sticks, spears and stones raised on high, shouting at the monkeys. It was as if they were intent on attacking an enemy fortress.

The monkey chief saw the royal force rush forward, roaring like a stormy sea, and showering his noble tree with arrows and stones, sticks and spears, like a barrage of thunderbolts. The monkeys could do nothing but shriek discordantly with fear as they turned to him with misery and distress writ on their faces. As he looked at them, a great compassion filled his mind.

The monkey chief was himself free of dejection, misery and anxiety. He comforted his clan and, having resolved to save them, climbed to the top of the tree with the intention of leaping across to the side of the adjacent hill. Although this would have required a series of jumps, such was the monkey chief's prowess that he sailed across like a bird – other monkeys would not have been able to do this even with two leaps.

After reaching the hillside, the monkey chief went up to a higher point where he located a large, strong and firmly rooted cane creeper of great length. Tying it securely to his feet, he leapt back to the banyan, but because of the distance and his feet being burdened, he could barely grasp the nearest branch of the tree with his hands.

Holding fast to the branch and stretching the creeper out forcibly, the monkey chief then signalled to his troop to quickly leave the tree. The frightened monkeys hastened to use the way which had thus been found and rushed across without any care that they were treading on their leader. Soon they had all escaped safely along the cane creeper. As for the monkey chief, though the incessant trampling had shorn the flesh from his frame, his mind retained its remarkable fortitude all the while.

The king and his men were utterly amazed to see this. 'Such courage and intelligence!' they cried. 'Such compassion for others without caring for oneself, would astonish even people who hear about it, not to speak of those who actually see it!'

'It is clear that this chief of the monkeys must be extremely tired,' the king told his men. 'He has been in the same position for a long time, and his body has been trampled upon and injured by the feet of his frightened troop. Obviously he is unable to extricate himself. Therefore spread a sheet below him quickly, and shoot off the cane creeper and the banyan branch with an arrow each at the same time.'

This was done, and the king had the monkey chief lifted gently from the sheet and placed on a soft couch. He had swooned and lost consciousness because of exhaustion and the pain of his injuries. These were attended to with ghee and other salves suitable for wounds. When his fatigue had lessened and he had recovered, the king approached him with curiosity, wonder and respect.

'You made a bridge of yourself to save the other monkeys,' said the king after he had enquired about the monkey chief's health. 'You had no pity for your own life. What are they to you, and you to them? Tell us, chief of monkeys, if you think it fit, for no small ties of friendship could impel the mind to do such a deed.'

The monkey chief lauded the king's kindness and cordiality as he duly introduced himself. 'These monkeys who are prompt to act on my orders,' he said, 'entrusted me with the burden of being their chief. I have accepted it as I love them like my own children. This, great king, is my connection with them. It has existed since long. Our living together has converted an amity based on the sameness of species into a family relationship.'

The king was amazed. 'The ministers and the others are there to serve the king's interest,' he protested, 'and not the other way round. Why, sir, did you sacrifice yourself for the benefit of your servants?'

'What you say is indeed statecraft, great king,' the monkey chief replied, 'but to me it seems difficult to follow. It is hard to ignore the intense and unbearable suffering of even a stranger, not to speak of one who is full of devotion and as dear as a brother. I was so pained to see the despair and distress overwhelming these monkeys because of this danger that I had no occasion to think of my own interest.'

The king observed that, despite his condition, the great one was jubilant. Marvelling greatly, he addressed him once more: 'You ignored your own comfort, and took upon yourself a disaster which threatened others. What profit, sir, have you thus obtained?'

'My body is indeed injured, O king,' replied the monkey chief. 'But my mind is at peace. I relieved the sufferings of those over whom I long ruled. I bear these afflictions with the same delight as heroes, who have vanquished their proud enemies in battle, wear the splendid marks of their valour like ornaments upon their bodies. My compatriots gave me many joys with great devotion. I received dominion from them, as well as honour and veneration. Today I am free of that debt.

'Therefore this suffering does not trouble me,' the monkey chief continued. 'Nor separation from my friends or the loss of my comfort. As for death, which approaches me in its course, its arrival will be like a great festival. I have the satisfaction of being free of the debt of past favours. My afflictions are at an end. My reputation is spotless. A king has praised me, and those who are grateful will count me among the virtuous. I have no fear of death. These are the benefits I have obtained from this adversity, O king.

'But the result would be opposite for a king without compassion for his subjects,' the monkey chief added. 'Devoid of virtues, his reputation ruined, he would become an abode of vice. Where can he go except into the flaming fire of hell?

'Thus have I shown you the powers of virtue and of vice, O mighty one,' he said further. 'Therefore rule your kingdom with righteousness. Fortune is fickle in its favours, like a woman. The king should be like a father. He should work for the happiness and benefit of all his people: the soldiers with their animals, the ministers, the citizens and those who are helpless, the shramans and the brahmins. Thus will increase his merit, wealth and glory, giving him joy both in this and the next world. With compassion for your subjects, O king, may you thus earn the sovereignty which the royal sages wielded in ancient times.'

The king listened to this with the utmost attention and devotion, like a disciple. And, after instructing him thus, the monkey chief gave up his body which was inert with pain, and ascended to heaven.

28

The Preacher of Forbearance

NOTHING IS INDEED UNENDURABLE TO THOSE WHO HAVE MADE forbearance a part of their life and are able to consider things tranquilly. Thus has it been heard:

The Bodhisattva was once an ascetic endowed with character and learning, with tranquillity, discipline and self-control. He had perceived that the householder's life offers little scope for the pursuit of righteousness. The life of the renunciant, on the other hand, is free of these evils. Abjuring material pursuits, he therefore took to it without reservation. He would preach forbearance and explain the righteous path. Eventually people came to know him as Kshantivadin, the preacher of forbearance, and his own family name went out of use.

The great soul lived in a forest region, at a spot delightful for its solitude. It was a place as charming as a garden, with flowers and fruit at all seasons and a lake of pure water adorned with pink and blue lotuses. The forest had the delightful splendour of Nandana, the garden of paradise. His presence made it as auspicious as a hermitage. The gods residing there respected him, and he would be visited by people who loved virtue and sought salvation. They came there in large numbers, and he would favour them with pious discourses, agreeable both to the ear and the mind.

Once the king of the country came to that forest with the ladies of his harem. He was a pleasure-loving ruler with amorous inclinations, and wished to amuse himself in the water because of the summer heat.

The king dallied with the girls as they shed their inhibitions in the groves and the arbours, under trees full of flowers, and in the water where the lotuses bloomed. He smiled at their charming diffidence as they were troubled by bees drawn by the perfume of their bath oils, the scent of wine and the fragrance of their garlands. For they could not have enough of the flowers which ornamented their ears and the wreaths in their hair, and he could not look enough at their wanton sport.

As he gazed at them, the glances of those girls flitted like bees from the arbours to the lotus blooms and thence to the flowering trees. Their merry talk, singing and dancing eclipsed even the bold intoxicating calls of the koels, the hum of the honeybees and the dance of the peacocks who, inspired by the deep thunder of the royal drums, had spread their feathers like dancers displaying their art in the king's honour.

Together with his harem, the king enjoyed the pleasures of that forest garden to his heart's content. At last, overcome with wine and the fatigue of dalliance, he lay down in a beautiful arbour on a fine bed spread with precious stuff, and fell asleep.

The girls, however, were still attracted by the beauties of the forest and not yet satisfied with what they had seen. Observing that the king was asleep, they spread everywhere in groups of their choice, the tinkle of their ornaments mingling with the lovely sound of their chatter. They wandered about as they pleased, followed by maidservants with golden parasols, fans, cushions and other emblems of royalty. Despite the efforts of their attendants, they greedily plucked pretty flowers and buds from the trees they could reach themselves. For, even though the floral garlands and decorations they wore were quite sufficient, such was their cupidity that they denuded every bush and tree on their way of its blooms and tender buds.

Thus did the royal ladies ramble through the forest, drawn onwards by its loveliness. At last they came to the hermitage of Kshantivadin. The officers of the harem were aware of the sage's eminence and the power of his penance, but they could not stop these wilful girls, who were the favourites of the king, as they went into the hermitage, attracted by its beauty.

There they saw the excellent sage, sitting under a tree in the posture of meditation. He looked tranquil and gentle, but his profound gravity inspired awe. He seemed to radiate the light of penance. Trained by meditation, his senses were undisturbed even by the presence of attractive objects in the vicinity. Auspicious and holy to behold, he was like dharma personified.

The royal ladies were overwhelmed by the lustre of his penance. Their caprices and their wanton, haughty ways disappeared at the very sight of the sage. Approaching him with respect, they sat around him modestly. He, on his part, greeted them with kind words and other courtesies due to guests. In response to their questions, he then welcomed them with a discourse on the righteous path.

'Born as an innocent human,' he said, 'if a person in full possession of his senses and organs is careless and does not do some good every day, he deceives himself, for his death is inevitable.

'No one can gain happiness in the next world by virtue of youth or beauty, noble birth, great power or prosperity, if he remains unadorned by charity, character and other merits. But if he has these, and abjures wicked ways, happiness will come to him in the hereafter as certainly as rain-swollen river waters flow into the sea.

'Even in this world what truly embellishes youth or beauty, noble birth, great power or prosperity, is virtue. A necklace of gold signifies no more than affluence. Trees are ornamented by flowers, rainclouds by lightning and lakes by lotuses on which honeybees hover, but for a human the real adornment is merit, properly acquired.

'People can be classed as high, low or average in terms of their health, beauty, wealth and birth. These differences are neither natural nor due to external causes. They are caused in fact by the individual's own past actions. This is the settled way of the world where life is transitory. Knowing this, eschew wickedness and adhere to good works. This is the road to happiness and glory.

'The wickedness within the mind is like a fire. It consumes what is good for oneself as well as for others. People who fear it should make an effort to avoid it by recoursing to other mental qualities. Just as a fierce fire abates on reaching the banks of a river full to the brim, so does the fire within when the mind recourses to forbearance which will serve it in both the worlds.

Forbearance fosters friendliness which prevents enmity. A forbearing person is loved and honoured. He is a happy person and, at the end, because of his merits, he goes to heaven as if it were his own home.

'Forbearance, ladies,' the sage concluded, 'is the ornament of the powerful, the foremost strength of ascetics, and a stream of water for the fire of hatred. It brings peace in both this and the next world. For the virtuous it is an armour on which the arrow-sharp words of the wicked are not only blunted, but often turn into flowers of praise, adding to the garlands of their glory. Forbearance destroys delusion – the enemy of virtue – and provides an easy way to salvation. Who should not try to acquire something so beneficial?'

Such was the pious hospitality which the great soul offered to the ladies. Meanwhile the king had woken up. Sleep had dispelled his fatigue, though his eyes were still heavy with a trace of wine, and his desire was roused. 'Where are the queens?' he said with a frown to the maidservants who guarded his bed. 'Sire,' they replied, 'they are gracing other parts of the forest to see its splendours.'

The king became eager to see the intimate and uninhibited laughing and jesting of his queens. He got up from the bed and went after them through the forest, accompanied by maidservants carrying his parasol and fan, his upper garment and his sword, and followed by liveried attendants of the harem with staffs of cane in their hands. Pursuing the trail of plucked flowers and scarlet betel juice stains wantonly left behind by the young women, he soon arrived at the hermitage.

There the king saw Kshantivadin sitting, surrounded by his womenfolk. The sight filled him with a terrible rage which was due as much to a past enemity,[1] as to the stupour of wine and a fit of jealousy. Unable to keep his composure, he lost all sense of decorum and decency. The evil of anger covered him with perspiration as he paled and trembled, his brow creased in a frown, his eyes red, rolling and staring. All his radiant grace and glory disappeared.

Rubbing together his hands adorned with finger rings, so that his golden bracelets shook, the king berated the sage. 'Ha!' he exclaimed. 'Who is this lowly butcher disguised as a sage, who belittles our majesty by casting eyes upon our harem?'

The eunuchs of the harem were alarmed to hear the king's words. 'Do not speak thus, sire!' they cried. 'This is the sage Kshantivadin. He has purified himself with a long life of vows, observances and penance.'

But the king's mind had turned perverse, and he paid no heed. 'Alas!' he said. 'So it is since long that this hypocrite has been cheating people with his crooked ways, passing himself off as a great ascetic! I will expose the true nature of his villainy and chicanery which he hides under a hermit's garb!' And, taking his sword from the attendant's hand, he advanced towards the sage as if he were an adversary, determined to kill him.

His eyes fixed upon the sage, he was about to fall upon him, when his womenfolk rushed to him, their hands folded in supplication, like lilies around the blooming autumn lotus.

The women surrounded the king. 'Do not, Your Majesty!' they cried. 'Do not act rashly. This is the reverend Kshantivadin!'

But evil had entered his mind. 'This man has obviously gained their affection,' he thought, and became even more incensed. 'This man speaks of forbearance,' he snapped, rebuking his women with a fierce frown for the temerity of their entreaty, 'but he does not practise it. That is why he cannot forbear to crave for the company of young women.

'What he says is at variance with what he does,' the king continued, 'and his wicked thoughts are even more at variance. He is a hypocrite. He has no self-control but sits here like a saint with an outward show of piety. What has he got to do in a hermitage?'

Their entreaty spurned, the ladies realized that anger had toxified the king's heart, and his fury was beyond persuasion. The scared and anxious harem officials signalled to them to withdraw, and they did so, their hearts full of sorrow and their heads bowed with shame, mourning for the sage.

'This ascetic is innocent,' they lamented. 'He is virtuous and mild. Even so, it is because of us that the king has turned against him. Who knows what path his anger will take? We are blameless but he may hurt us. He may even injure his own reputation and royal dignity apart from this sage's person and penance.'

But the ladies could do no more than grieve and sigh. After they had gone, the king angrily drew his sword and, threatening Kshantivadin, made as if to cut him down. His agitation increased on seeing that the ascetic even then remained calm and composed. 'This is the height of fraud!' he cried. 'He persists in deception and looks even at me as if he were a sage!'

Accustomed to forbearance, the ascetic was unperturbed by the king's offensive behaviour. He perceived within moments that it was due to anger and agitation that the monarch was acting so unbecomingly, devoid of decorum and courtesy, heedless of what was in or against his own interest. He marvelled at this but, filled with compassion, spoke some words to conciliate him.

'To be insulted is nothing unusual in this world,' he said. 'It is due to some fault in one's fate, and does not trouble me. What pains me is that I have been unable to offer you, even verbally, the proper reception due to visitors.

'Moreover, great king,' he continued, 'people such as you are the world's benefactors who bring evildoers on the right road. It does not behove you to act rashly. You should follow the path of reflection.

'Even something good can seem improper, and something wicked appear to be the opposite. The reality of what should be done cannot be discerned all of a sudden, without considering its particular purpose.

'A king needs to reflect upon what he must do. Having understood its reality, he should then do it with righteousness and prudence. In this way he gains virtue, profit and pleasure for his people without losing them for himself.

'Therefore calm your mind and do only that which adds to your glory. The misdeeds of the great get widely known, specially if they are unprecedented. You would certainly never tolerate that something prejudicial to proper order and deplored by all good men be done by anyone in a hermitage protected by your mighty arm. How, O king, can you do it yourself?

'If your ladies came by chance to my hermitage, what fault is it of mine that you are so beside yourself with rage? And even if it were my fault, O king, it would still become you to forbear and forgive. Forbearance is the greatest ornament of one who is powerful. It indicates that he is adept in guarding all his merits.

'Nothing adorns kings more than forbearance, not earrings which cast a shimmering blue glow upon his cheek, nor the gems glittering in his crown. Do not disregard it. Give up anger, which is always unworthy of being harboured, and guard forbearance as you would the earth. A gentle and respectful conduct with ascetics is beneficial for kings.'

But the king's mind was no longer open. Though the sage's words were conciliatory, he suspected something else in them. 'If you are not posing as an ascetic,' he asked, 'and if you are indeed engaged in vows and observances, why are you begging me for a safe conduct in the guise of a sermon on forbearance?'

'Listen, great king, to the purpose of my endeavour,' Kshantivadin replied. 'I do it so that your reputation should not be ruined on my account by it being said that the ruler killed an innocent brahmin renunciant. I am not afraid to die, for I am aware of my own conduct, and also know that death is inevitable for all creatures. I spoke to you about forbearance so that you should not suffer by injuring virtue, the source of happiness. Forbearance enables salvation. It is the fount of merits and keeps faults at bay. I told you about it because I was glad to give you this best of gifts.'

The sage's true and gentle words were like flowers. But the king disdained them. 'We will now see your love of forbearance!' he said angrily, and with his sharp sword he cut off the sage's right hand, which was a little extended to stop him, its long and slender fingers raised upwards.

It was as if a lotus had been severed from its stem. But Kshantivadin was steadfast in his vow of forbearance. The severance of his hand did not pain him as much as the terrible and immediate suffering which he knew would befall the king. 'Alas,' he said to himself, 'this man has crossed the limit of his own good. He is no longer fit for conciliation.' And, grieving for him as one would for someone sick given up by the physicians, he kept silent.

The king threatened him further. 'Give up this pretence of penance, and this villainous deceit!' he cried. 'Otherwise your body will thus be cut into pieces till you die!' But the ascetic said nothing, for he knew that the man had become obdurate and was beyond persuasion. The king then cut off in the same way the great soul's second hand, both his arms and feet, as well as his nose and ears.

Even when the sharp sword struck his body, the sage felt neither grief nor anger. He was aware that the dissolution of the body is inevitable. His forbearance towards others was habitual, and it remained unshaken even when his limbs were being severed. Nor was the good man perturbed at seeing this happen. He felt no pain because of his love. Yet he was in agony to see the king fallen from righteousness.

After committing this terrible deed the king was immediately seized by a fiery fever and, as he went out of the garden, the earth suddenly burst assunder and he was swallowed up by it. His disappearance into that flaming pit, which had opened up with a fearful noise, led to a great commotion everywhere.

The royal ministers were deeply agitated. Aware of the great power of the sage's penance, they concluded that the king had perished because of it. Worried and apprehensive that he may incinerate the whole country on account of the monarch's misdeed, they went with folded hands to propitiate him.

'You have come to this pass because of the king's delusions and rashness,' they pleaded. 'May he alone be consumed by the fire of your curse. Do not burn his city. Do not destroy innocent women and children, the old and the sick, the brahmins and the poor. You support virtue. Safeguard the king's realm and your own righteousness.'

Kshantivadin assured them. 'Do not be afraid,' he said. 'May you all have long lives. He did cut off my hands and my feet, my ears and my nose with his sword though I am just an innocent forest dweller. Even so, how can a person like myself ever think of hurting him? May the king live long and suffer no evil.

'A person subject to the torment of sorrow, sickness and death, in the grip of greed and hatred, and consumed by his own evil actions deserves to be pitied. Who should be angry with him? If it is possible, may the king's sin redound to me alone; for suffering, even of a brief duration, is intense and unbearable for those accustomed to comforts.

'The king destroyed his own good. If I am not able to save him, why should I disclaim my own inability and be angry with him? Even without him every born being would suffer death and other tribulations. It is birth alone which should be unendurable here, for if it did not happen, how and from where could unhappiness come?

'This worthless body has perished in many ways, through many aeons and a series of births,' Kshantivadin concluded. 'Why should I abjure forbearance at its dissolution? It would be like giving up a priceless jewel for the sake of a twig. I took the vow of renunciation, and lived in the forest, preaching forbearance. Soon I will die. Why should I give way to anger? So, have no fear. Go, and may all be well with you.'

Thus did that best of sages instruct all those people and make them his disciples in goodness. His fortitude unshaken due to his forbearance, he then departed from this earthly dwelling place and ascended to heaven.

29

The Horrors of Hell

THE TENETS OF FALSE BELIEF ARE CONDEMNABLE, BUT THOSE WHO
succumb to such faulty views deserve the special sympathy of
good people. Thus has it been heard:

Once the Bodhisattva obtained birth in Brahmaloka, the
highest heaven. While this was due to the good karmas he had
accumulated through the practice of mediation, even the great
bliss of Brahmaloka, which he had thus attained, did not dim
his eagerness to do good to others, which sprang from his
practice of compassion in previous births.

> Even sensual pleasures turn
> people careless, and they earn censure.
> But the virtuous will
> never hide their wish to still
> do good to others, even when
> the bliss of mediation they gain.

Once that great soul happened to look down at the earthly
region. It was full of many kinds of suffering and hundreds of

calamities, of disease and evil designs, violence and lust. There he saw Angadinna, the king of Videha, wandering in the wilderness of false belief.

The king had fallen into bad company and acquired wrong perceptions. 'There is no hereafter,' he had come to conclude, 'how can good or bad deeds bear fruit in that state?' As a result he had lost all enthusiasm for religious rites and become averse to charity, moral conduct and other good works. He held the pious in contempt and was indifferent to the scriptures in which he had no faith. Inclined to laugh at talk of the next world, he had no reverence for shramans and brahmins, and showed them scant courtesy. He was, instead, given up wholly to sensual pleasures.

The great-souled divine sage pitied the king whose flawed vision was bound to have bad consequences and bring disaster to his people.

One day, as the king sat alone in a beautiful arbour thinking of sensual pleasures, the Bodhisattva descended before him in a flame from Brahmaloka. He blazed like a ball of fire, glittered like a mass of lightning and shone with the intense brilliance of the sun. The king was overwhelmed by his splendour, and rose to greet him with folded hands. 'Who are you, sir?' he asked, looking at him respectfully. 'You shine with the lustre of the sun. Your feet are like lotus flowers, and they rest in the sky as if on the earth. Your appearance is delightful to behold.'

'O king,' replied the Bodhisattva, 'know me as one of those divine sages who attain Brahmaloka after defeating attachment and hatred, the two proud generals of an enemy army. They do so with the power of their mind's resolve.'

On hearing this, the king greeted him with kind words of welcome and the ritual offerings of water to wash his feet and

to indicate respect. 'Great sage!' he said, as he looked at the
visitor with wonder, 'your divine power is indeed marvellous.
You gleam like a flash of lightning. Without the support of any
building or wall, you walk in the sky as if it were the earth. Tell
me, how did you obtain this supernatural ability.'

'It is the fruit, O king,' replied the Bodhisattva, 'of the
pure conduct, meditation and self-restraint I practised in my
other births.'

'Is it true that there is a world hereafter?' the king asked.

'Yes, great king,' replied the Bodhisattva, 'there is another
world.'

'But, revered sir, how can we believe this?' the king asked
again.

'It is tangible, great king,' replied the Bodhisattva. 'It can
be grasped by direct perception and by other evidence. It can
be proved by logic. It is established by the testimony of reliable
persons and can be tested through scrutiny.

'Consider, sir,' the Bodhisattva continued. 'The heaven
adorned by the sun, the moon and the stars, the animals in their
great variety and shapes, are the world hereafter in a visible
form. You should have no doubts about this.

'Many remember their previous births through the practice
of meditation or the faculty of their memory. The world
hereafter can be inferred from this also. I myself have given
evidence of this here.

'It is only because intelligence existed earlier that it can
mature in the present. From this too one can infer the existence
of another world. The primeval intelligence of the child in the
womb is a continuation of this faculty in its previous birth.

'The faculty of perceiving an object of knowledge is called
intelligence. The primeval intelligence of the foetus
presupposes an object that it perceives. But that object cannot

be of this world as the foetus has no eyes or other sensory organs. This proves that it exists in the other world.

'One notices that children diverge from the nature of their parents and are different in their character and the like. As this cannot happen without a cause, it follows that the differences are due to habits acquired in other births.

'The mental powers of the newborn child are rudimentary, and its sensory organs are inert. Even so it makes an effort to take the mother's breast without any instruction. This shows that it is habituated from other births to practices suited to getting food, for practice alone could train it for such activities.

'But you may doubt this, sir, as you are not convinced about the other world. "The lotus flowers which open and close by themselves," you may argue, "are then also the proof of practices in other births. If this is not acceptable, how can the effort to take the breast be so attributed?"

'There is, however, no need for this doubt. In one case there is a regulation, the other none. One involves effort, the other does not. In the opening and the closing of the lotus one sees the regulation of time, but not in the child's effort to take the breast. On the other hand, there is no effort in the case of the lotus. Its opening is caused by the sun. In this way, great king, after a full consideration it is possible to believe that the other world exists.'

The king felt uncomfortable at this talk of the other world. The store of his sins was great and his mind was engrossed in false views. 'O great sage,' he said, 'if the next world is not just something to scare children with, and if you think it deserves my acceptance, then lend me five hundred coins of gold. I will return you a thousand in my next life.'

These were unbecoming words. The king uttered them brazenly, as was his habit, and poured forth the poison of false belief without hesitation. But the Bodhisattva's reply was most proper. 'Even in this world,' he said, 'those who wish to augment their money do not lend it to one who is wicked or incompetent, gluttonous or lazy. Money given to such a person will ruin him. On the other hand, if they see someone who is calm, modest and skilled in business, they will give him a loan even without witnesses, for it leads to prosperity.

'The same order, O king, applies to loans repayable in the hereafter. Your conduct is bad because of your false views. You are as such unsuited for a money transaction. For you will be consigned to hell on account of the cruel deeds flowing from your wrong beliefs. And, when you lie there, faint with pain, who would pursue you for a thousand gold coins?

'Which wise person would enter that world of deep darkness in order to get his money back? That is where the heretics dwell. It is a place where the sky maidens are covered in dark mantles unlit by the sun or the moon, and the starry firmament cannot be seen. An icy wind prevails there, painful and piercing to the very bone. Some wander for long within the bowels of that hell which is gloomy and overcast with a dense fog. They tug at the leather thongs of their rags, screaming as they fall over each other.

'Others run helter-skelter in the hell of flaming grass. They seek relief for their burning feet, but neither their sins nor their lives are near an end.

'The fierce servants of Yama[1] bind yet others and carve their limbs with sharp knives, like carpenters who delight in shaping fresh timber. Some of these people are totally stripped of their flesh so that only their bones remain. They are in agony, but cannot die because their past evil deeds keep them alive.

'Others are bound in blazing harnesses and have their mouths stuffed with thick, fiery bits. Lashed with whips of fire, they must draw flaming chariots for a long time over a burning iron surface.

'Some have their bodies ground under the mountain Sanghata, and are crushed to pieces by its impact. Their suffering is intense and unending, yet they do not die till their evil karma has been worked out. Some are pulverized with enormous flaming pestles in mortars glowing with fire, and yet stay alive.

'Yet others are torn apart by the servants of Yama who drag them with pitiless cries up and down trees of heated coral, prickly with sharp and flaming iron spikes. Others lie on huge piles of embers which smoulder like molten gold. All they can do is to writhe and moan as they suffer the consequences of their conduct.

'Some suffer the terrible agony of hundreds of sharp spears stuck into their bodies on a ground garlanded with flames. As they howl with their tongues hanging out, it is then that they are convinced that there is a world hereafter.

'Some are wrapped in burning sheets of iron. Others are boiled in pans of brass. Some are wounded with a shower of sharp weapons. Fierce animals tear off the skin and flesh of others. Exhausted, some enter the salt waters of the Vaitarani, the river of the netherworld. Its touch is as painful as that of fire. Their flesh wastes away in it, but not their life which is sustained by their wicked deeds.

'Sick with the torment of being burnt, some resort to the hell of unclean corpses, as to a lake. There they experience unparalleled suffering as their bones are eaten away by hundreds of worms.

'Some suffer for long the pain of fire. Surrounded by flames, their blazing bodies glow like hot iron. But they cannot turn to ashes, for they are held fast by what they did.

'Some are sliced with fiery saws, some with sharp razors. Some scream in anguish as their heads are crushed under swift blows of hammers. Some are impaled on thick spits and cooked on a smokeless fire. Others cry as they are compelled to drink molten flame-coloured iron. Yet others are attacked by powerful brindled dogs who tear off their flesh with sharp teeth so that they fall down, lacerated and weeping.

'Such are the terrible torments of hell,' the Bodhisattva continued. 'Impelled by your misdeeds, when you suffer them, you will be dejected, exhausted and beside yourself with grief.

'When you are in that sorry state, sir, who would ask you to repay the loan? You would be in such great pain that you would not be able even to reply. Pierced by icy winds, you would not have the strength even to groan. Or you would be screaming as you are torn assunder.

'Who should trouble you with a request for money when Yama's servants torment you in the next world, when you writhe inside a flaming fire, or when dogs and crows devour your flesh and blood? You would always be in agony under all kinds of torture: being struck or cut, beaten or cleft, burnt or pierced, ground or split. How could you repay my loan at that time?'

On hearing this fearful account of hell, the desire for emancipation arose within the king. He abandoned his attachment to false views and became convinced of the world hereafter. 'My mind is in a turmoil with terror,' he said, bowing to Bodhisattva. 'How will I avoid those tortures of hell? This doubt itself consumes me like fire.

'Wrong views had clouded my thinking,' the king continued. 'I was shortsighted and took the wrong road. You, O sage, know the right path. Attend to me now, and give me guidance and refuge. You have cleared my vision as the sun dispels darkness. In the same manner, show me the way so that I do not suffer in the hereafter.'

The Bodhisattva perceived that the king sought salvation. His views had been rectified, and he had become fit for the righteous path. Full of compassion, like a father for a son or a teacher for a pupil, he then instructed the monarch. 'The glorious way to heaven,' he said, 'is that followed by the kings of old. They loved virtue, behaved like good disciples with shramans and brahmins, and showed compassion for the people in their conduct.

'Vanquish injustice and overcome covetousness,' he added. 'Neither is easy to do, but in this way you will attain the golden-gated city of the king of heaven, which is resplendent with jewels.

'Your mind had been misled by wrong ideas. May it now be steadfast in the belief cherished by good people. Give up the former, which were propagated to please fools. You now wish to tread the right path. You have taken the first step towards it the moment you shed indifference to virtue.

'Therefore make wealth a means to virtue. Show mercy to people. Be steadfast in your conduct and self-restraint, so that nothing unpleasant befalls you in the next world. Let the light of your merit, O king, illumine your good works, so that they are pure and acceptable to the virtuous. Ruling thus, you will alleviate the people's suffering, promote your own good and earn great glory.

'Your body, which is the means to virtue, is like a chariot here. You are its rider. Let a righteous mind be its charioteer, friendliness its axle, charity and restraint its wheels, and the will to do good its shaft.

'Let control of the senses be the horses, heedfulness the strong reins and intelligence the whip. Make the scriptures the armament of the chariot, modesty its decoration, humility its pole and forbearance the yoke. Your skill will give it speed, and your steadfastness stability.

'Control bad language, and the chariot will not rattle. Speak sweetly, and its sound will be grave and deep. Maintain restraint and its joints will be firm. Abjure the crooked ways of wicked action, and it will go straight.

'It will be radiant with wisdom, with tranquillity as its flagstaff, glory its banner, and mercy its attendant. Riding in that vehicle, O king, you will succeed both here and in the hereafter. You will not go to hell.'

Thus did that great soul dispel the darkness of the king's wrong views with the brilliant light of his words. Having shown him the path of salvation, he vanished. As for the king, he had understood the reality of the accounts of the other world, and gained knowledge of views which are correct. Together with his ministers, townsmen and country folk, he devoted himself to charity, self-restraint and discipline.

Thus it is that the tenets of false belief are condemnable, but those who succumb to such faulty views deserve the special sympathy of good people. To listen to the preaching of the blessed dharma fills one with total faith: this is the conclusion to be drawn. Also, that to listen to another on this subject engenders belief in right views.

30

The Elephant

GOOD PEOPLE ESTEEM EVEN THEIR SUFFERING AS A GAIN IF IT benefits others. Thus has it been heard:

The Bodhisattva was once an elephant of great size in a forest full of fine young trees whose tops were hidden under flowers, fruit and tender leaves. Its ground was covered by their offshoots and all kinds of creepers and grass. Many hills added to its beauty. A home for wild animals, it also had a lake of deep, abundant water, and was surrounded on all sides by an immense arid wasteland which seperated it from human habitation.

Here the elephant led a solitary life of contentment and peace, enjoying water, leaves and lotus stalks like an ascetic. One day, while wandering on the border of the forest, he heard human sounds from the side of the desert. 'What can this be?' he wondered. 'There is no road through this region to any other place. Neither is it likely that anyone should cross this desert just for hunting, specially as catching elephants from our herd involves great toil and trouble.

'It is obvious,' he concluded, 'that these people have lost their way or have been badly guided. They may also have been banished by the king out of anger or because of some misconduct on their part. The sound I hear is gloomy and joyless. Its dominant note is one of distress, as if they are weeping. So let me find out.'

Drawn by compassion, the great soul proceeded in the direction from where the sound was coming. As the sad and piteous lamentation became clearer, he quickened his pace. Coming out of the dense forest, he saw seven hundred people in the desert. Weary with hunger, thirst and fatigue, they were looking towards the forest as if in supplication.

Those people also saw the elephant coming towards them like a mass of white mist or an autumn cloud driven by the wind. ' Alas, we are done for!' they thought on seeing him. But they were so sad and miserable, so dispirited with hunger, thirst and fatigue, that they made no attempt to flee even though they were terrified.

> They were overcome by distress,
> famished, thirsty, tired out:
> they did not try to run away
> even in that time of peril.

The Bodhisattva saw that they were scared. 'Do not be afraid! Do not be afraid!' he assured them, raising his trunk with its moist, broad and coppery tip. 'You have nothing to fear from me.' And, drawing near, be asked them kindly, 'Who are you, gentlemen? What has brought you into this state? You are pale with the heat and the dust, emaciated, sad and exhausted. From where have you come?'

He had spoken in a human voice which carried an assurance of security as well as goodwill. The men recovered their confidence. 'O lord of elephants,' they replied, saluting him, 'we were banished here by an angry king, even as our grieving kinsmen watched. But something must still remain of our luck and good fortune for us to have been noticed by you, sir, who are more than a friend or kinsman. To see you is auspicious, and now that we have done so, we know that our problems are over. Who would not be saved from adversity by seeing someone such as you, even in a dream?'

'Well, gentlemen, how many are there of you?' asked the noble elephant.

'The king had banished a thousand men,' they replied. 'But we had never experienced such suffering, and many perished, overcome by hunger, thirst and grief. Now, chief of elephants, seven hundred men remain. For them, who were also doomed, you have appeared as assurance personified.'

The great soul, who was compassionate by habit, grieved and shed tears on hearing the men. 'Alas,' he said sadly, 'how pitiless is the king! How shamelessly unmindful of the next world! How stricken, alas, are his senses by the glory of royalty which is as momentary as lightning! He does not see his own good! I think he does not understand that death approaches, nor heeds the evil consequences of sin. Alas, such kings cannot be helped, for they reflect but little, and do not listen to advice. Such cruelty to creatures, just for the sake of a single body which is perishable as well as subject to illness! Alas for such folly!'

As the lordly elephant looked at those men with tenderness and compassion, he began to contemplate. 'They are afflicted by hunger, thirst and fatigue,' he thought, 'and their bodies have become very feeble. Unless they have food, how will they cross this desert which extends for many miles and has neither water nor shade? Nor is there anything in our forest on which they could subsist without trouble, even for one day.

'But if they were to use my flesh for food,' he considered further, 'and my intestines as containers to carry water, they could cross this desert. Therefore I will make my body a means to save these people. It is subject to hundreds of ailments, all kinds of troubles and constant infirmity, and it is time it was put to use to benefit others. Besides it is hard to obtain human birth, a state in which it is possible to attain heaven and salvation. Let it not go waste for these people who, having come to me in my own home, are rightly my guests. Seperated from their kin and in trouble, they deserve my sympathy all the more.'

The wanderers were indeed weak with hunger and thirst. Bowing to the elephant with tear-filled eyes, they begged for water. 'For us who are without kindred,' some of them cried piteously, 'you are our kinsman, our recourse and refuge. Save us as you think best, great one!' Others, whose minds were more calm, enquired about a place where they could find water, and a way out of that impassable desert. 'Chief of elephants,' they said, 'tell us if there is a lake here, or a cool stream or waterfall, or a place with shady trees and grass on the ground. Be kind enough also to point out the direction in which you think this desert can be crossed. We have been wandering in it for many days, master, and you must get us out.'

The elephant's heart melted at these entreaties. Lifting up his trunk, which was like the great coil of a mighty serpent, he pointed to a hill where the desert could be crossed. 'Below that peak,' he said, 'there is a large lake of clear water adorned with pink and blue lotuses. Go, therefore, in that direction and dispel your fatigue caused by thirst and heat. Not far from the hill you will see the carcass of an elephant fallen from the top. Use its flesh for food, its intestines as containers for carrying water, and continue in that direction. In this way you will be able to cross the desert with the least trouble.'

Having thus assured and despatched the men, the elephant quickly climbed up to the summit of that hill by another path. There, with the intention of saving those people and the firm wish to obtain release from his own body, he made a formal resolution.

'This endeavour of mine,' he resolved, 'is meant neither to obtain emancipation for myself, nor sole sovereignty on earth. Nor is it made for the surpassing pleasures of paradise, or the splendour of Brahmaloka, or the bliss of salvation. I wish to save these people lost in the desert. If I earn even some merit from this, may I become the saviour of all the people lost in the wilderness of this worldly round.'

Having thus determined, that great soul let his body fall from the hillside in keeping with his intent. His joy was such that he gave no thought to the pain of crashing down the precipice to his death.

> He shone, while falling,
> like an autumn cloud;
> or the radiant disc, declining,
> of the moon about to set;
> or like a snowy mountain peak
> torn down by the fierce wind
> raised by mighty Garuda's[1] wing.
> The sound was like a thunderclap
> as he fell upon the ground,
> causing earth and hills to tremble,
> and shaking Mara[2] who was filled
> with the haughtiness of power.

On seeing this the forest deities were wonderstruck. Bristling with joy, they flung their arms upwards, their fingers stretching into the sky. Some showered the great one with fragrant flowers tinted with sandal powder, some with seamless celestial scarves embellished with gold, some with ornaments.

Some deities praised the great one out of devotion to him, filling the heavens with the sound of divine drums. Others adorned the trees with blossoms, fruit and new leaves out of season. An autumnal glow spread in all directions. The sun's rays seemed to slant, and the sea, its waves tossing, as it were, with eagerness to meet him, was filled with joy.

Meanwhile the men had reached the lake where they recovered from their thirst and fatigue. As had been mentioned by the great soul, they saw not too far away the body of an elephant recently dead. 'Oh, how similar it is to that chief to elephants,' they said to themselves. 'Indeed it may be the body of that great beast's brother, or of his son or some other relation. Even though crushed, it has the same form, shining with the splendour of a snow-covered mountain, or a host of lilies, or moonlight solidified. It is like his reflection in a mirror.'

Some men looked more carefully. 'As far as we can see,' they said, 'this is the same animal. His great beauty rivals that of the divine elephants which guard the world. He has obviously thrown himself down from the hillside in order to save us who were friendless and in distress. That noise we heard, like a thunderclap which shook the earth, was clearly that of his fall.

'It is the very same body,' they added, 'pale like a lotus stalk, covered with hair as fair as moonbeams, and marked by fine spots. It has the same tortoise-like feet with white nails, and the same backbone curved gracefully like a bow. The long and full face adorned with streaks of rut which perfumed the air, the high and handsome head never touched by any goad, and the ample neck are also the same, as are the pair of honey-coloured tusks. Reddened by the dust of the hillside, they were a mark of his pride. The trunk and its long tip, with which he showed us the way, is also the same.

'This is indeed most wonderful and marvellous,' they said further. 'He knew nothing about our antecedents, character or loyalty. He had not even heard about us. Yet he was so compassionate to us in our misfortune. Every reverence to that great being! He was someone else in the shape of an elephant, to have acted so virtuously in helping people like us who were overcome by fear, grief and despondency.

'In him, we see a proof of the popular saying that beauty cannot please without virtue. Oh, his goodness was in keeping with his form. He is content and his body, which had the splendour of a snowy mountain, now seems to be laughing.

'Who, therefore, will now be able to feed upon the flesh of this most virtuous being? Given to helping others, he was prepared to sacrifice his life for our benefit. It will only be proper for us to repay our debt of gratitude by cremating him with due rites and respect.'

As they spoke, these people were overcome by grief, as if they had lost a kinsman. Their voices faltered and their eyes filled with tears. Seeing them thus, some others, who were calmer and took other aspects into account, addressed them. 'This is not the way to revere or honour this best of elephants,' they said. 'We think that the proper way to do so is by accomplishing his purpose. This unknown friend gave up his body to save us because he held his guests to be even dearer. It will therefore be fitting to act in accordance with his intention. Otherwise his effort will have been to no purpose. Out of affection he offered all that he possessed to his guests. Who can let this hospitality be wasted by not accepting it? We should honour him, and secure our welfare, by following his word like that of a teacher. It is only after we have surmounted our present problem that we may revere this best of elephants by performing all the rites due to a deceased kinsman.'

Keeping in mind that great soul's intention to save them from the desert, the men then acted in accordance with his words. Feeding on his flesh and using his intestines to carry water, they proceeded in the direction he had indicated and came out safely from the desert.

Thus it is that good people esteem even their suffering as a gain if it benefits others. This should be recounted in praise of such people; also while discoursing on the Tathagata and listening with respect to the preaching of the righteous path. It should further be mentioned while describing how a goodly nature can be developed. With due practice, such a nature follows one in other births. This account should also be mentioned in pointing out the merit of practising charity. The habit of giving up material objects facilitates the abandonment of self-love.

As the Lord said at the time of his final release about the celestial flowers and music which accompanied it, 'O Ananda, the Tathagata[3] is not honoured by this.' To elaborate this it should be pointed out that true reverence is paid by accomplishing the intention, and not by perfumes, garlands and the like.

31

Prince Sutasoma

MEETING GOOD PEOPLE, NO MATTER HOW IT HAPPENS, IS conducive to spiritual improvement. One who seeks the latter should therefore recourse to virtuous company. Thus has it been heard:

When the Lord was a Bodhisattva, he was once born in the illustrious royal house of the Kauravas. It was a family famed for its brilliance and held in affection by the people for its adherence to virtue. It was, moreover, powerful and had subdued all its proud feudatories. The baby was radiant with merit and as beautiful as the moon. His father therefore named him Sutasoma, or moon-child.

The child grew up in course of time. He learnt the Vedas together with the auxiliary texts, and the sciences, including the higher ones. The people loved and respected him for he defended, promoted and nurtured merit like a brother and observed all the restraints prescribed in the scriptures.

The prince was endowed with character and learning, charity and mercy, self-control, forbearance and dignity. He was wise but humble, resolute but courteous, intelligent but modest. He had beauty, strength and renown, a clever mind and a good memory. Noting his ability to protect the people, and his elevated and benevolent nature, the king appointed him to the high rank of heir apparent.

Once Sutasoma went out to a wood to amuse himself. Escorted by a small troop of guards, he was in the course of visiting the parks around the city. It was the month of flowers. Spring had spread out a wealth of fresh and lovely foliage. The earth was covered with a mantle of grass, and the clear blue water of the lakes with dark and white lotuses. Honeybees hovered and hummed. Cuckoos and peacocks called. A soft breeze blew, fragrant, cool and pleasant. It was a delightful time.

Adorned with charming gardens and arbours, the wood was full of all kinds of trees bent under the weight of their blossoms. It echoed with the sound of the koel. The prince wandered there with his beloved wives, like one reaping rewards of past good deeds does in Nandana, the garden of paradise. He enjoyed its sylvan beauty as well as the luxury of the sweet music, the singing and voluptuous dancing of the women excited by wine.

There, he was approached by a brahmin versed in epigrams and well-said maxims. The learned prince loved such maxims of pious content. Anyone who came to him with these polished sayings was always received with praise and many honours. The brahmin too was given an appropriate reception, after which he sat down, entranced by the prince's comeliness.

Though the prince was at that time enjoying himself in keeping with his youth and his rich store of merits, he nevertheless felt a high regard for the brahmin who had just arrived. But, before the latter could recite some maxims and derive any benefit from his visit, there was suddenly a commotion which interrupted the music, frightened the women and spoilt the joy of the revelry.

'Find out what has happened,' the prince instructed the harem attendants kindly. They came back quickly, in great agitation, their faces overcast with fear and distress. 'Sire,' they said, 'the man-eater Kalmashapada Saudasa is here. He is another god of death. More cruel and fearsome than a demon, he has killed hundreds of men. His strength, energy and insolence are more than human, and he is a veritable terror for the world. He is coming towards this very place. The steadfastness of our guards has given way to fear. The chariots and horses, the elephants and warriors, are all in disarray. You must confront him, sire, or consider what will be best.'

'Who is this Saudasa?' Sutasoma asked.

'Sire,' the attendants replied, 'there was once a king called Sudasa who went out hunting and was carried away by his horse into a dense forest where he cohabited with a lioness. She became pregnant and in due course gave birth to a boy who was taken by some forest dwellers and brought before the king. As Sudasa was childless, he brought up the child Saudasa who succeeded to the kingdom on his father's death.

'The new king was addicted to eating meat on account of his maternal defect. Having tasted human flesh, he concluded that this was the tastiest meat of all, and began to kill and eat the denizens of his own city. They then prepared to put him to death. Afraid of this, Saudasa made a vow to the spirits who enjoy offerings of human flesh and blood. "If I am saved from this peril," he swore, "I will sacrifice a hundred sons of kings to the spirits." And, having been saved, he has been abducting royal prices by force. He has come here to abduct Your Highness also. Now that you have heard us, sire, we await your orders.'

As he was compassionate by nature, Sutasoma decided to cure Saudasa after hearing about his aberrations and wicked character. He was confident of his ability to do so, and received the intimation of Saudasa's arrival as gladly as if it were good news. 'This man lost his kingdom out of greed for human flesh,' he said firmly. 'He is like someone gone mad. No longer in control of himself, he has abandoned his duties and destroyed his own merit and reputation. He is thus in a pitiable condition.

'Where is the opportunity for me to display valour or give way to fear when he is in this state? I must destroy his wickedness without any effort at force. I should be sympathetic even if he were going away. But he comes to me on his own and it is proper that I should show him hospitality, for this is how one must act towards guests.'

'So, mind your duties, gentlemen,' the prince told the harem guards. He then assured and turned back the distressed young women who tried to block his way with tearful eyes and choking voices, and proceeded in the direction of the commotion.

There he saw Saudasa, sword and shield in hand, in hot pursuit of the fleeing royal force. A girdle was pulled tight over his dirty clothes. His hair, tied with a strip of bark, hung dishevelled and stiff with dust. A thick beard and whiskers darkened his face, and his fierce eyes rolled with anger. 'Ho, there!' the prince called out fearlessly. 'This is I, Sutasoma! Turn this way. What is the point of killing these poor people?'

His pride stirred by these words of challenge, Saudasa turned around like a lion and saw the Bodhisattva, unarmed, alone and gentle by nature. 'I too am hunting for you!' he cried. Without the least hesitation he then came forward suddenly, incensed, and swiftly placing the prince on his shoulder, ran off with him. Delighted at his great catch, he returned to his dwelling.

It was a fearful place. The ground was wet with blood and laden with corpses. Inauspicious cries of jackals seemed to warn others not to come near. Seen from afar by travellers, it petrified them with terror, for it was horrendous and sinister, with dancing demons and ghosts, and with trees discoloured by the smoke of cremation pyres, their leaves blood-stained by vultures and crows who sat on the branches.

Setting Sutasoma there, Saudasa rested for a while, his eyes transfixed by the prince's great beauty. Meanwhile the latter was reminded of the brahmin who had come to present his polished maxims. He had not been shown the due courtesies, the prince worried, and he must still be waiting in the garden, his heart full of hope. 'Alas, that brahmin came from afar, hoping to present his maxims to me. What will he do when he hears of my abduction? His hopes will have been dashed, and his great labour rendered fruitless. He will either sigh and grieve for me or curse his own fate.'

The great soul was compassionate by habit. As he worried thus, his heart sore at the brahmin's sorrow, tears welled up in his eyes. Saudasa saw them and laughed. 'Oh no, sir!' he said, 'among your many virtues you are famous for remaining clam. Yet you too shed tears on having come into my power. It has indeed been rightly said that patience is fruitless in adversity and learning useless in grief. There are none who will not shake when stricken. Tell me truly, for whom are these tears? For your own dear life or for your wealth, the means of your comfort? Or do you grieve for your kinsmen and your royal state? Is it that you remember your loving father or your weeping children?'

'These tears are not for my life,' Sutasoma replied. 'Nor are they for my parents, or even for my children, wives and kinsmen. Nor are they due to any recollection of the pleasures of power. My eyes are wet because I remembered that a brahmin had come full of hope with his maxims, and must now burn with despair on hearing that I have been abducted.

'You should, therefore, let me go,' he added, 'till the time I can reassure that dejected brahmin with due courtesies and hear his sweet maxims. After fulfilling my obligation towards him in this way, I will do the same for you by coming back here to give you satisfaction. Do not trouble yourself with any suspicion, O king, that this is a ruse for my escape. Men like me follow a path very different from that of others.'

'This is said most honourably,' Saudasa observed, 'but it is entirely beyond belief. Released from the jaws of death, who in his senses will go there again? Having evaded a fatal danger so difficult to avert, when you are safely back in your beautiful palace, what on earth would cause you to return to me?'

'The reason is obvious,' the prince replied. 'How is it, sir, that even then you cannot grasp it? It is that I have promised to come back. Do not think that I am some knave. I am Sutasoma. Out of greed or fear of death, some may abandon truth like a bit of straw. But, for good people truth is their life and wealth. They will not forsake it even in distress. Moreover, neither life nor mundane pleasures will protect from evil consequences one who is fallen from the truth. So, for their sake, who will give up truth which is the source of glory as well as happiness?

'Besides, what is it that make you suspect even me?' the prince continued. 'Virtuous conduct may be incredible in someone who is seen to act wickedly or never observed to make a good effort. I am a proud warrior. If I had been afraid, or attached to pleasures, or devoid of compassion, I would have approached someone famous for his ferocity like you, in armour, ready to fight. But I wish only to have a talk with you and, after rewarding that brahmin's labours, I will return to you on my own. People like me do not lie.'

Saudasa had no patience for Sutasoma's words which he considered contrived. 'He does indeed boast a great deal about his truth and rectitude,' he said to himself. 'So let me see his love of veracity and righteousness. Besides, what do I lose if he gets away? There are already a hundred princes in my power, and with them I can perform the sacrifice to the spirits as I have sworn to do.'

Having thought this over, he told the prince: 'Then go. We will see how upright you are. Go, and return quickly after doing what the brahmin wants. Meanwhile I will prepare your funeral pyre.'

Thus the prince, having given his word, went home where he was greeted by his household. He then sent for the brahmin and heard four verses from him. Delighted by the well-said maxims, he praised the brahmin duly and, valuing each verse at a thousand coins of gold, rewarded him with the wealth he had hoped for.

Now Sutasoma's father, the king, wished to avoid extravagant and uncalled-for expenditures. 'My dear,' he said to his son gently in the course of these proceedings, 'you should know the proper limit in rewarding such maxims. You have to look after many people, and sovereignty depends on a full treasury. I would think that it is more than enough to reward a well-said verse with a hundred coins. It is not proper to go beyond that. How long will the riches even of the god of wealth survive if he gives too much of it away? Wealth is the ultimate of effective means: nothing desirable can be attained without it. Fortune, like a harlot, does not even look at a king without an abundant treasury.'

'Sire,' replied the prince, 'if it were indeed possible to set a limit to the value of a well-said maxim, it is obvious that you would not blame me if I gave away even the kingdom for it. Such a verse is worth the flesh of one's body. Listening to it delights the heart, improves and illumines the mind and strengthens the love for salvation.

'A well-said maxim is a lamp which dispels the darkness of delusion, a treasure which thieves and others cannot take away, a weapon to assail the enemy which is infatuation, and a minister who counsels on policy. It is a friend steadfast even in adversity, a painless antidote for the malady of grief, a mighty army for defeating the forces of evil and a great reservoir of glory and wellbeing.

'Such maxims are thus well known for their many merits,' the prince added. 'I received them as gifts. How can I not honour the donor when I am able to do so? At the same time how can I disobey your command? Therefore I will return to Saudasa. I do not seek the toil of governance. Nor do I wish to incur the sin of going back on my pledge.'

These words alarmed the father who loved his son greatly. 'My dear,' he said earnestly, 'I said what I did only in your interest. Do not get angry. May your enemies fall into the hands of Saudasa. Even though you wish to keep your word and return to him as promised, I will not permit it. The scriptures say that there is no sin in falsehood to protect one's life or for the sake of one's parents and elders. Why should this precept be ignored?

'Those who are skilled in policy,' the father continued, 'point out that one based only on virtue but contrary to profit and pleasure is impolitic. For kings it can be disastrous. So do not insist on one which causes me grief and is against your own interest. But if, my dear, you consider that breaking your word will be dishonourable, incorrect and improper, then our mighty army is there to guard you. It has elephants and chariots, cavalry and infantry, and devoted and well-armed warriors who have won many battles. Go with it to Saudasa and overpower or slay him. In this way you will both keep your word and protect yourself.'

'Promise one thing, and do something else!' Sutasoma exclaimed. 'I cannot do this, sire. I cannot strike at those who are pitiable, mired in wickedness and heading for hell. Abandoned by their allies and helpless, they are my friends. Moreover, Saudasa treated me with a rare magnanimity. Though I was in his power, he trusted me and let me go. It is because of him, father, that I obtained these maxims. He is therefore my benefactor and deserves my sympathy in particular. Do not worry that anything bad will happen to me. What power will he have to harm me when I go to him thus?'

Having thus persuaded his father, the great soul turned back his loyal army as well as those who loved and stopped him. Alone and unafraid, free of distress and true to his word, he returned to Saudasa.

Saudasa saw the great one from afar. Long practice had rooted cruelty deep in his impure mind. Even so he was amazed and his respect for Sutasoma increased. 'Oh, Oh, it is a wonder of wonders!' he said to himself gladly. 'It is a marvel of marvels! The prince's nobility and veracity exceed that of both men and the gods. My nature is fierce and deadly. Yet he comes to me on his own, without any fear or agitation! What courage and admirable trueness to his word! Justly, indeed, has spread his fame, for he is prepared to give up his life and his kingdom for the sake of truth.'

As his heart thus filled with astonishment and admiration, the prince came up to him. 'Thanks to you, sir,' he said, 'I obtained a treasure of well-said maxims, rewarded the petitioner, and gladdened myself. Now I have come back. You can eat me, if you like, or use me as a victim for your sacrifice.'

'I am in no hurry to eat you,' replied Saudasa. 'Besides, this funeral pyre is still smoking, and flesh cooked on a smokeless fire is more tasty. Meanwhile, let me hear these maxims.'

'What will you do with listening to maxims in your present state?' Sutasoma responded. 'You have abandoned mercy towards your people for the sake of your belly. These verses praise virtue and that does not go with unrighteousness. You have forsaken the noble path and taken to the distorted way of demons. You are devoid of truth, what to say of virtue. What will you do with pious sayings?'

Saudasa was stung by this denigration. 'Don't speak like that!' he retorted. 'Tell me which king does not raise his weapon and kill deer in his pleasure park? And if I slay men similarly for food, am I then unrighteous and those deer slayers not so?'

'Those who bend their bows at frightened and fleeing deer are certainly not righteous,' Sutasoma replied. But a man-eater is even more condemnable than them. Human beings should not be treated as food. They are the highest of all creatures.'

Though he had been spoken to most severely, the fierceness of Saudasa's temperament was overcome by Sutasoma's friendly nature. 'O Sutasoma,' he said lightly, laughing at the prince's words, 'you are not skilled in ways of politics. I let you go, and you reached your home with all its royal splendours, Yet you have returned to me!'

'No,' said Sutasoma, 'I am indeed skilled in the ways of politics, for I do not wish to follow them. What is the point of such ways? They lead to deviation from what is right and bring no happiness. Moreover, those who are adept in them often reap disaster after death. So I set aside those crooked ways and came back, true to my word. Thus it is I who know politics, for I abjure untruth and delight in veracity. That is not a good policy, say the wise, which does not assure glory and happiness as well as profit.'

'What profit do you see in keeping a promise,' asked Saudasa, 'for the sake of which you have returned to me, forfeiting your dear life and leaving behind tearful kinsmen as well as the delightful pleasures which go with royalty?'

'Truth is the repository of many great merits,' Sutasoma replied. 'Listen, in brief, to what they are: The loveliness of truth surpasses the beauty of garlands, and its sweetness the best of flavours. It is greater than laborious penance and pilgrimage, for it yields merit without effort. It provides a path for glory to spread among men and permeate the three worlds. It is the gateway to heaven and a bridge to cross the worldly round.'

'Excellent! It is right!' cried Saudasa, bowing to the prince and looking at him with wonder. 'Other men who come into my power are so frightened and distressed that they lose all calm. But you, O king, have no fear of death!'

'Death cannot be avoided even with the greatest effort,' said the prince. 'What is the use of unmanly fear which cannot prevent it? Even cowards know it is a part of the worldly order, but they are troubled by their wickedness. They never tried to do good deeds, and are apprehensive of suffering in the next world. So they get paralyzed by the fear that they must die.

'As for me, I do not remember having ever done anything which should trouble my mind. My actions were pure. Why should one who does right fear death?

'I do not remember any visit of supplicants which did not gladden me. I was always content to give in charity. Nor do I recall, even after long reflection, ever having taken a step towards sin, be it in my thoughts. My path to heaven is thus clear. Why should I be afraid of death?

'I bestowed, as appropriate, much wealth on brahmins, on my kinsmen, friends and dependents, on the poor, and on the ascetics who adorn their orders. I built hundreds of beautiful temples and hospices, sacrificial and assembly halls, hermitages and wells for drinking water. I am thus satisfied and have no fear of death. You may use me for your sacrifice or indeed make a meal of me.'

The darkness of Saudasa's wicked nature was dispelled as he listened to these words. His eyes filled with tears of joy and his hair stood on end. 'Heaven forbid!' he exclaimed, gazing at the Bodhisattva with reverence. 'May anyone who wishes you ill swallow poison, O best of kings. May he eat an angry snake or a flaming iron ingot. May his head and his heart shatter in a hundred pieces.

'Yet you should tell me those fine maxims,' he added. 'My desire to hear them has become even keener. Your words gladden my heart like a rain of flowers. Moreover, sir, I have seen the ugliness of my deeds reflected in the mirror of dharma. My mind is eager for it, and may well be moved towards it.'

Sutasoma observed that Saudasa was now disposed to give ear to dharma, and his mind was ready to receive its message. 'It is fitting,' he said, 'that a seeker after dharma listen to its exposition in a suitable and appropriate manner. Look, the listener should sit modestly on a lower seat, enjoying as it were the sweetness of the words, his eyes full of love. His mind should be humble and attentive, happy and pure. He should listen with respect, like someone ill does the words of the physician.'

Saudasa then spread his cloak upon a rock and, seating the prince on this higher level, himself sat down on the bare ground in front. 'Speak, now, sir,' he said to the great one, looking intently at his face.

Sutasoma then spoke, his sweet and sonorous voice seeming to fill the forest as with the sound of a fresh raincloud:

> 'Keeping company with the good,
> that too by chance and only once,
> becomes a tie unbreakable:
> it does not need renewal.'

'Excellent! Excellent!' cried Saudasa, nodding his head and urging the prince. 'Go on, go on.'

Sutasoma then recited the second verse:

> 'From the good, don't keep away,
> but follow them with due humility:
> the pollen of their virtue's flower
> is bound to touch, and effortlessly,
> even those who stand nearby.'

'Virtuous man,' said Saudasa, 'rightly did you use your wealth! Rightly did you disregard the expense and reward the maxims so heartily. Go on, go on.'

Sutasoma continued:

> 'The cars of kings, and their own bodies,
> with gold adorned, and many jewels,
> must grow old and lose their beauty:
> but not the goodness of the good,
> for their love of virtues
> is always unperturbable.

'This is indeed a shower of nectar! Oh, I have been quenched!' cried Saudasa.

Sutasoma said:

> 'Far is heaven from this earth,
> and far the ocean's other shore,
> so too the hill where sets the sun
> from the mountain where it rises:
> but the virtues of the good
> from wicked folk are further still.'

Saudasa marvelled and rejoiced. Filled with affection and respect for the prince, he said, 'I am elated to hear these four sweet verses from you. The effulgence of their meaning surpasses the elegance of their words. As a reward for them I grant you four boons. Choose whatever you wish.'

'Who are you to grant boons?' Sutasoma said, his voice showing not the slightest trace of anger. 'You are a slave to your passion for wicked deeds, and have no power even over yourself. Averse to auspicious actions, what boon will you give to others. If I ask you for one, and your wish to give slackens, it would be an offence no kind person should like to provoke. It is enough that you want to give me a boon.'

Somewhat ashamed, Saudasa hung his head. 'Enough of your suspicions, sir,' he told the prince. 'I will give you these boons even at the cost of my life. Rest assured and choose what you wish for.'

'In that case,' said the prince, 'vow to speak the truth, give up violence towards other creatures, release all the people you have imprisoned and do not eat human flesh. Grant me, O hero, these four precious boons.'

'I grant you the first three, sir,' Saudasa replied. 'As for the fourth boon, choose another. Don't you know that I cannot give up eating human flesh?'

'Well, this is that I expected,' Sutasoma responded. 'Did I not say, who are you to grant boons? Moreover, O king, if you do not give up eating human flesh, how will you keep your vows of truth and non-violence? You said earlier that you would give me these boons even at the cost of your life, but that is proving otherwise. Where is your abstinence from injuring others if you kill men for their flesh? And, that being so, of what use are the three boons you give me?'

'How can I give it up?' Saudasa retorted. 'For it I renounced my kingdom, suffered living in the wilderness, ruined my reputation and destroyed my virtue!'

'That is precisely why you should give it up,' said Sutasoma. 'It has deprived you of virtue and profit, comfort and glory. It has been a disaster. Why should you not forswear it? Besides, it is only the mean-minded who repent after granting boons. How can you succumb to such baseness? And how can you enjoy yourself in this desolate forest, seperated from congenial kinsmen, children, and attendants, and from various royal pleasures like the sound of singing at night and the music of drums, as deep as the rumble of rainclouds?

'So, give up these wicked ways. You should know yourself. You, sir, are the son of Sudasa. At your disposal are various meats obtainable from the countryside, the lakes and the forests, checked by physicians and skilfully cooked. Use them to your heart's content, but please stop eating human flesh which is condemnable.

'You should not let yourself be overpowered by emotions,' the prince concluded. 'Alone you have defeated in battle many rulers and all their armies. Do not now be timid in fighting emotion. Follow the path of what is right and in your interest. You have to think of the next world also, and therefore must not do what may be pleasant but harmful. There is, on the other hand, a lovely path which leads to glory. Follow it, even if it may be displeasing, like you would take a medicine.'

Tears of joy welled in Saudasa's eyes and choked his voice as he fell before Sutasoma and embraced his feet. 'Who else but you,' he cried, 'would have shown compassion for a sinner like myself, as cruel as the messenger of death! Rightly does your fame pervade the whole world, together with the fragrance of your virtues and merits. You are my master, my guru, my very God. These words of yours I accept with bowed head. Henceforth I will not eat human flesh, Sutasoma, and whatever else you tell me, that I will do. Come, let us together release the princes I have abducted for the sacrifice. They are dejected, sad, and suffering on account of their confinement.'

'Very well,' Sutasoma replied, and the two went where the princes were imprisoned. 'Oh, we are free!' they exclaimed, rejoicing at the very sight of Sutasoma.

> Their smiling faces shone
> like lilies, when they open
> caressed by moonbeams
> at the start of autumn.

Sutasoma comforted the princes with kind words and had them swear that they would not harm Saudasa. He then released them and, followed by the princes, he returned together with that chief to his kingdom. There he duly honoured them all, and established Saudasa and the princes in their respective domains.

Thus it is that meeting good people, no matter how it happens, is conducive to spiritual improvement. One who seeks the latter should therefore recourse to virtuous company.

32

The Prince from the Iron House

T HE LURE EVEN OF SOVEREIGNTY CANNOT IMPEDE THE SPIRITUAL
progress of those whose hearts are filled with the desire for
salvation. One should, as such, understand this desire. Thus has
it been heard:

When the Lord was a Bodhisattva he saw that the world was
afflicted by hundreds of calamities such as illness, old age,
death and seperation from loved ones. It was unhappy and
unprotected, helpless and without guidance. Moved by
compassion, he resolved to save it. Exceedingly benevolent, he
ensured the welfare and the happiness of all the people, even
of those who were opposed or unknown to him.

Once he took birth in a royal family, highly regarded for its
modesty and decency. The good fortune of this house was
manifest in the love and support of its subjects, its ever-
increasing prosperity, and the subservience of its proud
feudatories. The Bodhisattva's birth invested both the family
and the capital with a festive slendour.

Within the palace, servants exulted in bright new garments
and brahmins were satiated with gifts. Outside, the city was

filled with the sound of drums, joyous dancing and abandon. The flow of song mingled with shouts of laughter. Full of satisfaction at the good news, the people embraced each other as they celebrated and offered good wishes to the king.

The gates of the city jail were thrown open and the prisoners released. Brocades and ornaments rained down from the mansions of the rich. Flags flew above and the ground below was strewn with flowers and coloured powders, and sprinkled with wine. Such were the delightful festivities in the capital that it seemed as if a river of felicity was streaming through it like the Ganges in full flow.

At that time it so happened that all the sons born to the king would die. Considering this to be caused by supernatural creatures, he had a special house built for the protection of this son. Made wholly of iron, it was beautifully embellished with figures wrought of gems, gold and silver. There he had all the rituals performed to counter and destroy demons, as foreseen in the occult sciences and prescribed in the scriptures.

In course of time the prince received the sacraments and learnt many sciences from professors versed in the Vedas, respected for their knowledge, and given to cogitation, restraint and discretion. He grew into a radiant youth, and his innate modesty made him deeply loved by all.

> It is because of virtue's splendour
> that people follow a good person,
> though he is unknown to them,
> not a kin and far away.
> But they see him as a dear friend:
> just as though they have no tie
> with the beaming autumn moon
> which spreads its smiles about the sky,
> but love it nevertheless.

Thus it was with the great one, as he enjoyed the heaven-like pleasures he had obtained effortlessly as a result of his accumulated merits. His father, who loved him dearly, felt assured and ceased to be anxious about his safety.

Once the prince wished to see the splendid displays arranged in the capital on the occasion of the Kaumudi festival.[1] Taking his father's permission, he mounted a fine chariot decorated with jewelled figures of silver and gold. Gaily coloured flags and banners fluttered above it, and its well-trained horses were dressed with golden trappings. Driven by a skilled charioteer, it was followed by armed attendants in bright attire. In it the prince proceeded through the city, accompanied by the pleasing sound of musical instruments.

The citizens and the countryfolk were enchanted to see the prince. Dressed in their best for the festival, their eyes rolling with curiosity, they responded to him with praise and adoration as they saluted him with folded hands and pronounced their blessings. He contemplated this charming spectacle but, though it was a joyous occasion, he was so given to the desire for salvation that it brought back to his mind the memory of his previous births.

'Pitiable is the world's condition,' he said to himself, 'and distasteful because it is so transient. Even the splendour of this Kaumudi festival will soon be no more than a memory. Yet, how heedless of danger are men! They pursue happiness without any care that all the ways are blocked by death. Which thinking person here has time for happiness? Illness, old age and death, all irresistible enemies, are ready to strike him and he cannot but go to the difficult world hereafter.

'Look at the clouds with their golden garlands of lightning. They rumble like the ocean and rain furiously. Yet they gather and then dissolve. Rivers break their banks and uproot trees with their strong currents, but in course of time are reduced to trickle, as if parched by some sorrow. The wind blows off crests from mountaintops, scatters clouds and stirs up the sea, but its force also dies down. Fire burns up grass with its fierce crackling flames, and then abates. The beauties of the forest appear and vanish with the passage of time. Which union does not end in seperation? What prosperity is not liable to calamity? People rejoice only because they do not perceive that change is the nature of the world.'

As he thought thus, the great soul's enjoyment of the festival was overtaken by his desire for salvation, and his mind turned away from the colourful crowds which thronged and adorned the capital, even though they were delightful. He could think only of returning to his palace, and this intensified his wish for salvation even more. 'Dharma alone is the refuge,' he reflected, 'for it is unconcerned with sensual pleasures,' and he made up his mind to embrace it.

At the first opportunity he went to the king and with folded hands begged permission to go away to a forest for penitents. 'I wish, for my own welfare, to take to the renunciant life,' he said, 'and seek the favour of your permission for it.'

The king, who loved his son, trembled at his words like an elephant struck by a poisoned dart. His mind was agitated by grief like the sea, though deep, is shaken by the wind. 'My son,' he said in a voice choked with tears, 'why have you decided so suddenly to leave us?' And he embraced the prince affectionately in order to stop him. 'Who has displeased you?' he asked. 'Who invokes death and his own destruction? Whose kin must shed tears of grief? Or is it that you apprehend or have heard of something wrong from my side? If so, tell me so that I may correct it, though I myself see no such reason.'

'You love me,' the prince replied. 'What wrong would you do me? And who else is capable of harming me or causing me grief?'

'Then why do you want to leave us?' asked the king tearfully.

'Because of the peril of death,' the great one replied. 'Consider, sire: From the very night that a person comes to stay in the mother's womb, he begins a ceaseless march, day after day, towards death. No one, skilful or strong though he may be, can escape old age or death. The whole world is infested by the two. That is why I wish to go to the forest and lead a virtuous life. I have decided to do so because, while proud and powerful princes can defeat vast armies arrayed with infantry and cavalry, chariots and elephants, they are unable to vanquish death, even though it is a solitary foe.

'Kings, protected by strong forces of horses and elephants, footmen and chariots, can succeed in escaping from their adversaries. But death subdued even Manu and other monarchs who were helpless before its greater power.

'Kings punish offenders in keeping with the offence. But they do not follow this policy in respect of death, that great offender and enemy. They bring offenders to heel by conciliation and other expedients. But death cannot be subdued by such means: its fierce pride is all the stronger with its long experience.

'Rutting elephants crush in battle gates of cities with their mighty tusks, as well as chariots, men and other elephants. Yet the same tusks, which break down walls, cannot push back death when it comes upon them. Skilled bowmen shoot down even enemies far away with their arrows, but not that old enemy – death.

'Lions bring down elephants, piercing their temples with sharp claws, and stun and scare other creatures with their roars.

Yet, faced with death, their pride and power vanishes and they fall asleep. Tigers drink the blood of frightened, fleeing deer, whom they catch swiftly and kill with a single thundering blow, as if in play. Yet they cannot show similar skills when confronted by death. And deer, though caught in the tiger's terrible claws, may still escape. But who can ever get away from the jaws of death, with its great tusks of illness, old age and suffering?

'Enraged snakes bite men with teeth full of fiery venom, flaming as it were with their wrath. But they lose this power in the face of death, even though it deserves to be killed because of its constant crimes. Physicians can neutralize the poison of an angry snake with charms and potions. But such means are of no avail against the strong and lethal fangs of the serpent death.

'Fierce, hideous demons catch men and deprive them of their vigour and life, yet they lose their arrogance and ferocity in the face of death. Exorcists restrain demons with talismans, medicinal herbs and the power of their penance, but the demon death cannot be thus restrained. Magicians mesmerize great crowds, yet even they cannot delude mighty death. Wizards appear and vanish, fly in the air or enter into the earth, by the power of their incantations; but they too lose it on encountering death. As for the haughty gods, they drive back proud ogres and are themselves driven back by the latter, yet the combined mighty forces of both cannot prevail against death.

'Those who counter poison with the charms they have obtained through penance,' the prince concluded, 'and excellent physicians who cure people's ailments, like even Dhanvantari, have all perished. Therefore I have decided to go away and practise virtue in the forest. I do so not out of anger, or any lessening of my love for you, but because death, that fierce enemy, is irresistible.'

'If it is so irresistible,' the king then asked, 'what assurance against death will you get by virtuous living in the forest? Will this enemy not come to you there? Have sages not succumbed to it in the jungle? Virtuous living is indeed possible everywhere. What then is the point of leaving your home?'

'Doubtless, death is the same for everyone,' replied the prince, 'whether they live at home or in the forest, are virtuous or wicked. But it causes no remorse to the righteous. Moreover it is easier to practise virtue in the forest.

'Consider, sir,' he continued, 'the home is also the abode of delusions, vanity and lust, greed and hatred, all of which are contrary to virtue. What scope is there to practise it at home? There, one is lured by many acts of wickedness. One is anxious to acquire things, and to guard what one has obtained. The approach of adversity and the expectation of prosperity makes one restless. How can a householder be at peace?

'But as a renunciant in the forest, one is happy, far from wickedness and free from the trouble of acquisition. Peace is one's only pursuit. The mind contented, one can attain bliss and virtue there, as well as glory. Virtue guards man, not wealth or power. Virtue gives happiness, not the possession of great riches. And death only gladdens one who is virtuous, because he has no fear of suffering in the afterlife. For, just as good and evil have different characteristics and definite functions, so does one lead to bliss and the other to torment in the next world.'

Thus did the great soul persuade his father and obtain his permission. Renouncing sovereignty as if it were straw, he then proceeded to the forest where he achieved an unprecedented state of meditation, and taught it to others before ascending to Brahmaloka.

Thus it is that the lure even of sovereignty cannot impede the spiritual progress of those whose hearts are filled with the desire for salvation. One should, as such, understand this desire. This should be recounted during discourses on the awareness of death. The thought that one must die one day arouses the desire for salvation.

33

The Buffalo

FORBEARANCE REQUIRES AN OCCASION FOR IT. THAT IS WHY GOOD people regard even those who trouble them as being useful. Thus has it been heard:

The Bodhisattva was once a wild buffalo bull in a certain forest region. His body rough with mud, he looked like a patch of dark cloud. It is difficult in the animal state, which is dominated by ignorance, to be aware of what is right. Yet even in that condition the great one was given to the practice of virtue on account of the keenness of his understanding.

It was the power of his karma which made him thus, for he was never lacking in compassion which had been a part of his nature since long. Without action there cannot be any rebirth; also, good deeds cannot bear evil fruit. It was because of a small misdeed that he had obtained an animal birth inspite of his virtues. The Lord has rightly said that the mystery of the fruit of karma is indeed beyond understanding.

The buffalo's natural goodness, and his merciful disposition which excluded all anger and violence, came to be known in the course of time to a wicked monkey. 'I have nothing to fear,' he thought, and began to torment the great one with all kinds of aggressive activities:

> Harsh insults and insolence
> mark the villain's actions
> towards the mild and merciful,
> for he fears not such people.
> But where he suspects
> even the slightest danger,
> he is servile and humble,
> his petulance at peace.

Sometimes, when the great one was drowsy or asleep, the monkey would suddenly jump upon him. Sometimes he would clamber over him as if he were a tree, and shake him violently. On other occasions he would stand before the buffalo and block the latter's way when he was hungry and looking to graze. Once he scratched the great one's ears with a piece of wood. He would also climb upon his head when he wanted to bathe in a pond, and cover his eyes with his paws. At times he would sit upon the buffalo's back and drive him perforce with a stick in imitation of Yama, the lord of the underworld[1].

The buffalo bore all this rude behaviour without any agitation or anger, indeed as if he considered it a favour. While it is the very nature of the wicked to act indecorously, this is deemed a good turn by the virtuous because it enables them to practise forbearance. But there was a yaksha[2] who saw the buffalo being ridden by the rascally monkey. Either because he could not bear to see such humiliation, or because he wished to understand the great one's nature, he stood in the way. 'Do not let this pass, sir!' he cried. 'Has this villainous ape purchased you as a slave or won you in a wager? Do you apprehend some danger from him, or do you not know your own strength, that you let yourself be insulted and ridden like this?

'The points of your horns are hard as adamant,' the yaksha added. 'Swiftly swung, they can pierce diamonds or cleave kingly trees like a thunderbolt. An angry kick from your feet could thrust them into the side of a mountain as if it were so much mud. Your strong and splendid body is as solid as a rock. Those who are naturally powerful are aware of your might. It would be difficult even for a lion to get the better of you. Why do you let this wretched monkey torment you as if you were powerless? Catch and crush him with your hooves, or deflate his impudence with your horns. When has a villain ever been cured by good behaviour and gentleness? He must be treated like the sickness of the phlegm, which requires bitter, hot and harsh remedies.'

The buffalo replied in mild words which displayed his forbearance. 'I know that this monkey is capricious and always rude,' he said, gazing at the yaksha. 'That indeed is the reason why it is proper for me to be patient with him. To act thus with the powerful, against whom it is impossible to retaliate, is hardly forbearance. And none is needed in dealing with the virtuous who are calm and decorous.

'It is only the strong who can tolerate the shortcomings of the weak,' the buffalo added, 'and it is better to put up with their insults than to lose one's virtues. Indeed bad behaviour by the weak provides the best opportunity for demonstrating virtue. Why should one lose patience on such occasions? It would, in fact, be the height of ingratitude if I did not show forbearance towards someone who acts as if to cleanse me of my sins without any care for adding to those of his own.

'In that case you will never be freed from his persecution,' said the yaksha. 'Villains have no respect for virtue. Who can control their rudeness without putting forbearance and humility aside?'

'The comfort derived or the discomfort avoided by hurting other is not suitable for one who seeks happiness,' replied the buffalo, 'for its result can never be satisfying. I have shown forbearance in trying to make this monkey come to his senses. If he does not, others who are less patient will stop him on their own. Treated by them more roughly, he will also behave better with those like me. Punished for his misconduct, he will not repeat it and I too will be freed from it.'

The yaksha was wonderstruck, and his heart filled with joy and reverence. 'Well said! Well said!' he exclaimed, nodding his head and waving his fingers as he praised the great one. 'Where does one see such a state of mind in animals, and such high regard for virtue? It is obvious that you have assumed this animal shape for some purpose, sir, for you must be a sage from some hermitage.' He then gave the buffalo a charm for his protection and, removing the wicked monkey from his back, disappeared forthwith.

Thus it is that forbearance requires an occasion. That is why good people regard even those who trouble them as being useful. This should be recounted during discourses on forbearance. It also shows the high inner awareness of the Bodhisattva even when he is born as a beast.

34

The Woodpecker

EVEN THOUGH INCITED, GOOD PEOPLE DO NOT ENGAGE IN
wickedness because they are unaccustomed to it. Thus has it
been heard:

The Bodhisattva was once a woodpecker of brilliant
plumage in a forest region. Even in that state of existence, he
was habituated to compassion and did not follow the normal
livelihood of woodpeckers which is marred by violence to other
creatures. He contented himself, instead, with a diet of tender
leaves of trees, their fragrant, sweet and tasty flowers, and fruit
of different flavours, scents and hues.

The woodpecker's care for other creatures was manifest. He
would admonish them suitably about the righteous path, help
those who were in distress, and dissuade the mean-minded
from acting improperly. Thus looked after by the great one, the
denizens of the forest thrived and flourished as if they had in
him a teacher or a friend, a physician or a ruler. Nurtured and
protected by his mercy, they multiplied both in numbers and
virtuous merit.

Sympathetic to all creatures, the great soul was once flying
around in another forest. There he saw a lion writhing in agony

as if struck by a poisoned arrow, his dishevelled mane soiled
with dust. Moved by pity, he approached the animal. 'What is
the matter, king of beasts?' he asked. 'I see that you are very
ill. Is it due to some excess in your exertions against elephants,
or to the fatigue of chasing deer? Or is it because of a hunter's
arrow or some sickness? Tell me, if you think it fit, and also
what needs to be done. You will surely be happy if there is
anything in my power, as a friend, to give you comfort.'

'Most virtuous and best of birds,' the lion replied, 'my illness
is not due to fatigue, nor to any disease or the hunter's dart.
There is a bit of bone which is stuck in my throat. It hurts me
terribly, as if it were a spear. I can neither swallow it nor spit
it out. This is the time for friends. Do whatever you can to make
me well.'

With his keen understanding the woodpecker at once
thought of a method to take out the bone. 'Open your mouth
as wide as you can,' he told the lion as he took a piece of wood
to act as a bar. And when the beast had done so, he placed the
wooden piece firmly between the two rows of his teeth and
went inside to the bottom of his throat. With his beak he then
caught hold of one end of the bone which was lodged
transversely there, and after loosening it, pulled it out by the
other end. After this he came out and removed the wooden bar
from the lion's mouth. No surgeon, however clever or adept,
could how done all this even with much labour. Yet he did it
effortlessly with the intelligence he had acquired through
hundreds of previous births.

Having thus assuaged the lion's pain and received his
thanks, the woodpecker took leave with a glad heart and
went home. On another day, as he flew about in search of food,
his beautiful wings outstretched, he could find nothing
suitable to eat. Tormented by hunger pangs, as he looked

around he saw the very same lion enjoying the flesh of a young deer freshly killed. His mouth, mane and paws spattered with blood, he looked like a patch of autumn cloud glowing in the light of dusk.

It is always disagreeable to ask for a favour, and the woodpecker could not bring himself to do so even though he had done one to the lion. Shame silenced his voice. Still, such was his need that, though embarrassed, he walked about before the lion. The villain saw him but made no move to invite him. Favours done to ingrates are as fruitless as the vidula reed, the seed sown on a rock, or an oblation offered into a fire gone cold.

The woodpecker concluded that he had not been recognized. Shedding some of his hesitation, he approached the lion like a ritual supplicant and, after pronouncing a suitable benediction, asked for alms. 'King of beasts,' he said, 'may all be well with you, who earn your livelihood by your own prowess. I seek the courtesy due to a supplicant which will bring you merit and fame.'

The lion was cruel, selfish and unmindful of noble conduct. Even though he had been addressed with a blessing, he looked askance at the bird from the corners of his angry bloodshot eyes, as if wishing to incinerate him. 'None of this!' he said. 'I do not care for unmanly mercy. I eat live deer. Is it not enough that, having entered my mouth, you came out alive? Are you so tired of life that you insult me once again with your entreaties? Do you already wish to see the next world?'

The lion's harsh retort left the woodpecker crestfallen, and he flew up into the sky. A forest deity who was either indignant at the dishonourable manner in which the great one had been treated, or wished to know how patient he could be, also flew with him. 'Best of birds,' he said, 'you helped that villain, but he has been discourteous to you. How can you put up with this despite your capabilities? Why do you ignore what this ingrate has done? Though he is strong, you can pounce upon him and blind him with your beak, or take away the meat even from his teeth. Why do you tolerate his insolence?'

Though the woodpecker had been insulted by the lion and was now being incited by the forest deity, he nevertheless manifested the goodness of his nature. 'Do not speak thus,' he said, 'this is not the way of those such as me. Good people are moved, not by any wish for gain, but by mercy for those who are suffering. Whether the latter recognize this or not, it should give no cause for anger.

'One who is ungrateful,' the great one continued, 'deceives only himself. No one expecting a favour in return will ever help him again. But one who helps others will get for certain the fruit of his good deeds in the next world as well as glory in this one. Moreover, to help others as a duty can give no cause for regret. To do so for something in return is no more than giving a loan, and to harm another because of his ingratitude is to besmirch one's own repute and virtue.

'If someone is weak-minded enough to be ungrateful,' the woodpecker added, 'he will not attain the splendour of virtue. But is it appropriate for an intelligent person to tarnish his own reputation by retaliating? To me the proper course seems to be that if a person shows no signs of friendliness despite being helped, one should dissociate from him gently, without any harshness or anger.'

The forest deity was delighted at these well-said words. 'Well spoken! Well spoken!' he cried effusively as he praised the woodpecker. 'Though you do not wear matted hair and garments of bark,' he said, 'you are, sir, a seer who knows the future. You are a sage. Garb alone does not make one, but saintliness comes from merit.' And glorifying him thus, the dcity disappeared.

Thus it is that, even though incited, good people do not engage in wickedness because they are unaccustomed to it. This tale should be recounted in praise of the virtuous. Also, while discoursing on forbearance it must be emphasized that its practice reduces reproachful enmity, and makes one loved and adored by the many. It should be recounted further in elaborating on awareness: thus do the wise preserve their virtue and glory. Likewise in glorifying the Tathagata, and in describing the cultivation of good nature which, nurtured well, does not diminish even in an animal state.

Notes

Introduction

1. A.B. Keith, *A History of Sanskrit Literature,* London, 1920; M. Winternitz, *History of Indian Literature, Vol. II,* Calcutta, 1933. S.N. Dasgupta, ed. *History of Sanskrit Literature, Vol. I,* Calcutta, 1947. Hereafter referred to respectively as Keith, Winternitz and Dasgupta.
2. Winternitz. Some of the frescoes depict scenes and verse inscriptions from tales 2, 8, 13, 22 and 26, as noted in J.C. Mishra, ed. with Hindi translation and introduction, *Jatakamala,* Varanasi, 1989. Hereafter referred to as Mishra.
3. These are *Jatakamalatika,* perhaps, eighth century AD; *Jatakamalatika* by Dharmakirti; and *Jatakamalapanjarika* by Viryasimha. The first is extant in Sanskrit and the other two only in Tibetan translations. Peter Khoroche, *Towards a New Edition of the Jatakamala,* Bonn, 1987. Hereafter referred to as Khoroche.
4. Winternitz.
5. J.S. Speyer, tr. *Jatakamala of Aryasura,* London, 1895. Reprinted Delhi, 1971. Hereafter referred to as Speyer.
6. Speyer. Mishra.
6A. *Subhashita Ratnakosha* of Vidyakara, v. 1292, and *Subhashitavali* of Vallabhadeva, v. 272.

7. Speyer.
8. Mishra, names them as: *Subhashitaratnakarandakakatha, Paramitasamasa, Pratimokshasutra Paddhati, Bodhisattvajataka Dharmagandi*, and *Supathanirdesa Parikatha*. The last three are extant only in Tibetan translations.
9. Speyer. Lama Chimpa and A. Chattopadhyaya, tr. *rGya-gar-chos-'byun*, (History of Buddhism), Simla, 1970.
10. Keith. Dasgupta.
11. Mishra.
12. In W.T. de Barry, *Sources of Indian Tradition, Vol. I*, New York, 1958. Hereafter referred to as de Barry.
13. In A.L. Basham, ed. *A Cultural History of India*, Oxford. 1975.
14. These are: generosity (*dana*), moral conduct (*shila*), patience (*kshanti*), courage (*virya*), meditation (*dhyana*), wisdom (*prajna*), skill in means (*upayakaushalya*), strength (*bala*), determination (*pranidhana*), and knowledge (*jnana*). de Barry.
15. Speyer.
16. de Barry.
17. As first noted by Hendrik Kern, these are tales 1, 8, 10, 12, 13, 17, 18, 23, 24, 29, 30 and 31 in the text translated here.
18. Khoroche.
19. In his foreword to Speyer's translation.
20. Khoroche.
21. Mishra.
22. E.B. Cowell, ed. *The Jataka*, 6 vols. Cambridge, 1895–1907.
23. *Jatakamala*, ed. with introduction and Hindi translation, by S.N. Chaudhari, Delhi 1971 and by J.C. Mishra, Varanasi, 1989.
24. Speyer.
25. Keith. Dasgupta.

Prologue

1. i.e. to attain their own emancipation.
2. *Sarvajna* in the original. An epithet of the Buddha. It also refers to his knowledge of his previous births, a recurring feature in these tales.

1. *The Tigress*

1. The Buddha, the dharma or faith enunciated by him, and the sangha or the monastic order he established.
2. The celestial tempter or personification of earthly desires in Buddhist philosophy and mythology. Vanquished by the Buddha, whom he sought to tempt with his arguements, threats and baits of sensory pleasures, he appears also in several jataka stories.

2. *The Shibi King*

1. A superior breed of elephant with a particular odour.
2. A popular epithet of the Buddha, literally 'he who has thus come.'

3. *A Bit of Gruel*

1. The highest category of saint in Buddhist terminology, who is exempt from further rebirth.

4. *The Merchant Prince*

1. A Buddha who has attained enlightenment for himself, but does not seek to teach others
2. cf. tale 1, note 2.

7. *The Hermit*

1. This could be the hermit's patronymic, his actual name being Agastya which figures only in this jataka's original title.

8. *King Maitribala*

1. A kind of supernatural beings.
2. Yakshas were believed to stutter and lisp when beginning to speak in a human language.

3. The reference is to his five former associates, who were the first to be taught by the Buddha when he commenced his ministry at Sarnath.

9. Prince Vishvantara

1. cf. tale 2, note 1.
2. In formal affirmation of a decision.
3. These supernatural beings appear in several *jatakas*. They could be fierce, as in tale 8, or benign as here.
4. cf. note 2 above.
5. cf. tale 1, note 2.
6. A class of demigods.

10. The Sacrifice

1. The reference here is to tonsure, fasting and similar rituals associated with a sacrifice.

11. Shakra

1. cf. Tale 3, note 1.
2. This verse is reproduced in Vallabhadeva's anthology. cf. introduction, note 6A.
3. cf. Tale 2, note 2.

13. The Enchantress

1. Held on the occasion of the full moon in autumn.
2. Moonlight personified.
3. Dharma, artha, kama, that is, virtue, wealth and pleasure.

14. Suparaga the Navigator

1. Sometimes identified with the island of Sumatra. Bharukaccha is also mentioned in the Mahabharata but its location is uncertain.
2. Three groups of gods in the Vedic pantheon.

3. The plural usage indicates belief in many Buddhas, past, present and future, which is also reflected in the invocation at the beginning of the prologue and in tale 7.
4. *Kalyanamitra*, an epithet for the Buddha.

16. The Fledgeling Quail

1. The two stanzas can be perused in the Aryasthaviriyaka Nikaya. Hendrik Kern put this portion of the text, including the two verses, within brackets. Speyer considered them as interpolations, mentioning their similarity to verses 244 and 245 in the *Dhammapada*.

17. The Pitcher

1. A reference to the fratricidal war in the Yadava clan, well known in Indian mythology and mentioned in the *Mahabharata*.

18. The Renunciant

1. Buddhist monks.

19. The Lotus Stalks

1. The four Vedas are well known. The Upavedas or auxiliaries are also four: *Ayurveda, Dhanurveda, Gandharvaveda* and *Sthapatyaveda*, dealing respectively with medicine, military science, music and mechanics. The Vedangas or supplements are six: *Shiksha, Kalpa, Vyakarana, Nirukta, Chhanda* and *Jyotisha*. These are concerned respectively with pronunciation, ritual, grammar, etymology, prosody and astronomy, knowledge of which was considered essential for proper recitation of the liturgy and performance of sacred ceremonies. All these are generally referred to as auxiliaries or supplements in this translation.
2. cf. tale 9, note 3.

3. This paragraph is a translation of the tale's final three verses. They indicate that the Buddha himself commented on this story. The persons named were his disciples and contemporaries, of whom Shariputra, Maudgalyayana and Ananda are well known. Speyer considered these verses to be a later interpolation.

22. The Two Swans

1. Ananda was one of the Buddha's foremost disciples. Speyer considered this sentence a later interpolation.

23. Mahabodhi the Renunciant

1. This and the next two sentences are taken from a verse included in the amendments suggested by Khoroche to Kern's text. cf. introduction, notes 3 and 20. This is the sole change included in this translation.

24. The Great Ape

1. Identified by Speyer with *Diosperos Embryopteris,* an evergreen tree the fruit of which is very sour but edible and considered a food for the poor.

25. The Sharabha Antelope

1. A kind of antelope. The name is also used for a mighty eight-legged mythical beast.

26. The Ruru Deer

1. The plants mentioned in this paragraph are well known in India, but most have no equivalent names in English.
2. The deer and antelope types named here remain unidentified.
3. The *Mrigashiras* or Deer's Head is one of the twenty-seven celestial constellations recognized in Indian astronomy.

28. The Preacher of Forbearance

1. In a former existence. The Pali version of this story mentions that this king was, in a subsequent life, Devadatta, the kinsman, contemporary and adversary of Gautama Buddha.

29. The Horrors of Hell

1. The presiding deity of the netherworld.

30. The Elephant

1. The divine eagle.
2. cf. tale 1, note 2.
3. The legend is that celestial music sounded and heavenly flowers rained down to honour the Buddha as he passed away. The disciple Ananda, cf. tale 22, note 1, was present at the time.

32. The Prince from the Iron House

1. cf. tale 13, note 1.

33. The Buffalo

1. Yama is depicted in mythology as riding upon a buffalo.
2. cf. tale 8, note 1.